"I have ver__ __ with that s__ __ rushed into your arms—and into your bed—without a second thought."

"I was very fond of that girl." Regret edged Egan's voice.

Fond of. Fond of. The words rang out inside Maggie's head like a blast from a loudspeaker. Oh, yes, he had been *fond of* her. And she had *loved* him. Madly. Passionately. With every beat of her foolish young heart.

And now, everything that was female within her longed to lean on him, to seek comfort and support in the power of his strong arms and big body. She was so alone and had been for what seemed like a lifetime. And who better than her son's father to give her the solace she desperately needed at a time like this?

But would Egan love and protect her...even though she had kept his son a secret all these years?

Dear Reader,

As you have no doubt noticed, this year marks Silhouette Books' 20th anniversary, and for the next three months the spotlight shines on Intimate Moments, so we've packed our schedule with irresistible temptations.

First off, I'm proud to announce that this month marks the beginning of A YEAR OF LOVING DANGEROUSLY, a twelve-book continuity series written by eleven of your favorite authors. Sharon Sala, a bestselling, award-winning, absolutely incredible writer, launches things with *Mission: Irresistible,* and next year she will also write the final book in the continuity. Picture a top secret agency, headed by a man no one sees. Now picture a traitor infiltrating security, chased by a dozen (or more!) of the agency's best operatives. The trail crisscrosses the globe, and passion is a big part of the picture, until the final scene is played out and the final romance reaches its happy conclusion. Every book in A YEAR OF LOVING DANGEROUSLY features a self-contained romance, along with a piece of the ongoing puzzle, and enough excitement and suspense to fuel your imagination for the entire year. Don't miss a single monthly installment!

This month also features new books from top authors such as Beverly Barton, who continues THE PROTECTORS, and Marie Ferrarella, who revisits THE BABY OF THE MONTH CLUB. And in future months look for *New York Times* bestselling author Linda Howard, with *A Game of Chance* (yes, it's Chance Mackenzie's story at long last), and a special in-line two-in-one collection by Maggie Shayne and Marilyn Pappano, called *Who Do You Love?* All that and more of A YEAR OF LOVING DANGEROUSLY, as well as new books from the authors who've made Intimate Moments *the* place to come for a mix of excitement and romance no reader can resist. Enjoy!

Leslie J. Wainger
Executive Senior Editor

Please address questions and book requests to:
Silhouette Reader Service
U.S.: 3010 Walden Ave., P.O. Box 1325, Buffalo, NY 14269
Canadian: P.O. Box 609, Fort Erie, Ont. L2A 5X3

BEVERLY BARTON

EGAN CASSIDY'S KID

INTIMATE™ MOMENTS®

Published by Silhouette Books
America's Publisher of Contemporary Romance

To Billy Ray Beaver, D. G. Hatch
and every man and woman who served their country
during the Vietnam War years. And to their families.

Special thanks to Malaina for permitting me to use her
heartfelt poetry that so beautifully expresses the
emotions shared by many veterans.

 SILHOUETTE BOOKS

ISBN 0-373-27085-2

EGAN CASSIDY'S KID

BEVERLY BARTON

has been in love with romance since her grandfather gave her an illustrated book of *Beauty and the Beast*. An avid reader since childhood, Beverly wrote her first book at the age of nine. After marriage to her own "hero" and the births of her daughter and son, Beverly chose to be a full-time homemaker, aka wife, mother, friend and volunteer. The author of over thirty books, Beverly is a member of Romance Writers of America and helped found the Heart of Dixie chapter in Alabama. She has won numerous awards and made the Waldenbooks and *USA Today* bestseller lists.

Prologue

After all these years, he finally had what he wanted—the perfect ammunition to use against his worst enemy. At long last, he could make Egan Cassidy pay. All he had to do to bring Cassidy to his knees was kidnap Bent Douglas.

General Grant Cullen, the supreme leader of the Ultimate Survivalists, leaned back in his swivel chair and grinned. Revenge was sweet. Hell, just the contemplation of revenge was sweet.

He had waited nearly thirty years for this day and he was going to savor every minute of it.

"I want champagne," Cullen told his right-hand man, Winn Sherman. "Send one of the boys to the wine cellar. This is a celebration!"

"Then your phone call was the news you've been waiting for?" Winn asked.

"Oh, yes." Grant rubbed his hands together gleefully. "I've been searching a lifetime to find a way to destroy Egan Cassidy. I knew that sooner or later the way in which

I could inflict great suffering on him would be revealed to me."

"And the way has been revealed, sir?"

Grant laughed. "Mmm-mmm…" He licked his lips and sighed. "I could have killed Cassidy years ago, but I wanted more. I need to see him suffer, to see him lose everything, the way I did. And now it's going to happen."

"I thought you'd told me that Cassidy had nothing to lose, except his life."

"Ah, but that's the joy of it. He does have more to lose—much more—and he doesn't even know it," Cullen said.

"Then this last private detective uncovered something you can use against Cassidy?"

"Indeed he did. He came upon some information that none of the other idiots I hired ever discovered."

Grant couldn't remember when he'd felt more alive. More exhilarated. Pure pleasure wound its way through his mind and body as he fantasized about the moment he would rip out Cassidy's heart.

"It seems that for the past fourteen years Cassidy has paid for flowers to be placed on the grave of Bentley Tyson III, a former Vietnam vet, from some Podunk little town in Alabama," Grant explained. "When I learned that bit of information, I knew that Tyson had meant something to Cassidy. So I had my detective investigate a little further. Seems Tyson saved Cassidy's life in Nam."

Winn frowned. "I'm afraid I don't understand. What good is this information if Tyson is dead?"

"Tyson had a younger sister."

"I see, sir. What significance—?"

"Maggie Tyson Douglas has a fourteen-year-old son."

"I don't follow you, sir," Winn admitted sheepishly.

"Tyson's sister and nephew wouldn't mean anything to Cassidy, would they?"

"Oh, yes, but they do, my friend. They do. They mean more to him than he realizes. Especially the boy." Euphoria unlike any he had ever known suffused Cullen's very soul. "After we've arranged to bring Bent Douglas here for a little visit, I plan to telephone Cassidy and tell him just how important Maggie Douglas's child is to him."

"I'm confused, sir." Winn's cheeks flushed with embarrassment. "You're inviting this boy here to the fort?"

Cullen shot to his feet, clamped his hand down on Winn's shoulder and smiled broadly. "We're going to insist the young man come for a visit. You see, Colonel Sherman, Bent Douglas is Egan Cassidy's kid and the man doesn't even know it."

Chapter 1

"Don't eat so fast," Maggie Douglas scolded. "We aren't running late this morning. We have plenty of time to get you to school early for your student council meeting."

"I'm hungry, Mama," Bent replied, his mouth half-full of cereal. "Is my grilled cheese sandwich ready, yet?"

Using a metal spatula, Maggie sliced the sandwich in two, then lifted it from the electric skillet and laid it on her son's plate. For the past six months the boy had been eating her out of house and home. No matter how much he ate, he remained famished. She smiled, remembering how her father had teased her brother when he'd gone through his ravenous period at about the same age Bent was now.

Maggie wanted to ruffle her son's hair, the way she'd done when he was younger. But another change that had occurred in the past few months was Bent's obsession with his hair and clothes. He wore his silky black hair in the latest style: short, moussed and sticking straight up. And his baggy jeans and oversize shirt looked as if they'd been purchased at a secondhand store, despite their hefty price tags.

Bent lifted a sandwich half and stuck it into his mouth. His gaze met Maggie's just as she rolled her eyes heavenward. He munched on the grilled cheese, swallowed and then washed it all down with a large glass of orange juice.

Bent wiped his mouth with the back of his hand. "Go ahead and ask me."

"Ask you what?"

"Ask me if my legs are hollow." Laughing, Bent shoved back his chair and stood. "You know you said Grandfather used to tell Uncle Bentley that he ate so much his legs had to be hollow."

"I don't need to ask you. I've come to the conclusion that all teenage boys have hollow legs and sometimes—" she reached up and pecked the top of his head "—hollow noggins, too."

"Ah, gee, Mama, don't start that again. Just because I want to go to Florida with the guys this summer doesn't mean I'm stupid."

Maggie looked up at her six-foot son and a shudder rippled along her nerve endings. Dear Lord, the older he got, the more he resembled his father. And the stronger the wild streak in him grew. A yearning for adventure and excitement that was alien to Maggie. She'd always preferred safety and serenity.

"You're too young to go off with a bunch of other boys, without a chaperone." She and Bent had been batting this argument back and forth for weeks now. She had no intention of allowing her fourteen-year-old child to spend a week in Florida with five other boys, ranging in age from fourteen to eighteen.

"Chris's big brother is going along to chaperone us."

Bent picked up his clear vinyl book bag from the kitchen counter.

"And how old is Chris's big brother?" Maggie downed the last drops of lukewarm coffee in her mug, set the mug aside and grabbed her purse off the table.

"He's twenty," Bent said, as if twenty were an age of great wisdom and responsibility.

Maggie snatched up her car keys and headed toward the back door. "Let's go. If I have to drop you off a block from the school, then we'd better head out now so you'll have time to walk that extra block."

Bent grabbed Maggie's shoulder, then leaned over and kissed her cheek. "You're the absolute best mom. Some mothers wouldn't understand why a guy my age would be embarrassed to have his mommy drive him to school every day."

Maggie caressed her kissed cheek. Those sweet moments of little-boy affection were few and far between these days. Her only child was growing up—fast. Each day she noted some small change, some almost indiscernible way he had transformed from a boy into a young man.

"Buttering me up won't work, you know." She opened the kitchen door and shooed him outside. "You aren't going to Florida this summer, unless you go with me."

Bent shrugged. "If you say so."

He let the subject drop, but Maggie knew the issue was far from dead. Her son was a good kid, who'd given her very little trouble over the years, but she knew that the wanderlust in him would sooner or later break her heart. She could protect him, now, while he was still underage, but what would happen once he reached eighteen?

Ten minutes later, Maggie pulled her Cadillac over to the curb, one block from Parsons City High School. "Do you need any money?"

Bent flung open the door, glanced over his shoulders and smiled. Even his smile reminded her of his father's.

"Got plenty," Bent said. "You just gave me twenty Monday, remember?"

Maggie nodded. "Have a good one. And don't be late this afternoon. You're getting fitted for your tux at four-thirty so you need to meet me at the bookstore by four."

He slid out of the car, then leaned over and peered inside, his smile unwavering. "I'll meet you at the bookstore no later than four." With that said, he slammed the door and walked down the sidewalk.

Maggie watched him for a few minutes, then eased the car away from the curb and out into traffic. Another perfectly ordinary day, she thought, then sighed contentedly. Perhaps her life wasn't perfect, but it was good. Maybe she didn't have a special man in her life and hadn't had anyone since her divorce from Gil Douglas four years ago, but she was content. She had the most wonderful child in the whole world, a job she loved, enough money for Bent's college as well as her old age and both she and Bent were blessed with excellent health. What more could a woman want?

A sudden, unexpected memory flashed through her mind. Her heartbeat accelerated. Heat flushed her body. Why had she thought about *him?* she wondered. She had tried to forget, tried not to ever think about that week they'd spent together and the way she had felt when she was with him. Fifteen years was a long time. Long enough for her to have gotten over her infatuation. So, why had she been thinking about Egan Cassidy so often lately? Was it because Bent had grown up to be a carbon copy of him?

She couldn't help wondering where Egan was now. Was he even alive? Considering his profession, he could have been killed years ago. Emotion lodged in her throat. Despite the fact that a part of her hated him, she couldn't bear the thought that he might be dead. As surely as she hated him, she still cared. After all, he was Bent's father.

"Psst... Hey, kid, are you Bentley Tyson Douglas?" a deep, masculine voice asked.

Bent jerked his head around, seeking the man who had called out to him. "Who wants to know?"

A big, burly guy wearing faded jeans and an army fatigue shirt stepped out from behind a car in the parking lot at Bent's right. "I'm a friend of a friend of your old man's."

Bent inspected the rather unsavory-looking character, from his shaggy dark beard to his scuffed leather boots. Bent very seriously doubted that this man was a friend of anyone Gil Douglas referred to as even an acquaintance. His adoptive father was one of the biggest snobs in the world. He probably wouldn't let a guy who looked like this man did walk his dog.

"So? What do you want?" Bent asked.

"I got a kid fixing to start school here next year," the man said, easing closer and closer. "Thought maybe you could tell me about the teachers and stuff like that."

Bent glanced into the mostly empty parking lot. It'd be another twenty minutes or so before the majority of his fellow students would start arriving. The only cars already here belonged to a few teachers on early duty and the other student council members. But right this minute, he didn't see another soul around. Instinct warned him not to trust this man. Maybe he was selling dope. Or maybe he was just a nutcase. Whatever, there was something all wrong about him.

Across the street, on the school grounds, Bent noticed a couple of students entering the building, but they were too far away to hear him if he yelled.

What are you afraid of, Douglas? he asked himself.

You're not some little kid. You're a pretty big guy, so if this man tries anything funny, you can handle him, can't you?

"Look, I haven't got time to talk," Bent said, taking several steps backward until he eased off the sidewalk and into the street.

The man grinned. Bent didn't like that sinister smirk. Just as he started to turn and make a mad dash toward the schoolyard, he heard the roar of a car's engine. Before he had a chance to run, the big man moved in on him. Tires screeched. Someone grabbed him from behind. A hand holding a foul-smelling rag clamped down over his nose and mouth. With expert ease, the two men lifted him and tossed him into the back of the car.

The last thing Bent remembered was the car speeding away down the street.

"So how does mama bear feel about her cub going to his first prom?" Janice Deweese stacked the tattered books into a neat pile, being careful not to crease any of the loose pages. "And with an older woman!"

"Grace Felton is only two years older than Bent," Maggie corrected. "She's hardly an older woman. Besides, I've known Grace's parents all my life and—"

"She's quite suitable for Bent."

"Lord, did I sound that snobbish?" Maggie stood perched on a tall, wooden ladder placed against the floor-to-ceiling bookshelves at the back of the room.

"I did hear a hint of Gil Douglas in that comment." Janice eyed the books in front of her. "Should I start on these today or wait until tomorrow? Repairing all eight of them will require a great deal of patience."

Maggie checked her wristwatch. "Since it's nearly four, why don't you wait and get started on that job first thing in the morning. Bent should be here soon and I'll need you to close up shop for me today.''

"Have you two settled your trip-to-Florida argument?'' Janice slid off the stool behind the checkout counter and stretched to her full five-foot height.

"As far as I'm concerned it's settled.'' One by one, Maggie placed the recent shipment of books, which were collections of first-person Civil War accounts, into their appropriate slots on the shelves. "Bent is too young to go off to Florida with a bunch of other teenage boys. He'll have time enough to indulge his adventurous streak after he turns eighteen.''

"Bent's a great kid, you know. I don't think you need to worry too much about him. You've done a wonderful job of raising him without a father,'' Janice said.

"But Bent has a father who—''

"Who wasn't much of a parent, even before you two got a divorce. Let's face it, Maggie, you've brought up your son with practically no help from Gil Douglas.''

"Gil tried.'' Maggie wished she could have loved Gil the way a woman should love her husband. Perhaps if she had, Gil might have been a better father to Bent. In the beginning, he had made a valiant effort, had even adopted Bent. But a man like Gil Douglas just wasn't cut out to raise another man's son.

"Face the truth, Maggie. Gil couldn't get past the fact that you were engaged to him when you had your little fling with Egan Cassidy.''

Maggie tensed. "I've asked you not to mention his name.''

"Sorry. I didn't mean to dredge up bad memories.''

That was the problem, Maggie thought. The memories weren't bad. They were bittersweet, but not bad. Nothing had prepared her for an affair with a man like Egan. She had been swept away by a passion unlike anything she'd known—before or since.

"It's all right," Maggie said. "Just try not to forget again."

The bell over the front door jingled as a customer entered. Both Janice and Maggie glanced at the entrance. Mrs. Newsom, a regular patron who collected first editions and had a passion for books of every kind, waved and smiled.

"You two just keep on doing whatever you're doing," Mrs. Newsom said, her sweet grin deepening the laugh lines around her mouth. "I just came to browse. I haven't been by in several days and I'm having withdrawal symptoms." Her girlish laughter belied the fact that she was seventy.

Maggie climbed down the ladder, shoved it to the end of the stacks and emerged from the dark cavern of high bookshelves into the airy lightness at the front of the store, where the shelves were low and spaced farther apart. She checked her watch again. Four o'clock exactly. Bent should arrive any minute now. Her son was always punctual. A trait he had either inherited or learned from her.

Bent regained consciousness slowly, his mind fuzzy, his body decidedly uncomfortable. Where was he? What had happened? He attempted to move, but found himself unable to do more than twitch. Someone had bound his hands and feet. He tried to call out and suddenly realized that he'd also been gagged.

The guy in the school parking lot and someone who'd come up from behind had drugged him and tossed him into a car.

Bent looked all around and saw total darkness. But he felt the steady rotation of tires on blacktop and heard the hum of an engine. He was still in a car, only now he was inside the trunk.

Obviously he'd been kidnapped. But why? Who were these guys and what did they want with him? His mother's finances were healthy enough for her to be considered wealthy by some standards, but he knew for a fact that her net worth was less than a million. Her bookstore, which specialized in rare and out-of-print books, barely broke even, so she relied on interest and dividends from her investments for her livelihood. So why would anyone kidnap him when there were kids out there whose parents were multimillionaires? It just didn't make sense.

Bent had heard about young boys and girls being kidnapped and sold on the black market, so he couldn't help wondering if his abductors planned to ship him overseas. The thought of winding up on an auction block and being sold to the highest bidder soured Bent's stomach. Or he could end up in some seedy brothel, a plaything for dirty old men. A shiver racked his body. He'd rather die first!

But he had no intention of dying or of being used as a sex slave. He'd find a way to get out of this mess. He wasn't going to give up without one hell of a fight!

"I can't understand where Bent is," Maggie said, checking her watch again. "It's ten after five. He always calls if he's running late and he hasn't called."

Janice grasped Maggie's trembling hands into her steady ones and squeezed tightly. "He's all right. Maybe he forgot. Or he could be goofing off with the guys or—"

Maggie jerked her hands free. "Something's wrong. He's been in an accident or... Oh, God, where is he?"

"Do you want me to check the hospital? I can call the ER."

"If he'd been in an accident, the police would have contacted me by now, wouldn't they?"

"I think so. Yes, of course they would have."

Maggie paced the floor, her soft leather shoes quiet against the wood's shiny patina. "I'm going to call some of his friends, first, before I panic. He usually catches a ride with Chris or Mark or sometimes Jarred."

"So call their houses and find out if maybe he's with one of them. And if he just forgot about calling you, don't give him a hard time."

"Oh, I won't give him a hard time," Maggie said. "I'll just wring his neck for worrying me to death."

Setting her rear end on the edge of her desk in the office alcove, separated from the bookstore by a pair of brocade curtains, Maggie lifted the telephone and dialed Chris McWilliams's number first.

Fifteen minutes and six calls later, Maggie knew what she had to do. Janice stood at her side, a true friend, desperate to help in any way she could. With moisture glazing her eyes, Maggie exchanged a resigned look with Janice, then lifted the receiver and dialed one final number.

Paul Spencer, Parsons City's chief of police answered. "Spencer here."

"Yes, this is Maggie Douglas. I'd like to report a missing child."

"Whose child is missing?" he asked.

"Mine."

"Bent's missing?" Paul, who'd gone to high school with Maggie, asked, a note of genuine concern in his voice.

"I've contacted all his friends and even talked to Mr. Wellborn, the school principal. Although I dropped him at school this morning—early—for a student council meeting, he never arrived. No one has seen him all day. Oh, God, Paul…help me."

"Are you at home or at the shop?"

"I'm still downtown at the shop."

"Stay where you are. I'll be right over. As soon as you fill out the N.C.I.C form, we'll get it entered into the computer. But I'll go ahead and have a couple of men start checking around to see what they can find."

"Thank you." The receiver dangled from Maggie's fingers. Every nerve in her body screamed. This couldn't be happening. Not to her child. Not to Bent, the boy she loved more than life itself.

Janice took the telephone from Maggie and returned the receiver to its cradle, then she wrapped her arms around her best friend. Maggie hugged Janice fiercely as she tried to control her frazzled emotions. This was a parent's worst nightmare. A missing child. She kept picturing Bent hurt and alone, crying for help. Then that scenario passed from her mind and another quickly took its place. Bent kidnapped and abused—perhaps even killed.

Maggie clenched her teeth tightly in an effort not to scream aloud.

Egan Cassidy poured himself a glass of *Grand cru* Chablis as he watched the salmon steak sizzling on the indoor grill. As a general rule, he dined alone, as he did tonight. Occasionally he had beer and a sandwich at a local bar with another Dundee agent. And once in a blue moon he actually took a woman out to dinner. But as he grew older, he found his penchant for solitude strengthening.

He liked most of his fellow Dundee agents, but except for two or three, they were younger than he. Perhaps the age difference was the reason he had very little in common with most of the other employees of the premiere private security and investigation firm in the Southeast, some said in the entire United States.

And as for the ladies—he'd never been a womanizer, not even in his youth. There had been special women, of course, and a few minor flirtations. But it had been years since he'd dated anyone on a regular basis. He had found that most of the women close to his age, those within a ten-year-span older or younger, were often bitter from a divorce or desperate because they'd never married. And he found younger women, especially those in their twenties, a breed unto themselves. Whenever he dated a woman under thirty, he somehow felt as if he were dating his daughter's best friend. Of course, he didn't have a daughter, but the fact was that at the ripe old age of forty-seven he easily could have a twenty-five-year-old daughter.

Egan turned the salmon steak out onto a plate, then carried the plate and the wine to the table in his kitchen. Although the kitchen in his Atlanta home was ultramodern, his table and chairs were antiques that he'd brought here from his apartment in Memphis. Over the years, while he'd traveled the world as a soldier of fortune, he had always returned to the States, so he'd maintained a place in his old hometown. But two years ago, after joining the Dundee Agency, he'd bought a home in Atlanta and moved his furniture, many priceless antiques, into his newly purchased two-story town house.

The salmon flaked to the touch of his fork and melted like butter when he put it into his mouth. He ate slowly, savoring every bite. He enjoyed cooking and had found that he was a rather good chef.

Egan poured himself more Chablis, then stood, picked up the bowl of fresh raspberries on the counter and headed for the living room. He could clean up later, before bedtime, he thought. As he entered the twenty-by-twenty room, he punched a button on the CD player and the strains of the incomparable Stan Getz's saxophone rendition of

"Body and Soul" filled the room. The stereo system he and his friend and fellow Dundee agent, Hunter Whitelaw, had installed was state-of-the-art. The best money could buy. Everything Egan owned was the best.

Easing down into the soft, lush leather chair, he sighed and closed his eyes, savoring the good music as he had savored the good food. Maybe growing up on the mean streets of Memphis, with no one except an alcoholic father for family, had whetted Egan's appetite for the good things in life. And maybe his lack of a decent upbringing and his brief tenure in Vietnam when he'd been barely eighteen had predisposed him for the occupation to which he had devoted himself for twenty-five years. He'd made a lot of money as a mercenary and had invested wisely, turning his ill-gained earnings into quite a tidy sum. He had more than enough money, so if he chose to never work again, he could maintain his current lifestyle as long as he lived.

Two hours later, the kitchen cleaned and the bottle of Chablis half-empty, Egan made his way into his small home office. The bookshelves and furniture were a light oak and the walls a soft cream. The only color in the room was the dark green, tufted-back leather chair behind his desk. This was the one room in the town house that his decorator hadn't touched. He smiled when he remembered Heather Sims. She'd been interested—very interested. And if he had chosen to pursue a relationship with her, she would have been only too happy to have filled his lonely hours with idle chitchat and hot sex. Three dates, one night of vigorous lovemaking and they had parted as friends.

Egan sat, then opened his notebook and picked up a pen. No one knew that he wrote poetry. Not that he was ashamed, just that to him it was such a private endeavor. At first, it had been a catharsis, and perhaps even now it still was.

With pen in hand, he wrote.

because he was eighteen
he was considered
man enough to fight old men's wars...

The ringing telephone jarred him from his memories, from a time long ago when he'd lived a nightmare—a boy trapped in the politicians' war, a boy who became a man the hard way.

Egan lifted the receiver. "Cassidy here."

"Well, well, well. Hello, old friend."

Egan's blood ran cold. He hadn't heard that voice in years. The last time he'd run into Grant Cullen, they'd both been in the Middle East, both doing nasty little jobs for nasty little men. When had that been, six years ago? No, more like eight.

"What do you want, Cullen?"

"Now, is that any way to talk to an old friend?"

"We were never friends."

Cullen laughed and the sound of his laughter chilled Egan to the bone. Something was wrong. Bad wrong. His gut instincts warned him that this phone call meant big trouble.

"You're right," Grant Cullen agreed. "Neither of us has ever had many friends, have we?"

Cullen was playing some sort of game, Egan thought, and he was enjoying himself too damn much. "You want something. What is it?"

"Oh, just to talk over old times. You know, reminisce about the good old days. Discuss how you screwed me over in Nam and how I've been waiting nearly thirty years to return the favor."

"You want me, you know where to find me," Egan said, his voice deadly soft.

"Oh, I want you all right, but I want you to come to me."

"Now why the hell would I do that?"

"Because I've got something that belongs to you. Something you'll want back."

"I don't know what you're talking about." Egan clutched the phone tightly, his knuckles whitening from the strength of his grasp.

"Remember Bentley Tyson III, that good ol' boy from Alabama who saved your life back in Nam?"

"How the hell do you know about Bentley?"

"You've been paying for flowers to be put on his grave every year ever since he killed himself fifteen years ago."

"Get to the point," Egan snapped, highly agitated that a man like Cullen would even dare to say Bentley's name. Bentley, who'd been a good man destroyed by an evil war.

"The point is I know that when you paid your condolences to Tyson's little sister fifteen years ago, you stayed in Parsons City for a week. What were you doing, Cassidy, screwing Maggie Tyson?"

Egan saw red. Figuratively and literally. Rage boiled inside him like lava on the verge of erupting from a volcano. How did Cullen know about Maggie, about the fact that he'd spent a week in her home?

He's guessing about the affair you had with her, Egan assured himself. He wants to think Maggie meant something to you, that she still does.

"I don't know where you got your information," Egan said. "But you've got it all wrong. Bentley's little sister was engaged to a guy named Gil Douglas and they got married a few months after Bentley's funeral."

"Oh, I know sweet Maggie was engaged, but she didn't marry Gil Douglas until five years later. What Maggie did a few months after Bentley's funeral—nine months to be exact—was give birth to a bouncing baby boy.''

Egan felt as if he'd been hit in the belly with a sledge-hammer. His heartbeat drummed in his ears. He broke out in a cold sweat. No, God, please, no! He'd spent his entire adult life looking over his shoulder, waiting for Grant Cullen to attack. He had denied himself the love and companionship of a wife and the pride and joy of children to protect them from the revenge Cullen would be sure to wreak on anyone who meant a damn thing to Egan.

"What's the matter, buddy boy, didn't sweet Maggie tell you that you have a son?''

"You're crazy! I don't have a son." *He couldn't have a child. God wouldn't be that cruel.*

"Oh, yes, you do. A fine boy of fourteen. Big, tall, hand-some. Looks a whole hell of a lot like you did when you were eighteen and you and I were buddies in that POW camp.''

"I do not have a son," Egan repeated.

"Yes, Cassidy, you do. You and Maggie Tyson Doug-las.''

Cullen laughed again, a sharp, maniacal sound that sliced flesh from Egan's bones.

"You're wrong," Egan said, his statement a plea to God as well as a denial to Cullen.

"Run a check. Your name is on his birth certificate. And one look at a photograph of Bentley Tyson Douglas will confirm the facts.''

"I don't believe anything you've told me. You're a lying son of a bitch!''

"Well, believe this, buddy boy. As we speak, your son is in my hands. I had him flown in from Alabama this afternoon. So just think about that for a while. And you have a good night. Bye now.''

Chapter 2

It couldn't be true. Maggie's child couldn't be his. She would never have kept the boy a secret from him all these years. Not Maggie. She would have come to him, told him, expected him to do *the right thing*.

Don't be an idiot, Cassidy, an inner voice chided. You ended things with her rather abruptly once you realized she was in love with you. You gave her a hundred and one reasons why a committed relationship between the two of you would never work. You broke her heart. Why would she have come to you if, later on, she'd discovered she was carrying your child? You had made it perfectly clear that you didn't love her or want her.

And there was another reason he couldn't be the father of Maggie's child—he had used condoms when he'd made love to her. He never had unprotected sex. The last thing he'd ever wanted was to father a child—someone Cullen could use against him.

His thoughts swirled through time to the week he'd spent

with Maggie Tyson. She had been in mourning, torn apart by Bentley's suicide. And she'd reached out to someone who had known and cared for her brother. Someone who had lived through the same hell, who understood why Bentley had been so tormented. She'd realized that Egan was on a first name basis with the same demons that had haunted her brother for so many years, had shared the same nightmares that finally had driven Bentley to take his own life. Maggie had reached out to Egan and, for the first time in his life, he had succumbed to the pleasure of giving and receiving comfort.

But the connection he and Maggie had shared quickly went beyond sympathy and understanding, beyond a mutual need to mourn a good man's untimely death. Passion had ignited between them like a lightning strike to summer-dry grass. An out-of-control blaze had swept them away.

Suddenly Egan remembered—he hadn't used protection the first time he made love to Maggie!

He paced the floor, calling himself all kinds of a fool and finally admitting that the only way to find out the truth was to telephone Maggie. *God help us all if her child is my son and Grant Cullen really has kidnapped him.*

Maggie escaped into the powder room, locking the door behind her. She needed a few quiet moments away from the crowd that had gathered at her house. All her friends, aunts, uncles and cousins meant well, as did Bent's friends and their parents, who were congregated in her living room. Paul Spencer had stopped by less than an hour ago to give her an update on the local manhunt for Bent. No one had seen the boy all day and there wasn't a trace of him or the book bag he'd been carrying. It was as if her son had dropped off the face of the earth.

The agony she'd felt earlier had intensified to such an

unbearable degree that she wondered how she was able to function at all. But somewhere between the moment she realized that Bent was missing and this very second, a blessed numbness had set in, allowing her to operate with robotic efficiency.

If only she could shut down her mind, stop all the horrific scenarios that kept repeating themselves over and over in her head.

She held on to the hope that Bent was still alive and unharmed. That any minute now he would walk through the front door with a perfectly good reason for where he'd been and why he had worried her so.

She could hang on to her sanity as long as she could believe that her son was all right. If anything happened to Bent...if she lost him...

Maggie rammed her fist against her mouth to silence a gut-wrenching cry as she doubled over in pain. No! No! her heart screamed. This wasn't right. This wasn't fair. Bent was all she had. He was her very life. If she lost him, she would have nothing.

Her son deserved to live and grow up to be the man she knew he could be. He had a right to go to college and get a job and find a girlfriend. To marry and have children. To live a normal life and die in his sleep when he was ninety.

As Maggie slumped to her knees in the small powder room, she prayed, trying to bargain with God. *Let him be all right. Let him live and have a long, happy life and you can take me. Take me now and I won't care. Just don't let my precious Bent suffer. Don't let him die.*

A loud tapping at the door startled Maggie. She'd been so far removed from the present moment that she had forgotten she had a houseful of concerned friends and relatives. The tapping turned into repeated knocks.

''Maggie, honey, there's a phone call for you,'' Janice

said. "I told him that now wasn't a good time for you, but he insisted. Mag, it's Egan Cassidy."

"What!"

"Do you want me to ask him to call back later?"

"No." Maggie lifted herself from the floor, stared into the mirror over the sink and groaned when she saw her pale face and red eyes. "I'll be there in a minute. I'll take the call in the den. Would you make sure no one else is in there."

"Sure thing."

Maggie turned on the faucet, cupped her hands to gather the cold water and then splashed her face. After drying her face and hands, she unlocked the door and stepped out into the hall. She made her way through the throng of loving, caring, wall-to-wall people, as she headed toward the den. Slowed down by hugs and words of encouragement, it took her quite some time to finally reach the small, cosy room that she considered a private sanctuary.

Janice waited by the mahogany secretary, the telephone in her hand. Maggie hesitated for a split second, then took the phone, breathed deeply and placed the receiver to her ear. Janice curled her fingers into a tiny waving motion as she started to leave the room, but Maggie shook her head and motioned for her friend to stay.

"This is Maggie Douglas." She was amazed by how calm her voice sounded.

"Hello, Maggie. It's Egan Cassidy."

"Yes, Janice told me."

"I know you're probably puzzled by this phone call."

"Yes, I am. After fifteen years, I never expected to hear from you." Why was he calling now? she asked herself. Today of all days?

"I need to ask you some questions," Egan said.

"About what?"

"About your son. You do have a son, don't you? A fourteen-year-old son named Bentley Tyson Douglas."

"What do you know about Bent?" She couldn't hide the hysteria in her voice. Had Egan found out that he had a son? Had he somehow talked Bent into going away with him? Was that why Egan was calling, to tell her that he had claimed his son?

"Then you do have a son?"

"Yes, I—is Bent with you? Did you find out that—"

"Bent isn't with me," Egan told her. "But your son is missing, isn't he?"

"If he isn't with you, then how do you know—"

"How long has he been missing?"

"Since this morning. I dropped him off at school and no one has seen him since."

"Damn!"

"Egan, please, tell me what's going on. How did you know about Bent and how did you find out he was missing?"

Long pause. Hard breathing. Although they were physically hundreds of miles apart, Maggie could feel the tension in Egan, could sense some sort of emotional struggle going on inside him.

"Egan, you're frightening me."

"I'm sorry," he said, his voice deep and low and the sentiment truly genuine. "Maggie, I need to know something and it's important that you tell me the truth."

The rush of blood pounded in her head. Her heartbeat accelerated rapidly. Adrenaline shot through her like a fast acting narcotic. "Ask me."

"Is Bent my son?"

Maggie closed her eyes. A tear escaped and trickled down her cheek. Janice rushed to her side and draped her arm around Maggie's waist.

"Are you all right?" Janice whispered. "Do you want me to talk to him?"

Maggie shook her head, then opened her eyes, her vision blurred by the sheen of moisture. "Yes, Bent is your son."

Egan groaned. Maggie bit down on her bottom lip. The sound from Egan that came through the telephone was that of a wounded animal. A ferocious hurt. An angry growl.

"Listen to me very carefully," Egan said. "I know what has happened to Bent—"

Maggie cried out.

"Don't panic. For now, he's safe. Do you hear me? He hasn't been harmed. But in order to keep him safe, you're going to have to let me handle things. Do you understand?"

"No," Maggie said. "No, I don't understand anything. Where is Bent? What's happened to him?"

Janice gasped. "He knows where Bent is?"

"Who's that?" Egan asked. "Who's there with you?"

"Janice Deweese. In case you've forgotten, Janice is my dearest friend and my assistant at Rare Finds."

"Then you can trust Janice?"

"Yes, of course I can trust her."

"With your life? With Bent's life?"

"Yes."

"I assume you've alerted the local authorities," Egan said. "But what I'm going to tell you, I want you to keep it to yourself. Or at least between you and Janice."

"God in heaven, Egan, will you just tell me what's going on?"

"Bent's life could depend on your following my instructions, on letting me handle things without involving any law enforcement other than the ones I chose to bring in on this."

"Bent's life could—" Maggie choked on the tears lodged in her throat. Her son's life was in danger and Egan knew from what or from whom that danger came. How was it possible that Egan was involved in Bent's disappearance when he'd never been a part of Bent's life? She didn't understand any of this. Nothing made sense. It was as if she'd suddenly passed through some invisible barrier straight into the Twilight Zone.

"Maggie!" Egan demanded her attention.

"I don't understand anything. None of this makes any sense to me. Explain to me what's happening. Where is Bent? Why…why—"

"Don't do anything. And don't speak to anyone else tonight. If there are people in your house, get rid of them. I'll fly into Parsons City tonight and I'll explain everything to you when I get there."

"Egan, wait—"

"I'll get your son back for you, Maggie. I'll bring him home. I promise you that."

"Egan!"

The mocking hum of the dial tone told Maggie that Egan had hung up. She slumped down in the chair at the secretary, covered her face with her hands and moaned.

Janice knelt in front of Maggie, then pried Maggie's hands from her face. "What's going on?"

"I'm not sure," Maggie admitted. "Somehow Egan found out that Bent is his son and he knows that Bent is missing. Egan said…he said that he knew what had happened to Bent and that he wanted me to let him handle everything. He promised me that he'd bring Bent home."

"Is Bent with Egan?"

"No, I don't think so." Maggie stared straight through Janice. "Egan is coming here tonight to tell me what happened to our son."

Bent glared at the plate of food his jailer had brought to him several hours ago. He was hungry, but he hadn't touched the fried chicken, mashed potatoes and green beans. He had no way of knowing whether or not his food had been poisoned. But why his captors would choose to poison him, he didn't know. They could easily have killed him a dozen different ways by now.

Although they had taken his book bag and his cellular phone, they hadn't robbed him of either his wallet or his wristwatch. And other than drugging him initially in order to kidnap him and keeping him bound and gagged in the car and then on the airplane, his abductors hadn't laid a finger on him. Of course, they had blindfolded him when they'd taken him off the plane.

He had heard one of them, the guy who'd approached him in the school parking lot, tell the other one, a younger, more clean-cut man, that *the general* didn't want the kid hurt.

"He's waiting for the kid's old man to show up first."

Bent didn't understand. What did his father have to do with his kidnapping? He hadn't seen Gil Douglas in over a year. And he hadn't spoken to him in three months. After his parents' divorce his relationship with his dad had slowly deteriorated. And it wasn't as if his father was rich. Gil spent every dime he made, as a chemical engineer, on his new wife and two-year-old daughter.

Nope, it didn't make any sense at all that his dad was involved in any way, shape, form or fashion with his kidnapping.

So what was going on? He had been abducted, flown across country to only God knew where and was being kept prisoner in a clean, neatly decorated bedroom and served a decent meal on a china plate.

Bent checked his watch. Fifteen after nine. He'd been missing for more than twelve hours. His mother must be out of her mind with worry. She'd probably called the police and had every friend and relative in Parsons City out scouring the countryside for him. And what had she done when no one had been able to find him? His mom would stay strong and hopeful. And she would go to her kitchen to think and plan. He could picture his mother now, in their big old kitchen, baking. For as long as he could remember, his mother had baked whenever she was upset, depressed or needed to make a decision.

Boy, what he'd give for some of her delicious tea cakes. And a glass of milk. And his own bed to sleep in tonight.

Eaten alive by frustration and an ever-increasing fear, Bent tried the door again. Still locked. Stupid! He scanned the room, searching for any means of escape. There were no bars on the two windows, both small rectangular slits near the ceiling. He shoved a chair against the wall, climbed onto the seat and peered out the windows. The moonlight afforded him a glimpse of the shadowy, enclosed courtyard below and the two men who seemed to be guarding the area. Scratch the idea of climbing out the windows.

He heard voices in the hallway, but couldn't make out the conversation. His heartbeat increased speed. Sweat dampened his palms. What if they were coming for him? What if—

Footsteps moved past the door. Silence. Was someone standing outside the door guarding him? Had another someone stopped by to issue orders?

Bent balled his hands into tight fists and beat on the door. "Let me out of here! Why are you doing this? What are you going to do with me?"

He pummeled the door until his fists turned red, until they ached something awful. And he hollered while he banged on the hard wooden surface—hollered until he was hoarse. But no one replied. No one released him. It was as if no one could hear him.

Anger boiled inside Bent, mingling with fear and frustration. He kicked the wall, denting the Sheetrock with his toe. Damn! He couldn't blast his way out of here. He was stuck, trapped, caught.

Bent flung himself down on the neatly made bed, shoved his crossed arms behind his head and glared up at the ceiling. He had to find a way to get out of here, to free himself from his captors. But how? He didn't know. But there had to be a way. He sure as hell wasn't going to give up! Not now. Not ever.

"Are you sure you don't want me to stay with you?" Janice asked as she stood on the front porch with Maggie. "I can spend the night."

"No, Egan said to clear the house. He doesn't want anyone here when he arrives." Maggie hugged her arms around her as she waited for her friend to leave.

"Why do you trust him? He's the man who ran out on you and left you pregnant."

"Egan never made me any promises."

"No, but he didn't have a problem taking advantage of you, did he? He sweet-talked his way into your bed, made you fall in love with him and then told you that he wasn't interested in a committed relationship."

"None of that matters now," Maggie said. "All that's important is that he knows what's happened to Bent and he's promised to bring my son home to me."

"And you believe him?"

"Yes, I do."

"Aren't you the least bit suspicious? You haven't heard from the guy in fifteen years and suddenly, on the very day

Bent disappears, he calls to tell you he knows Bent is his son.''

"Yes, of course I'm suspicious. But I know—I know!—that Egan is as concerned about Bent as I am. I could hear it in his voice. He was in pain.'' Maggie looked out over the front yard. Streetlights on either end of the block illuminated the manicured lawn and flower beds. She and Bent did all the yard work themselves—a mother and son project.

Janice gave Maggie a tight hug, then released her and walked down the porch steps. "I'm a phone call away. I can be back here in five minutes.''

"Go on home and get some rest. Call me in the morning, if you haven't heard from me before then.''

"Okay. And don't worry about the bookstore. I'll take care of things there.''

Maggie remained on the porch until Janice backed her car out of the driveway, then she turned and went inside the house. In the foyer, the tick of the grandfather clock's pendulum kept time with her heartbeat. As she made her way through the living room and dining room and into the kitchen, she found herself wishing Janice and the others hadn't cleaned up after themselves. If they had left dirty glasses and nasty ashtrays, at least she'd have something to do, something to occupy her mind while she waited.

She had thought of nothing else for the past two hours except the fact that Egan Cassidy knew what had happened to Bent. She had gone over at least a dozen possibilities, but not even one plot line was based in reality. Her mind had run the gamut from Bent having left home to find his biological father to someone from Egan's mercenary world having kidnapped Bent to hold him for ransom.

Maggie found herself alone in the kitchen, her favorite room of the house. All her life, since early childhood when she had hovered at her grandmother's side and watched her beloved MaMa create mouthwatering meals, Maggie had found her greatest solace in this room.

She had redecorated the kitchen and the master bedroom shortly after her divorce, needing to wipe away any memories of Gil. Forgetting her five-year-marriage to her childhood friend had been easy enough, especially when he had remarried so quickly. In less than six months after their divorce was final. Even then, realizing that he'd probably been unfaithful to her for quite some time, she still couldn't blame him for the demise of the marriage. How could she hold him at fault when he had always known that he was her second choice, that Bent's father was the one man she had truly loved?

Rummaging in the cabinets for the ingredients to MaMa's tea cakes—Bent's favorite—Maggie let her mind drift back to the first time she ever saw Egan Cassidy. Oh, she'd heard about Egan for years. Bentley had talked about his old war buddy, when he was sober as well as when he was drinking. Her brother had admired and respected Egan in a way he had no other man. Several times over the years, Bentley had gone to Memphis to visit Egan, to share a few days of wine, women and song. But Egan had never come to Parsons City. Not until Bentley died.

Three weeks after Bentley's funeral she'd gone to the cemetery to put fresh flowers on the grave. Just as she rose from her knees, she noticed someone behind her. The stranger stood by the willow tree at the edge of the Tyson plot. He didn't say anything, didn't make a move to come toward her. But when she passed him, she looked into his intense dark eyes and saw the pain.

"Did you know my brother?" she asked.

"You're Maggie, aren't you?"

"Yes." She felt drawn to this man, as if he existed solely to comfort her.

"I'm Egan Cassidy. I didn't find out about Bentley until yesterday," he explained. "I've been out of the country on business."

"I called and left several messages. And when I didn't hear from you, I wrote."

"I'm sorry I wasn't here for the funeral."

"He killed himself." She heard her voice, heard her state the undeniable fact and yet she felt as if someone else were speaking. "He took his pistol, put it in his mouth and pulled—" She burst into tears.

Egan wrapped his arms around her and eased her up against his body, encompassing her in a tender, comforting embrace. "I should have been here for you. Bentley was the best friend I ever had. I owed him my life."

Maggie had clung to Egan, feeling safe and secure. And knowing that this man shared her grief. Bentley's Vietnam comrade understood as no one else did what it had been like for her brother. How he had used alcohol as a crutch to get him through each new day.

She had taken Egan Cassidy home with her and he had stayed for seven days. That had been almost fifteen years ago and she hadn't seen him since.

Maggie mixed the ingredients together with expert precision. She needed no recipe. Indeed, she could prepare these little cakes with her eyes closed. Eggs. Butter—real butter. Flour. Milk. And vanilla. She would make fresh coffee when Egan arrived and serve him tea cakes and coffee in the living room, just as she'd done that day, long ago, when she had opened her home and her heart to Bentley's friend.

At eleven o'clock, Maggie put away her cooking utensils, stored the tea cakes and the raisin-nut bread she had prepared and tidied up the kitchen. Just as she untied the strings on her apron, the doorbell rang. She jumped as if she'd been shot.

Calm down, she cautioned herself. It took every ounce of her willpower not to fall completely apart, not to scream and cry until she was totally insane. But she couldn't come unglued. She had to remain strong and in control. For her own sake and for Bent's sake.

Maggie hung the yellow gingham apron on the back of the Windsor chair at the table, squared her shoulders and marched hurriedly through the house. Before she reached the front door, the bell rang again. He was impatient, she thought. But then, he always had been.

Peering through the glass panes, she saw Egan Cassidy standing on her porch. Big. Tall. Lean. Just as he'd been fifteen years ago. She opened the door.

"Maggie." He studied her face as if he were trying to memorize it, as if he had forgotten how she looked and never wanted to forget again.

"Come in, Egan."

His short, jet-black hair was now laced with silver and he wore a neat, closely cropped beard and mustache that gave him a roguish appearance. An aging desperado. A renegade who lived by his own rules.

Khaki slacks covered his long legs, a brown tweed jacket clung to his broad shoulders and a navy blue cotton shirt covered his muscular chest. His appearance belied the dangerous warrior within him.

"Are you alone?" he asked.

"Yes, I'm alone," she told him. "I did as you asked and sent everyone home. Janice wanted to stay, but—"

Egan lunged toward Maggie, grabbed her shoulders and shoved her gently back into the foyer. He kicked the door closed with his foot. Maggie gasped when she looked up into his eyes and saw fear. Never in her wildest imagination could she have pictured Egan Cassidy afraid of anything or anyone. He was the type of man who put the fear of God into others. But he was invincible, wasn't he? He had not only survived Vietnam, but he had somehow managed to remain sane and return to warfare on an international level as a soldier of fortune.

What—or who—was Egan afraid of?

She trembled, her whole body convulsing in one long, uncontrollable shiver. If Egan was afraid, then she had reason to be terrified.

"Why didn't you tell me that I had a son?" he demanded.

"What?" She tried to pull free of his tenacious hold, but he held her fast.

"If I'd known about Bent, I could have found a way to protect him, to protect both of you!"

"I don't understand, dammit. What are you talking about? Why would Bent and I need protection?"

"Why didn't you tell me?" he asked again.

Maggie had never thought this day would come. Not really. Oh, she had once fantasized that Egan would learn about Bent and how he would come to her, profess his undying love and claim her and her son for his own. But those daydreams had died a slow, painful death. After waiting five years for Egan's return, she had finally agreed to marry Gil. Another monumental mistake she'd made.

"Why would I have told you? You'd made it perfectly clear that you and I had no future. You didn't want any type of commitments in your life. No wife. No children. That is what you said, isn't it?"

Egan released his grip on her shoulders, but quickly draped his arm around her and led her into the living room.

She went with him quite willingly, not having the strength to argue.

"God, Maggie, I'm so sorry." He stepped away from her and gazed into her eyes. "You'll never know how sorry I am. You're the last person on earth I'd want to hurt. I can't blame you for not telling me about Bent. But heaven help me, I wish you had."

"Would it have made a difference?"

"More than you know."

"More than—are you saying that you would have cared, that you would have wanted to be a part of our lives?"

"I'm saying that if I had known I had a child, I would have found a way to prevent what happened to Bent."

"What—what happened to Bent?"

"A man who hates me, a man with whom I endured months of hell in a Vietcong POW camp, a man who has spent over twenty-five years searching for a way to destroy me, has kidnapped our son."

Chapter 3

Maggie couldn't feel her body. Numbness claimed her from head to toe. She could hear the roar of Egan's words as he continued speaking, but she couldn't understand what he was saying. Suddenly the room began to spin around and around. Maggie reached out, grasping for Egan, but before she could grab him, she fainted dead away.

Egan caught her before she hit the floor, lifted her into his arms and carried her to the sofa. By the time he laid her down and placed a pillow under her head, she opened her eyes and moaned.

"Oh, God." She tried to sit up, but Egan placed his hand in the middle of her chest and forced her to lie still.

"Are you all right?" He hovered over her, wishing so damned hard that he didn't have to put her through the nightmare that lay ahead of them. It was unfair that Maggie was suffering because of him.

"I'm all right." When she looked into his eyes, she smiled weakly. "Really. I'm okay. I don't know what happened. I've never fainted before in my entire life. Not even when I was pregnant with— Oh, God! Bent!'' She reached up and grasped the front of Egan's shirt. ''Bent's been kidnapped by someone who wants to destroy you. This man knows…he knows that Bent is your son. But how?''

Egan helped Maggie to sit up, then eased his big, lanky frame down beside her on the tan-and-cream striped sofa. He ran his hand across the smooth silk fabric, but what he wanted to do was pull Maggie back into his arms. Comfort her. Tell her how sorry he was that this had happened. Beg her to forgive him.

''You put my name on your son's birth certificate,'' Egan said. ''Cullen got hold of a copy. And he also has pictures of Bent. He told me that the boy looks a lot like I did when I was eighteen.''

Maggie nodded. ''Bent does resemble you. He's only fourteen and already six feet tall. He has your gray eyes. Your black hair.'' Maggie's quivering hand lifted ever so slowly and reached out toward Egan's face. ''Why, Egan, why?''

They stared into each other's eyes, each seeking understanding, each sharing a realization that no parent should have to accept.

''He—he…this man you call Cullen, he's going to kill Bent, isn't he?''

Maggie's hand dropped to her side. She sat very still. Egan could hear the sound of her breathing. Silence hung between them like a heavy veil.

''I won't lie to you, Maggie.'' He had never lied to her. Never pretended to be anything other than what he was. Never made her promises he knew he couldn't keep. ''I'm sure that's Cullen's plan.''

Maggie gasped loudly and the agony on her face was

almost more than Egan could bear. For just a split second he had to close his eyes and shut out the sight of her.

"But Cullen won't harm Bent," Egan said. When Maggie's eyes cleared and she looked to him for hope, he amended his statement. "Not yet. He'll want me there. To watch."

Egan shot up off the sofa. How the hell had this happened? He'd been so careful all these years, making sure no woman became important to him, so that Cullen wouldn't have anyone to use against him. He had given up what most men wanted—a wife, children, a real home—in order to prevent this very thing from ever happening.

Pacing the floor, he forked his fingers through his hair and cursed under his breath. "I'll move heaven and earth to stop Cullen," Egan vowed as he halted his prowl and faced Maggie. "I'll find a way to save Bent."

Squaring her shoulders, Maggie lifted her chin and glared at Egan. "What did you do to this man to make him hate you so much? Can't you undo whatever it is you did?" Although she sat perfectly still, her hands folded primly in her lap, there was just a hint of hysteria in her voice. "You can't let him kill…kill my…" Tears glazed her soft, brown eyes.

Egan rushed to her, dropped down on one knee and grabbed her hands. "If I'd only known about Bent, I could have—"

Maggie jerked away from him, shoved him aside and rose to her feet. "Don't you dare blame me for this! You keep saying if only you'd known about Bent, as if it's my fault that he's been kidnapped by some lunatic who wants to punish you." She pointed directly at Egan, who rose from his knees to his full six-foot-three height.

"I didn't mean to imply that this is your fault."

"Then why don't you place the blame where it belongs,'' she glowered at him, anger and hatred gleaming in her eyes, turning them from brown to black. "You're the reason my son was kidnapped, the reason his life is in danger. You—" she jabbed her finger into the air, pointing it in his direction and then at herself "—not me."

"Maggie, let me explain." He held open his hands, the very act a plea for her understanding.

"Explain what? That you've lead such an unsavory life, such a wicked life, that you have evil men, capable of murder, searching for ways to punish you." Maggie flew toward him, her arms lifted, her hands cupped into taut fists. "The hard, cruel world you chose to live in, the ungodly way you chose to make a living is the reason Bent's life is in danger." Maggie hurled her fists into Egan's chest. "You've never cared about anyone—ever! You've lived only for yourself, never wanting or needing me or my child. You don't deserve to be a father!"

Her slender, white fists flayed him repeatedly. He barely felt the blows in a physical sense, but emotionally he felt as if Maggie had stripped him down to his bones, with one angry, cutting accusation after another.

He stood unmoving, allowing her to vent her frustration, to beat her fists against his chest until she was spent. He deserved her hatred. She was right. It *was* his fault that Cullen had kidnapped Bent.

When Maggie's blows lost their strength and she seemed barely able to raise her hands, Egan wrapped his arms around her. If only she would allow him to hold her, to comfort her, then perhaps he could find some small amount of comfort himself. Her head lay against his chest as she sucked in her breath, gasping for air. Uncertain how to proceed, Egan lifted one hand to her head and caressed her hair. He remembered how much he had loved Maggie's long, mahogany-red hair.

"I'm sorry," he whispered. "I'd give anything if I could have spared you."

As if suddenly realizing that the man who held her was the enemy, Maggie disengaged herself from his embrace and shoved him away. "I don't want your apologies. Saying I'm sorry now is too little, too late. All I want from you is for you to save Bent."

"I'm going to do everything—" Egan's cellular phone rang.

Maggie jumped. "Would he call you on your cell phone?"

"No. There's not any way he could get this number. All the phones issued to Dundee agents have restricted numbers and operate with a scrambling security frequency."

Maggie laughed, the sound harsh and brittle. "You're still in the cloak-and-dagger business, aren't you?"

"Look, I need to get this," Egan said, then removed his small cell phone from the clip on his belt. "Yeah?"

"Egan, I've called in our top six men," Ellen Denby, the CEO of the Dundee agency, said. "And I've put in a call to Sam to alert him that you're going to need not only manpower, but that he'll need to use all his connections to make sure we head up this operation and we get full cooperation from the FBI. By the way, are you already in Alabama?"

"Thanks for handling things for me," Egan said. "And, yes, I'm in Alabama, with the mother of my child."

"Any word from the kidnapper?"

"Not yet. But it's only a matter of time."

"I've already called in a few favors of my own," Ellen told him. "I'll have a dossier a foot thick on Grant Cullen by morning. I'll know what toothpaste he buys and how many times a day he uses the john."

"Have the men on standby," Egan said. "As soon as

we hear from Cullen, I want to move in quick and hit him hard.'' When Egan heard Maggie gasp, he glanced across the room at her and their gazes locked. ''My one and only objective is to rescue my son. Getting Cullen will be a bonus.'' Egan saw the startled look on Maggie's face, the shock in her eyes, the very minute she realized that in order to save Bent, Egan might have to annihilate his abductor.

''When you're ready to move, just let me know,'' Ellen said.

''You're the best, Denby.''

''Yeah, and don't you ever forget it.''

Egan hit the Off button and returned his cell phone to its nest on his hip. ''I work for a private security and investigation firm based in Atlanta,'' he explained to Maggie, who was staring at him questioningly. ''I've been with them for a couple of years now. Most of the agents are former special forces or former lawmen, all highly trained professionals. My boss has just called in the top six men at Dundee's to be ready to act on my command, once we hear from Cullen.''

''You're planning Bent's rescue as if it's a commando attack, as if this man Cullen is going to tell you where he has Bent and invite you to come and get him.'' Maggie flung her hands out on either side of her body in an are-you-insane? gesture. ''This is my child's life we're talking about. I'm going to call the FBI right now. I've had enough of this craziness.''

Maggie swerved around and headed toward the white and gold telephone sitting atop the chinoiserie cabinet positioned along the back wall. Egan reached her in three giant strides and grabbed her arm just as she lifted the receiver.

''Put the phone down.'' His voice brooked no refusal.

Maggie glared at him, hesitating to obey his command.

When he tightened his hold on her arm, she winced. "Why should I listen to you? Why should I do what you tell me to do?"

"Because handling this situation my way is the only chance we have of getting our son back alive."

Maggie continued staring at Egan, but she gradually lowered her arm and replaced the telephone receiver. "So, what do we do now?"

Egan released her and when she rubbed her arm, he realized he might have held her too tightly. "Did I hurt you?"

"No, not really. You just don't know your own strength."

"You've got to believe me, Maggie, I'd never intentionally hurt you."

"That's debatable," she told him. "But it isn't important. Not anymore. But you didn't answer my question, what do we do now?"

"We wait."

"Wait for what?"

"Wait for Grant Cullen to call us and give us his demands."

Grant Cullen strolled the grounds of his secluded Arizona camp, hidden away in the mountains southeast of Flagstaff. It had taken him years to build and stock his retreat and to man it with his own army. His troops, though few in number, were well-trained young men—schooled personally by him. Two dozen well-trained and obedient followers were worth more to him than a hundred ordinary men.

He had founded the Ultimate Survivalists thirteen years ago when he had realized that eventually he and other brave souls would have to defend themselves against an ever strengthening left-wing, liberal government. There were many men such as he who felt it their God given right to govern their own lives without interference from Uncle Sam. The time would come when chaos would reign and only those who had prepared themselves for the confrontation would survive. When martial law was declared and men were stripped of their rights and their weapons, he and his followers would be prepared to fight to the death.

He had spent a lifetime acquiring the means to secure land in the United States and create a hideaway where he could retreat after every mercenary mission. He and Egan had been in the same line of business, ever since they'd returned from Nam. The only difference was that he hadn't been choosy about the people who hired him. He had no allegiances to any country, not even his own. He hired out to the highest bidder and did whatever nasty little chore that needed to be done.

And all the while he had been planning and preparing, he had known this day would come. The day of reckoning. The day he would finally have the revenge that was long overdue.

His rottweilers, Patton and MacArthur, trotted on either side of him, two ever-alert canines with the same killer instincts he himself possessed. And like the men under his command, obedient unto death.

After sunset, even springtime in the mountains maintained winterlike temperatures and tonight was no exception. A cold north wind whipped around Grant's shoulders. He breathed deeply, dragging in as much fresh, crisp air as his lungs would hold. Invigorated by thoughts of triumph over his nemesis, he experienced a feeling of pure happiness that he hadn't known since before Nam. Before having been a POW. Before having had his promising military career destroyed by an eighteen-year-old recruit with a Boy Scout mentality.

Grant Cullen had been the son, grandson and great-grandson of West Point graduates and no one had been prouder than he the day his name was added to that family tradition. And no one had been more willing to serve his country than he. Everyone who knew him had been certain that he would one day be a great general, just as his heroes, George Patton and Douglas MacArthur had been.

But Egan Cassidy had ruined any chances he'd had of a distinguished military career. Once Cassidy had exposed him as a traitor, even his own father had turned against him. It had been his word against Cassidy's until that snot-nosed Vietcong major had been captured and had collaborated Cassidy's story.

Revenge had been a long time coming, but finally Cassidy was going to get what he deserved. He was going to learn what real suffering was all about.

Grant entered the two-story fortress through the wrought-iron gates that opened up into an outdoor foyer. Two guards, one outside the gate and one inside saluted him when he passed by. He marched into the interior entrance hall, the rottweilers at his heels.

"Winn! Winn!" Grant called loudly. "Where the hell are you?"

The stocky, hard-as-nails Winn Sherman, stormed down the long corridor that led from Grant's office and met his commander halfway. "Yes, sir!" He clicked his heels and saluted.

"Bring the boy to my office." Grant checked the time. "In exactly forty-eight minutes. I'll be making a phone call precisely at three o'clock and I want young Bent Douglas to say a few words to the folks at home."

The corners of Winn's thin lips curved into a smile.

Grant liked his protégé, a man who shared Grant's thoughts and beliefs. A man he trusted as he trusted few others.

"You will personally be in charge of Cassidy's son from now until…" Grant laughed heartily, as he contemplated the various ways he could kill the boy—slowly and painfully while his father and mother watched.

In her peripheral vision Maggie saw Egan down the last drops of his third cup of coffee and then set the Lenox cup on the saucer that rested on the silver serving tray. The grandfather clock in the foyer struck the half hour. Maggie lifted her head from where it rested on the curved extension of the wing chair. Instant calculations told her it was now two-thirty. Her muscles ached from tension. Her frazzled nerves kept her on the verge of tears at any given moment. And her heart ached with a burden almost too great to bear. No mother should ever have to endure what she was being forced to endure.

But she had never been a pessimist or a quitter or a whiner. She wouldn't—couldn't—give up hope. She had to trust Egan, had to believe that he could do what he had promised—save their son. But who did he think he was, some kind of superhero? Maybe he was a rough, tough, mean son of a bitch. Maybe he did know a hundred and one ways to kill a man. And maybe he did have an elite force of Dundee agents prepared to do battle with him. But did that mean he could rescue Bent?

She watched Egan as he treaded across the Persian rug centered in the middle of the living-room floor. Weariness sat on his broad shoulders like an invisible weight. He plopped down on the couch and tossed aside a white brocade throw pillow, which landed on its mate at the opposite end of the camelback sofa. Bending at the waist, he dangled his hands between his spread legs and gazed down at his feet. He repeatedly tapped his fingertips together and patted his right foot against the hardwood surface, just inches shy of the large, intricately patterned rug.

Her feminine instinct told Maggie that Egan was suffering in his own strong, silent way. He hadn't shed a tear. Hadn't shown much emotion at all, except anger. And he most certainly hadn't fainted, as she had. But she knew he was in pain. In some strange way she could feel his agony and understood that he probably could feel hers just as intensely.

Was he feeling guilty? she wondered. He should feel guilty! Because of something in his past, her son's life now depended upon the whims of a madman.

A part of Maggie hated Egan, more than she'd ever thought possible to hate anyone. But a part of her pitied him and shared his grief. And yet another part of her, a small, nagging emotion buried deep inside, still cared for him.

You fool! she chastised herself. This is the man who broke your heart. He left you and never looked back. He didn't want you and he wouldn't have wanted Bent. The only reason he wishes he'd known of his son's existence is so he could have figured out some way to have protected Bent from Grant Cullen.

Don't you ever forget what kind of man Egan is. You were naive enough once to think that your love could change him, could liberate him from the bonds of a lonely, unhappy existence.

"Would you like me to make some fresh coffee?" she asked.

Egan's head snapped up; his eyes focused on her. "Yeah, sure. And maybe something to eat, for both of us. I'll bet you haven't had a bite since lunch yesterday, have you?"

"I'll fix you something," she said. "I don't think I could eat anything."

"Why don't I go into the kitchen with you and we'll fix something together, and then I want you to try to eat something. You can't help Bent by making yourself sick."

I can't help Bent at all, she felt like screaming. But she held herself in check, suppressing the urge to rant and rave.

Egan stood, walked over to her and held out his hand. She stared at his big hand, studying his wide, thick fingers, dusted with dark hair just below the knuckles. A tingling awareness spread through Maggie as she recalled exactly how hairy Egan was. Dark curls covered his muscular arms and long legs. Thick swirls of black hair coated his chest, narrowing into a V across his belly and widening again around his sex.

Sensual heat spread through Maggie, flushing her skin and warming her insides. *How could she be reacting to Egan sexually at a time like this?* her conscience taunted. What sort of power did this man have over her, that after fifteen years, she was still drawn to him in the same stomach-churning, femininity-clenching way?

Apparently tired of waiting for a response from her, Egan reached out, grasped her hand and hauled her to her feet. She wavered slightly, her legs weak, as she stood facing him, her gaze level with his neck. He had once teased her about being tall and leggy.

I'm a leg man, he had said. *And you, Maggie my love, fulfill all my fantasies.*

Without asking permission, Egan slipped his arms around her waist and held her, but didn't tug her up against him. "You haven't changed much, Maggie. You're still... You're even more beautiful than you were the first time I saw you."

She told herself to move away from him, to demand that

he release her and never touch her again. But she knew that all she had to do was slip out of his hold. His grip on her was tentative, featherlight and easily escaped.

Everything that was female within her longed to lean on him, to seek comfort and support in the power of his strong arms and big body. She was so alone and had been for what seemed like a lifetime. And who better than her son's father to give her the solace she so desperately needed at a time like this?

Don't succumb to this momentary weakness, to the seduction of Egan's powerful presence and manly strength, an inner voice warned. *If you do, you'll regret it.*

She lifted her gaze to meet Egan's and almost drowned in the gentle, concerned depths of his gunmetal-gray eyes. "I have changed," she told him. "I have very little in common with that starry-eyed, twenty-three-year-old girl who rushed into your arms...and into your bed, without a second thought."

"I was very fond of that girl." Regret edged Egan's voice.

Fond of. Fond of. The words rang out inside her head like a blast from a loudspeaker. Oh, yes, he had been *fond of* her. And she had *loved* him. Madly. Passionately. With every beat of her foolish, young heart.

Maggie eased out of his grasp. He let her go, making no move to detain her flight. When she turned and walked away, he followed her.

"You put on the coffee," she said, her back to him. "And I'll make a couple of sandwiches."

Egan went with her into the kitchen and although the room had been redecorated since his weeklong visit years ago, the warm hominess mixed quite well with the touch of elegance, just as the decor had back then. Creamy cabinetry, curtains and chairs contrasted sharply to the earth-brown walls, the brown-and-tan checkered chair cushions and dark oak of the wooden table.

He went over to the counter at the right of the sink and there, where she had always kept it, he found the coffee grinder. "You still keep the beans in the refrigerator?"

"Yes." She didn't glance his way. Instead she opened the refrigerator, retrieved the coffee beans and held them out to him, without once looking at him.

He grasped the jar, accepting her avoidance without comment, and pulled out a drawer, searching for a scoop. Then he asked her a question that had been bothering him. Tormenting him actually—ever since Cullen had told him that Maggie had married and divorced the man who had been her fiancé before Egan became her first lover.

"What happened with Gil Douglas?"

Maggie almost dropped the head of lettuce she held in her hand, but managed to grab the plastic container before it hit the floor. "Gil and I married when Bent was five." *After I'd given up all hope that you'd ever return to claim your son and me.* "Gil and I managed to hold things together for five years and then we divorced."

Beginning and end of story! Egan thought. Her meaning had been so clear that she might as well have made the statement.

"Gil adopted Bent?"

"Yes." Maggie retrieved the makings for their sandwiches and dumped the ingredients on the work island directly across from the refrigerator.

Where was Bent right now? her heart cried. Was he hungry? Was he hurt? Was he frightened? Did he know that the lunatic who had kidnapped him intended to murder him?

"Are Gil and Bent close?" Egan asked. "Do they have a good father-son relationship?" His feelings were torn be-

tween hoping Gil was such a great dad that his son didn't
need him and wishing that he would have the opportunity
to be a real father to Bent.

"Is Gil here, now, waiting with me, out of his mind with
worry?" she asked, not the least bit of anger in her voice,
only a sad resignation. "That should tell you what sort of
relationship they have."

"I assume Bent knows Gil isn't his father." Egan waited
for her to respond. She didn't. "Does he know...? Have
you ever told him...? What I'm trying to say is—"

"He knows his father's name is Egan Cassidy. Like you
said, your name is on his birth certificate." She opened the
cellophane-wrapped loaf and pulled out four slices of wheat
bread. "I'm afraid that I mixed truth with fiction when I
told him about his conception." She unscrewed the mayonnaise jar. "I told him that you and I had loved each other,
but that we had ended our affair before I knew I was pregnant."

Egan ground the coffee beans to a fine consistency, mea-
sured the correct amount, then dumped them into the filter.
"What else did you tell him about me?"

Maggie searched a drawer in the island and brought out
a knife, which she used to spread the mayonnaise on the
bread. "I told him that you were a soldier of fortune who
worked all over the world and that we had agreed there was
no way a marriage between us would ever work."

Egan filled the coffee carafe from the jug of spring water
that rested on a stand in front of one floor-to-ceiling window. "You were generous, Maggie. More generous than I
deserved."

She washed the ripe tomato, placed it on the cutting
board and sliced through the delicate skin. "I didn't lie for
you, Egan. I lied for Bent's sake."

Bent, her precious baby boy, who was alone and afraid.

And probably asking why this had happened to him. Oh, God, where was he? And why hadn't Grant Cullen contacted Egan? What was he waiting for? But she knew, as did Egan, that the man was prolonging their torture, savoring each moment he could make Egan suffer.

"Will Bent hate me when we meet?"

"You mean *if* you meet, don't you?" Her hands trembled. The knife slipped and sliced into her finger. She cried out, startled by what she'd accidentally done to herself.

Egan rushed to her side, grabbed her hand and turned on the faucets of the island sink. Holding her injured finger under the cool running water, Egan said, "Cry, dammit, Maggie. Go ahead and cry!"

She snatched her hand from his and inspected the wound. Enough to require a bandage but not stitches, she surmised. "I'll just wrap a piece of paper towel around it to stop the blood flow. Later, I'll put a bandage on it."

He stood by and watched her as she doctored her own cut, all the while wishing she would allow him to do it for her.

"Bent is safe," Egan assured her. "And he'll remain safe until Cullen has me right where he wants me."

"Then don't go." Maggie shook her head, realizing how irrational her thoughts had become. "Don't listen to me. I don't know what I'm saying."

Tears glistened in Maggie's eyes. Egan wished to hell she'd just go ahead and break down. He'd rather see her screaming and throwing things than to see her like this. Deadly calm. Numb from pain.

If only she would let him hold her. But he knew better than to try again. Every time he got too close, she shoved him away. He was the one person on earth who could even begin to understand the agony she was experiencing, and yet he was the one person she wouldn't allow herself to turn to for comfort.

The telephone rang. Egan froze to the spot. Maggie cried out, the sound a shocked, mournful gasp.

Egan walked over to the wall-mounted, brown telephone that hung between two glass-globed, brass sconces. With his stomach tied in knots and his hand unsteady, he lifted the receiver. Maggie hurried to his side.

"Cassidy here."

Maggie grabbed his arm.

"Hello, buddy boy," Grant Cullen said. "I've got somebody here who wants to talk to his mama."

Chapter 4

Egan placed the receiver to Maggie's ear. Her inquiring gaze searched Egan's eyes, and then suddenly she heard the sweetest sound on earth.

"Mama."

"Bent!"

"I'm all right, Mama. They haven't hurt me. Don't worry—"

"Bent? Bent?"

Another voice, one she didn't want to hear, spoke to her. "Maggie, put Cassidy back on the phone."

"No, please, let me talk to Bent," Maggie said. "Whatever reason you have to hate Egan, don't take your revenge out on an innocent boy. Bent doesn't mean anything to Egan. They don't even know each other." Tears welled up in her eyes.

When Egan yanked the phone away from her, Maggie crumbled like a broken cookie, her nerves shattered. Before he returned the receiver to his ear, he grabbed her around the waist and hauled her to his side. Holding her securely, he spoke to Cullen.

"Name the time and the place," Egan said.

Cullen chuckled. Egan's stomach churned. Salty bile rose in his throat.

"Maggie seems a tad upset," Cullen said. "I suppose she's worried about her son. So, how does it feel, big man? I'm holding all the cards and there's no way you can win."

"Name your terms." Egan tried to keep his voice calm. The last thing he wanted was for Cullen to pick up on the panic he felt. The bastard fed off other people's misery.

"I could just kill the boy right now," Cullen said, every word laced with vindictive pleasure. "That way your son would be dead and your woman would hate you until her dying day."

"You want more than that, don't you, Cullen? I can't believe you'd be satisfied with such a paltry revenge."

Maggie's wide-eyed stare momentarily broke Egan's concentration. He realized that she was on the verge of losing it completely. She'd taken just about all she could stand. Without giving his actions a thought, he pressed his lips to her temple and kissed her tenderly. She melted against him, her arms clinging, her body shaking, as she buried her face against his chest.

"You know me too well, buddy boy," Cullen said. "After Nam my pretty little wife left me and took my kid with her. My father never spoke to me again and even disinherited me. I left the army in disgrace. And I owe all those good things to you." Cullen chuckled again. "Now, it's payback time. And payback is going to be a bitch."

"Just name your terms. What, where and when. And I'll be there."

"You and Maggie."

"No," Egan said. "Not Maggie. Just me."

Maggie lifted her head, puzzlement in her eyes. He shook his head, cautioning her to keep quiet.

"You bring your woman or there is no deal. I'll put a gun to your boy's head and blow his brains out. Do I make myself perfectly clear?"

"Perfectly." Egan narrowed his gaze, frowning at Maggie when he noticed she had opened her mouth to speak.

"You haven't done something stupid, like calling in the feds, have you?" Cullen asked.

"Maggie notified the local authorities, but no one else." He kept his gaze focused on her face. She had to keep quiet and let him handle things from here on out. She only suspected what they were up against with Grant Cullen, but he knew. God help them, he knew!

"Good. I figured you were too smart to screw up like that. As long as you keep using your brains and following orders, Bent stays alive. Screw with me and he's dead!"

Egan heard the snap of Cullen's fingers. His own heartbeat thumped an erratic *rat-a-tat-tat,* the sound humming in his ears.

"Your game, your rules," Egan said. He rubbed Maggie's back, trying to soothe her, but at his touch she tensed even more.

"Got that damn straight."

"What do I have to do?" Egan asked.

"All you have to do is come get your son. You want to see him, don't you? Flesh of your flesh. Bone of your bone. The fruit of your loins."

"Yeah, sure, I want to see him."

"Then why don't you and Maggie hop a plane and come on out to Arizona for a visit. It'd be nice if you could get here within forty-eight hours. That way the boy would still be alive when you get here."

"Forty-eight hours. I think that can be arranged."

Maggie glared at Egan and he understood she wanted to speak, wanted to ask questions, but wisely remained silent.

"Won't be as easy as you think, buddy boy," Cullen told him. "My place is rather secluded. Can't get here except on foot. Of course, I've got my own helicopter pad, but I don't want you flying in. You might bring company with you and we wouldn't want extra visitors showing up, now would we? If that were to happen, I'd have to execute your son immediately."

"I understand. So, where exactly are you located?"

"Fly into Flagstaff, then take Highway 40 southeast. When you come to a town called Minerva, go to Schmissrauter's Garage and ask for directions to the general's fort. You can take a Jeep part of the way in, then you'll have to switch to horseback. But I want you and Maggie to walk in, so leave your horses."

Instantly Egan began calculating the scenario, trying to figure out the best plan of action. But any way you looked at it, the chances of rescuing Bent and his getting Maggie and himself out alive were—with the aid of the Dundee agents—fifty-fifty. If he discounted himself, then the odds rose to maybe sixty-forty in their favor.

"Anything else I should know?" Egan asked.

"That's about it...except...I'm looking forward to meeting your son's mother. Figure I'll enjoy getting to know her and I'll make sure she enjoys getting to know me."

Egan clenched his teeth together. Even knowing what Cullen was doing, why he was taunting him with images of Maggie being raped, it took every ounce of Egan's willpower to keep from telling the slimy bastard to go straight to hell. At that precise moment, he knew that if he ever got his hands on Cullen, he would kill him.

The dial tone hummed in Egan's ear. He replaced the receiver, then turned and pulled Maggie into his embrace.

No one was going to hurt this woman more than she'd already been hurt. If he had to move heaven and earth to protect her and their son, then that's what he'd do. If it meant dying to save them, then he would gladly lay down his life.

Do you hear me, God? Are you listening? Do we have a bargain? My life for Maggie's life and Bent's?

Maybe he'd better improve the odds, he thought. More than likely his soul was going to burn in hell anyway, so maybe he should be making his bargain with Lucifer instead of the Almighty.

You want my soul, Old Scratch? I'm willing to make a bargain with you, too, if that's what it takes to save Maggie and Bent.

"Egan?" Maggie's voice rasped with emotion.

He looked down into her eyes, into those beautiful, warm brown eyes and his only thought was how dear and good and loving Maggie was.

His lips took hers in a breath-robbing kiss as his arms tightened around her. Equal parts of frustration and desire dictated the intensity of the kiss. As if her body had never forgotten the feel of his, Maggie responded. Her breasts pressed against his chest as she fitted herself snugly to him. When she opened her mouth to him, he accepted the invitation.

Egan kissed her until they were both breathless, then he laid his forehead against hers and whispered into her mouth, "I care, Maggie. I did then and I do now."

Turning her head so that she couldn't see the expression in his eyes, she hunched her shoulders and slid out of his embrace. "What about Bent? My son is the only thing that matters to me. I don't care about you or me or how either of us feels about the other."

How could he blame her for the way she felt? She was

a mother whose only child had been kidnapped by a psy-
chotic son of a bitch who had every intention of killing the
boy.

"I know where *our* son is," he told her. "And you and
I are going to get him and bring him home."

Bent understood things a lot better now. Now that he
knew when the man in charge said "your father," he
wasn't talking about Gil Douglas. He was referring to Egan
Cassidy, who was nothing more to Bent than a name on
his birth certificate.

His being kidnapped was connected to some sort of
grudge this man had against Egan Cassidy. Bent realized
that he was simply a pawn in a game between two mer-
cenaries. A prize to be won. Or lost.

While two burly guards flanked him on either side, Bent
studied his abductor. Six feet. Maybe six-one. Somewhere
in his early to mid-fifties and in great physical shape for
an old guy. There was definitely a crazy look in his blue
eyes, as if he were spaced out on speed. He laughed too
much. And a nervous twitch pinched his left cheek and
blinked his left eye from time to time.

He wore army fatigues and his men called him General.
His grayish-brown hair had been cropped short like a GI
from an old fifties movie. And he strutted around as if he
were king of the world.

The general looked directly at Bent, then pointed his index finger at him. Bent swallowed hard. Show no fear, he
told himself. Show no fear. But how the hell did he do that
when he was so scared he was about to wet in his pants?

"Your old man's on his way here."

"I guess you're talking about Egan Cassidy, aren't
you?" Bent asked.

"Yeah. So you know who your father is? What did your mother tell you about my old buddy, Cassidy?"

"Nothing," Bent said. "Just that he fought in Nam with my uncle Bentley and that he became a mercenary after the war."

"Then you don't know that your old man is one of the toughest sons of a bitch that ever lived. His own life never meant spit to him, so just killing him was never an option." The general approached Bent, a sick smile on his face. "I've waited over twenty-five years to find his Achilles' heel." The general jabbed his finger into Bent's chest. "And here you are, the answer to my prayers—Egan Cassidy's kid, all mine to do with what I will."

Bent lunged at the general, but before he could touch him, the two guards grabbed Bent and jerked him back away from their leader.

"If Egan Cassidy is the hard-ass you say he is, he'll storm this place and kick your butt!" Bent shouted.

The general laughed long and hard and loud. Then as his laughter died down, he clamped one large, hard hand over Bent's shoulder and looked him square in the eye.

"You're just like your old man. God, would he be proud of you."

Joe Ornelas answered the phone on the third ring. "Yeah, Ornelas here."

"Joe, this is Egan Cassidy. Has Ellen been in touch with you?"

"She called me about an hour ago. Hey, man, I'm really sorry about your kid."

"Thanks," Egan said. "Ellen is using the Dundee jet so we can be in Arizona as quickly as possible. Cullen's given us a forty-eight-hour deadline and the clock is ticking."

"I'm already packed," Joe told him. "Ellen and I figured you'd need somebody familiar with the lay of the land, who just happened to be a pretty good tracker.''

''She explained to you why you can't go all the way in with Maggie and me, didn't she?''

''Sure did. All I'll do is get you there, then I'll join forces with our guys who'll be coming in by helicopter, within a few miles of Cullen's fort,'' Joe said. ''Ellen put together Whitelaw, O'Brien, Parker and Wolfe for this operation.''

''Counting you, that's only five men. I asked for six.''

''You'll have six. Ellen's taking this one on personally.''

''Why am I not surprised?''

Cassidy had never known a woman quite like Ellen Denby. She was equal parts femme fatale and highly trained commando. Every man who worked for Dundee liked and respected the CEO of the agency.

Although she was everybody's buddy in a social setting, she kept her private life strictly private. And if there was a man in her life, she kept him private, too.

''We'll all be aboard the jet when we pick up you and Ms. Douglas. We can work out our plan of attack and rescue on the way to Flagstaff. Ellen's already pulled in a few favors and gotten maps that pinpoint Cullen's fort, so we won't have to wait for directions in Minerva.''

''I take it that somebody's been keeping tabs on Cullen,'' Egan said. ''I assume Ellen didn't give away any secrets in order to acquire info.''

''Nobody's going to get in our way,'' Joe assured him. ''This is going to be our party, even though the feds have been invited along.''

''If one thing goes wrong—''

''We'll get your kid out alive.''

''Joe?''

''Yeah?''

"I don't factor into this rescue operation. Our only objective is to get Maggie and Bent to safety. You got that?"

"Yeah, sure. If it comes down to it, you're expendable."

"Make sure the others understand."

"Yeah. I will."

Maggie dug into the back of her closet, searching for a pair of old jeans that she used when she worked in the yard. Egan had told her she'd need an outfit to wear on the plane trip to Flagstaff and the Jeep ride to Minerva. Something comfortable and practical. Then she'd need jeans, shirt and jacket to change into for the horseback ride and final trek to Grant Cullen's hideaway.

"The last thing I want to do is take you with me," Egan had told her. "But your being with me is one of Cullen's demands. And for now, we have no choice but to play this game by his rules. Do you understand?"

She'd nodded her head and said yes, that she understood. She understood more than Egan realized. The two of them would walk into the lion's den alone and be taken captive by the man who was holding Bent. Their lives would depend on six Dundee agents who would storm the fort and, God willing, save them. Egan hadn't told her what their odds were, but she could guess. He hadn't explained any details or implied that there was even the remotest possibility that he and she and their son could all die, but she knew.

"Got any old boots?" Egan asked.

Gasping, Maggie jumped at the sound of his voice. She had left him downstairs to make a phone call ten minutes ago and his unexpected appearance in her bedroom unnerved her. It had been fifteen years since Egan had been in this room, but she could remember, as if it were yesterday, the long nights and sweet mornings they had shared in her bed.

Nothing in this room was the same, not even the bed. When she married Gil, she had redecorated before he had moved in with her and Bent. And then she'd redecorated again after her divorce. The bed she had shared with Egan was now stored in the attic.

"Boots?" she asked.

"Where we're heading we're going to run into some pretty rough territory. And in the mountains, it'll be cold at night. I want you to wear some heavy socks and some sturdy boots. If you don't have any, we'll have to find you some."

"I have hiking boots," she told him. "Bent and I go to the Smoky Mountains at least once a year to hike the trails. Twice a year, some years. We've done that ever since he was five. Of course, back then we took easy trails and I made it more of an adventure than a real hike."

At the thought that Bent and she might never hike together again, might never share another Smoky Mountain vacation, Maggie's stomach twisted into knots. Her gaze locked with Egan's and she realized he could read her thoughts. But what was he thinking? she wondered. About all the years he had missed with his son? Or that now he was aware of the fact he had a child, he might never get the chance to know him?

"Good," Egan said. "A pair of boots that have already been broken in will be a lot better for your feet."

"I'm almost finished packing." Maggie diverted her attention from the man in her bedroom to a search through her closet. "I'll have to dig the boots out. They're in the back here somewhere." She dove into the walk-in closet, down on her knees, scrambling around, searching through the boxes stored there.

Egan tried not to look at her, did his level best not to notice how curvaceous her hips were or how long her legs were. At thirty-eight, Maggie was a gorgeous woman. In some ways more beautiful than she'd been at twenty-three. Just the sight of her excited him, aroused him. And now, more than then, something about her brought out all his possessive, protective instincts. The primitive man within him recognized her as his mate—his woman.

He had known his share of women, but no one had ever touched his soul. Only Maggie. He supposed that was one of the reasons he had run from her fifteen years ago. Why he had cut their affair short. Because he'd known that he wanted more from her than a brief, no-strings-attached relationship. He could never have had what he'd wanted most—a lifetime with Maggie. He had walked away before it had been too late—before Cullen had learned about their relationship. He had thought that by leaving her, he was protecting her.

Why the hell hadn't he been honest with her back then? Why hadn't he told her about Cullen? If she had known the danger existed, she would have come to him when she'd found out she was carrying his child.

"Here they are." Maggie emerged from the closet, a pair of scuffed, well-worn boots held high, as if they were a prize catch. After tossing them into her unzipped overnight bag, she lifted her underwear and socks off the bed where she had laid them out and then stuffed them into a large side pocket.

"We're going to fly into Flagstaff on the Dundee jet," Egan said. "Six agents will be going with us, but only one—Joe Ornelas, a former Navajo policeman—will be making the trip to the fort with us."

"Aren't you concerned that Grant Cullen will somehow

learn about your plans to storm his fortress? Shouldn't we be more worried about secrecy?''

"Cullen will be expecting an attack," Egan told her. "There's not a chance in hell that we'll take him by surprise."

"I thought he told you that we had to come alone, that we couldn't involve anyone else."

"He did."

"Then I don't understand—"

"Just trust me, Maggie. Believe that I know what I'm doing."

"I'm trusting you with the most precious thing in the world to me. My son's life."

"Our son," Egan corrected. "I might have only known about Bent's existence for less than twenty-four hours, but that doesn't make him any less my son."

Maggie nodded agreement, but quickly whirled around and began searching inside her closet again. Egan wandered around the large, airy bedroom. A row of three tall windows, curtains drawn back, lined the back wall and overlooked the side yard. Early-morning sunlight slipped into the room and lightened the soft pink walls to a pale blush. A beige cotton throw hung over the arm of a floral-upholstered settee at the foot of the bed. This had been the room he had shared with Maggie, but that wasn't the bed. If not for the distinct architecture of the room itself, he wouldn't have recognized it. She had changed everything, including the furniture.

As Egan sauntered past a writing desk in front of the windows, he noticed several volumes held upright by fleur-de-lis brass bookends. Curious as to why these particular books warranted a special place atop her desk, in her bedroom, Egan removed one thin volume. For a split second his heart stopped.

I Remember. By Nage Styon.

One by one he removed, examined and then returned to its place each of the six volumes of poetry. Memories. Cries from the heart. The soul's torment. A vein opened and words were written in the author's blood.

He was the class of sixty-three
full of hopes, dreams, and ideas for his future
but returned with death, nightmares, horrors,
the blood of friends on his hands,
the smell of rot encrusted in his memory,
something in the jungle stalking his soul...

Did Maggie have any idea who the author was? Egan wondered. Or had she purchased these specific books and kept them close to her because they helped her understand her brother and the hell he had lived through in a faraway country when he'd been not much more than a boy and she only a small child? When a publisher had bought Egan's first volume of poetry, he had insisted on using a pseudonym. Had Maggie deciphered the thinly veiled transposition of letters that formed the name Egan Tyson? Although he wrote the poetry, he believed that the sentiments expressed came from Bentley's soul as well as his own, so he used both his name and his deceased friend's name.

"Have you ever read Nage Styon?" Maggie asked.

Egan almost dropped the book he held, but managed to clutch it to his chest. "Yes, I've read all these volumes. I see you have everything he's written."

"I ordered his first book twelve years ago, when it was first published and I've been a devoted fan ever since." Maggie folded her faded jeans and laid them alongside her boots inside the vinyl overnight bag. "Whenever I read his poetry, I cry," she admitted. "I think about Bentley. And

I think about you." She took a deep breath. "And all the other young men who had their lives forever changed by that war."

"All those young men, those who are still alive, are all old men now," Egan said, unable to discern whether or not Maggie knew the truth about the author. "Most of them are older than I am and not a one of them has ever forgotten. Grant Cullen sure never forgot what happened in that POW camp."

Egan could sense Maggie tense when he mentioned Cullen. He should tell her about those months he and Cullen had been together, prisoners of the Vietcong. She had a right to know why her son had been kidnapped, why Cullen planned to kill all three of them.

He had never told anyone the whole story and never would. Only in the deepest, darkest recesses of his soul did the complete memory of those months remain. But he could tell her the basic facts, the simple truth of why for the past twenty-eight years he had spent his life waiting, looking over his shoulder, wondering when and where Grant Cullen could attack. Never had he considered the possibility that Cullen's *day of reckoning* would involve Maggie and her child.

"Did the war mess up Cullen's mind?" Maggie asked, as she walked over to Egan and took the book of poetry from him. Her fingers touched his briefly during the exchange. A whisper touch. Fleeting, yet tremendously powerful.

"Cullen was pretty messed up before he ever went to Nam."

She placed the book with the others and straightened the row. "Why does he hate you?" she asked.

"Because I destroyed his military career. Cullen was a West Point graduate, just like his father and grandfather before him."

"How did you destroy his career?"

"Short and simple. During our detainment in a POW camp, Cullen betrayed his fellow soldiers and his country. And he did it to save his sorry hide and make his life in prison easier. He willingly traded information he possessed for favors and later on he exposed a planned escape. The only reason I wasn't killed along with the other men that day was because I was being *interrogated* at the time it happened."

"Oh, Egan." Maggie grasped the edge of the writing desk, her knuckles bleached from the pressure.

"Later, when we were free, I gave a full account of Cullen's actions to my CO. It was Cullen's word against mine, until a Vietcong major, one of the officers at the camp, was captured by our side and collaborated my account of the events."

"Cullen has hated you all these years," Maggie said. "He has wanted to pay you back because you told the truth about what he did."

"Yeah, and now he thinks he's found a way to exact revenge."

"By killing your son." Maggie's face paled.

"I won't let that happen." Every muscle in Egan's body tightened, every nerve tensed. He thought he knew what torture was, thought he had experienced the worst in that Vietcong POW camp. But he'd been wrong.

Maggie held out her unsteady hand, an offering of care and comfort and unity. Egan clasped her hand in his. With the newborn morning sun washing light and warmth over them, they stood together, their eyes speaking a silent language. The heart's language. A mother and a father praying for the strength and courage—and the chance—to save their son's life.

Chapter 5

The testosterone level aboard the Dundee jet was off the Richter scale. Maggie had never been surrounded by so much high-octane masculinity. As she watched Ellen Denby's total ease commanding these ultramacho guys, she envied her greatly. What gave a woman as beautiful as Ellen the ability to give-and-take with these men as if she were just one of the boys? There was not a trace of unease or unsureness in Ellen. Every one of the agents showed her the greatest respect and accepted her orders without blinking an eye. Despite the comradery and familiarity that existed among them, not one man treated Ellen like they would have any other woman. And Maggie figured that it wasn't easy for them, considering Ellen's obvious physical attributes. A to-die-for body and a face like an angel.

"Care for some coffee, Ms. Douglas?" Jack Parker approached, a mug of freshly made brew in his hand. "Sugar, no cream. Right?"

"Why, yes, thank you, Mr. Parker." Maggie accepted

the white mug that bore a gold-and-blue Dundee Agency emblem.

Jack sat beside her. "Call me Jack. And I can't take credit for remembering how you like your coffee, even though I fixed you a cup right after we first boarded. Egan reminded me to add the sugar."

Maggie glanced toward the table where Egan, Joe Ornelas and Ellen huddled over topographical maps of Arizona, taking special interest in the areas south and east of Flagstaff. She had heard them talking about mountains and gorges, about the Tonto National Forest, East Sunset Mountain, West Sunset Mountain, Clear Creek and something called the Mogollon Rim.

"Would you like a sandwich to go with that?" Jack asked.

Maggie smiled at the charming and attractive man who had undoubtedly been assigned the task of keeping an eye on her. He'd been quite attentive during the entire flight and she could see why he'd been chosen as her baby-sitter. Jack Parker possessed a magnetic personality. And he was good-looking in a rugged, John Wayne sort of way.

"Thanks, I'm not hungry. But you could do something else for me, if you would." She lifted the mug to her lips and took a sip of the strong, sweet coffee.

"Name it, lovely lady, and it's yours."

"Tell me something about yourself and these other Dundee agents who will be risking their lives to save my son."

Jack's broad smile vanished, replaced by a sadness in his golden eyes. "Not much to tell. I suppose Egan's already told you that we're a bunch of former government agents, military men and law enforcement officers. I can assure you that we're not a group of amateurs."

"I realize that y'all are highly trained professionals."

"As for me, I'm just a good ol' boy from Texas," Jack

told her. "I used to work for the DEA before I suffered a severe case of burnout."

"And the others?" she asked, genuinely interested, as she continued sipping her coffee.

"Sleeping beauty over there—" Jack inclined his head toward Matt O'Brien, who relaxed nearby, his eyes closed, his breathing soft and even "—is a former cowboy."

"Is he from Texas, too?"

Jack chuckled. "No, ma'am, he wasn't that kind of cowboy. Pretty boy Matt used to be a member of the Air Force's Green Hornets Squadron. He'll be piloting the chopper that'll take us into Grant Cullen territory."

"Oh, I see." Maggie studied the long, lean Matt, who was, by anyone's standards, a devastatingly handsome man.

Jack glanced at the big, six-foot-four bear of a man who sat across from Matt, his blue-gray eyes riveted to the pages inside a file folder that Ellen Denby had handed him when they'd first boarded the jet. "Then there's Hunter White-law, a Georgia boy and an army man who was part of the *publicly unacknowledged* Delta Force."

"Mmm… I have heard of the Delta Force," Maggie said. "I thought it might not actually exist, except in the movies."

"Oh, it exists," Jack said, then turned his attention to the Native American standing at Egan's side. "Our ace tracker and wilderness expert is Joe Ornelas. He used to be a Navajo policeman."

"Yes, Egan told me that Mr. Ornelas would be our guide."

Finally, as she finished the last drops of coffee, Maggie's gaze settled on the tall, quiet man who sat alone, apart from the others. She had noticed that he'd said very little to anyone since the agents had boarded the plane. He, too, seemed immersed in reading the contents of a file folder.

"That's Wolfe," Jack told her. "David Wolfe. Don't know anything about him…except that Sam Dundee, who owns our agency, personally hired him. Unfriendly cuss. Stays to himself. Doesn't socialize. But he's an expert marksman. He can shoot a gnat off a horse's as—er…a horse's ear from a mile away."

"I suppose a talent like that could come in handy, couldn't it? Especially on an assignment that requires…" Maggie swallowed the lump in her throat. When they went in to rescue Bent, there was bound to be shooting. Probably a lot of shooting. And someone might get killed. One of these men. Or one of Grant Cullen's soldiers. Or even Egan or Bent.

"Try not to think about what's going to happen," Jack said, his voice low and soft and soothing, as he took the empty coffee mug from Maggie's unsteady hand. "Just concentrate on the fact that come this time tomorrow, you'll have your son back with you, all safe and sound."

"You're right. That's exactly what I must concentrate on, if I'm going to keep my sanity."

"Are you sure I can't get you something to eat?" Jack asked. "If you don't want a sandwich, let me get you one of those pastries and another cup of coffee."

"I'm fine, but thank you all the same."

Before Jack could respond, Ellen Denby approached and gave him a nod of dismissal. He patted Maggie's hand and offered her a weak smile. She responded with a fragile smile of her own, then turned to Ellen who quickly took the seat Jack had just vacated.

"How are you holding up?" Ellen asked, her voice naturally throaty and sexy.

"I'm all right."

"Sorry that I haven't had a chance for us to get better acquainted, but since we pulled this operation together pretty damn fast, we needed the time in flight to finish plotting our course of action.''

''I understand.''

''I know this is rough on you, Maggie, but you've got to realize how difficult this is for Egan.''

Maggie's head snapped up. She glared at Ellen. ''If you're referring to the fact that he blames himself for the situation Bent's in, then yes, I do realize how difficult this is for him. But I think you should understand something, Ms. Denby. A part of me wants Egan to blame himself, because however irrational it may sound to you, I blame Egan. He should have told me about Grant Cullen when we…when… He should have told me fifteen years ago.''

''You're right, he should have,'' Ellen agreed. ''And you should have told Egan that he had a son. The way I see it, there's more than enough blame to go around.''

''Yes, you're quite right.''

Ellen's gaze softened as she looked Maggie directly in the eye. ''We're going to rescue Bent. You have to hold on to that thought.''

Maggie nodded. ''How long have you known Egan?''

''Only since he came to work at the Dundee Agency,'' Ellen replied. ''Why do you ask?''

Maggie nervously rubbed her fingertips up and down her thigh, her short, manicured nails scraping over the cotton knit fabric of her tan slacks. ''Despite the fact that he is the father of my child, I really don't know anything about the man Egan is today. I suppose I thought that if you knew him well—''

''There isn't a special woman in his life. I know that for a fact.''

''I wasn't asking about his love life.''

''Yes, you were.'' Ellen's facial expression didn't alter

in the least. "You wouldn't be human if you weren't curious."

"That's all it is—just curiosity."

"Hmm-mmm. Well, Egan's life isn't exactly an open book. He's a fairly private man, but there's one thing all of us at Dundee's know about him—he's a very lonely man."

"Lonely?"

"Yes. Lonely in a way I can't even begin to describe. Egan is a good man, who does his job well. He's friendly with me and all the other agents, but he keeps everyone in his life at arm's length. He doesn't allow anyone to get too close."

"Because of Grant Cullen," Maggie said. "He's never allowed himself to have established friendships or committed relationships of any kind because Grant Cullen could have used anyone Egan cared for against him."

"Didn't take you long to figure that out, did it? You're a smart lady, Maggie, so you should understand that what Egan is going through right now is every bit as bad as what you're going through. Worse, if that's possible. And believe me, I do know that no one can love a child more than his mother."

Maggie clenched her teeth together in an effort not to cry. She hated the thought of showing such a feminine weakness in front of a tough-as-nails woman like Ellen Denby.

Ellen sat beside Maggie throughout the rest of the flight, occasionally engaging her in conversation, but mostly just offering her female companionship and comfort. Maggie realized that Ellen understood that a mother's love was incomparable to any other love, an emotion so strong and pure that since time immemorial, mothers have not only killed to protect their young, but they have often died to protect them. Just as the males of the species have done to protect their mates.

Why was Ellen so astute about the depth a mother's love? Maggie wondered. Had she simply assumed this was true or did she know firsthand?

When they arrived in Flagstaff, having landed at Pulliam Airport, Ellen and all the agents, except Egan and Joe, left in a rental car for a private airstrip, where, Maggie had been told, they would inspect the helicopter Matt O'Brien would use to take them within hiking distance of Cullen's hideaway before nightfall.

Egan hoisted Maggie's overnight bag, along with his own, over his shoulder and led her to the parking deck where a late-model SUV was waiting for them. Joe Ornelas opened the unlocked vehicle, slipped his hand under the floor mat on the driver's side and lifted a key. After they stored their bags in the back, on top of a stack of provisions, Egan settled Maggie in the front seat and took the key from Joe, who climbed in the seat directly behind Maggie. Egan slid behind the wheel, started the engine and maneuvered the SUV out of the deck and onto the road leading from the airport.

"We're about forty miles from Minerva," Joe said, as he removed a map from the black leather briefcase he carried. "We take Interstate 40 toward Winslow, but we exit off at Cedar Hills and then it's two-lane all the way in to Minerva."

"Maggie, do you need to stop for anything before we leave Flagstaff?" Egan asked, but didn't glance her way.

"No, I'm fine," she replied.

"Then we should be in Minerva in less than an hour."

Thirty-seven minutes later, they reached the downtown area of a small, isolated town perched halfway up the mountain. Time seemed to have stopped here sometime in the early twentieth century, Maggie thought, as she watched tree-lined Main Street unfold in front of her. The tallest structure in town appeared to be the two-story, corner brick that had apparently once housed a hotel. Glancing down alleyways, she noted the sidewalks turned into wide stretches of old asphalt and some weathered, wooden hitching posts remained intact, a reminder of a bygone era.

Joe pointed out Schmissrauter's Garage, a crumbling stucco building with an attached front porch constructed of unfinished logs. A couple of antique gas pumps stood out front on the cracked pavement. Silent sentinels of another time.

Egan drove on past the place where he was supposed to make contact with the person possessing the directions to Cullen's fort.

"Aren't we stopping?" Maggie asked.

"No," Egan said.

Egan pulled the SUV to a halt in front of the only restaurant in town. "We'll park here." Miss Fannie's was housed in a tin-roofed, clapboard house that hadn't seen a fresh coat of paint in two decades "You two go in and order dinner, while I walk over to the garage and take care of a little business."

Maggie grasped Egan's arm. "Isn't Joe going with you?"

"I can handle this alone," he told her, then glanced over his shoulder at Joe. "After we eat, we'll head out immediately. I want to be within five miles of Cullen's fort before we make camp tonight."

Joe only nodded, but the minute Egan exited the SUV, Joe jumped out and opened Maggie's door for her. After he helped her disembark, he escorted her into Miss Fannie's. The place reminded her of a little café in Parsons City where her father had taken her when she was a little girl for the best greasy hamburgers in the world. Oiled wooden floors, marred with wear. Bead-board ceilings from which rickety fans dangled. A long counter, with a row of round stools, the seats covered with cracked, faded red vinyl. Pete's Café hadn't existed, except in her memory for over thirty years, but this place brought her memories to life.

They seated themselves at a table near the door. A fat, middle-aged waitress with teeth as yellow as her bleached hair handed them each a well-worn menu.

"What'll it be folks?" the woman asked, eyeing them suspiciously.

"Why don't you order for all three of us, Maggie?" Joe suggested.

"You folks lost your way or something?" Their waitress scratched her head with the nub of the pencil she held in her hand. "We don't get many strangers in these parts."

"Mr. and Mrs. Cassidy are here in Arizona to do some hiking. They hired me as a guide," Joe explained.

"Where's her husband?" She inclined her head toward Maggie.

"At the garage," Joe said. "He'll be on over soon."

Nervously Maggie scanned the menu, all the while wondering if any of the other patrons in Miss Fannie's might be spies for Grant Cullen. The old coot at the counter, slurping down soup? Or the Native American couple at a back table? Or maybe the three men feasting on gravy-smothered fried steaks? Hadn't the possibility that one of Cullen's men could be watching them crossed Joe's mind? What if this whole town was under Cullen's control? *Stop it!* a strong-willed inner voice demanded. *You can't let your imagination run wild with you like that.*

"Three cheeseburgers, three orders of fries and three large colas, please," Maggie ordered, then looked to Joe for approval.

He smiled, and for the first time since she'd been in his presence, she realized what a beautiful man Joe Ornelas was. Not in the classically handsome way some men were, but in a bronze-sculpture way, with a muscular physique and a magnificent profile.

The waitress's sausage-link fingers clasped her pencil tightly as she hurriedly scribbled down their order. "We got some homemade apple pie. It's mighty good."

"All right. We'll take three pieces." Maggie handed her menu to the waitress and Joe followed suit.

Minutes ticked by. Neither she nor Joe bothered with making small talk. Maggie checked her watch continuously. Where was Egan? What was taking him so long? Had something gone wrong?

Fifteen minutes later, Joe got up and walked over to an old jukebox in the corner of the restaurant. He dropped in several coins, then selected the songs.

Three things occurred simultaneously. The waitress brought their order and placed the food on the table. Hank Williams's distinctive voice wailed the lyrics of "I'm So Lonesome, I Could Cry." And Egan Cassidy sat down beside Maggie.

She wanted to ask him what had happened, if everything was all right, but she didn't. Instead she said, "Did Bentley ever tell you about the hamburgers at Pete's Café?"

The edges of Egan's lips curved up in a hint of a smile. "Yeah, he sure did. Hamburgers. Cherry Cokes. Root beer floats. He said his old man used to take him there—take both of you there."

"This place reminds me of Pete's."

"We couldn't save Bentley." Egan laid his hand over

Maggie's where it rested atop the table. "But we are going to save his namesake."

Maggie wished she could cry. Longed to weep until she was spent. But the tears wouldn't come anymore. It was as if fear had numbed her completely and dried up all her tears.

"Let's eat." Egan picked up his burger, ketchup oozing down the sides of the bun, and took a huge bite.

The food was greasy, but good. Unfortunately Maggie had to force down what little she ate. She noticed that both Egan and Joe left over half their burgers and fries untouched and all three of them did little more than taste the pie.

Egan paid the bill, leaving the waitress a nice tip, and the three of them used the rest rooms and changed into their battle gear. Rugged outerwear and boots, suitable for a horseback ride and eventually a hike in wilds of the Arizona mountains. Within ten minutes, they climbed into the SUV and headed out of town on a dusty dirt road that led higher into the mountains. No one spoke for a good ten minutes.

"I told the guy at the garage that I had a guide who was going part of the way with us," Egan said. "I'm sure he'll report that bit of news to Cullen."

"But Cullen told you that we had to come alone, didn't he?" Maggie watched as Egan's jaw tightened. "What if he gets upset that we—"

"Don't worry," Egan said. "As long as you and I go in alone, everything will be fine."

Maggie nodded. *Oh, please, God, let Egan be right about Grant Cullen.*

"Remember, this is all a game to Cullen." Egan glanced her way, then quickly returned his focus to the winding road ahead of them. "He's trying to figure out what I'll do, what I've got planned. He thinks he has me right where he wants me, but at the same time, he'll wonder if we'll really come in alone and whether or not I'll have a team waiting to attack.''

"He'll be prepared, then," Maggie said. "What's to stop his men from gunning down the Dundee agents?"

"We have a secret weapon." Egan stole a quick glance in the interior rearview mirror at Joe. "A way to get in Cullen's stronghold without storming the place. But even with that advantage, this is a risky operation. I won't lie to you, Maggie. Anything can happen when all hell breaks loose. But the Dundee squad knows that their first priority is to get you and Bent out safely."

Grant Cullen ate the last bite of bloody steak, then downed the last drops of Cabernet Sauvignon. With a wave of his hand, he commanded that his wineglass be filled again. Sawyer MacNamara obeyed instantly, then stepped back, standing at attention and waiting. Waiting for *the general* to drink himself into a stupor. For the past month, Sawyer had been assigned as one of Cullen's bodyguards. He and two young idealistic morons rotated duty every eight hours. He considered himself damn lucky to have gotten this close to the commander in chief so quickly. After all, he'd just been inducted into this secret order six months ago.

Sawyer had realized immediately that Grant Cullen, although a highly intelligent man, was insane. Perhaps not clinically insane, but insane by the average person's standards. The man had taken money he'd earned through a lifetime of illegal dealings all over the world and built himself a fort high in the Arizona mountains. And once he had completed his stockade, he had set about collecting himself a small group of followers, whom he'd trained in warfare. Cullen's group called themselves the Ultimate Survivalists.

It had taken Sawyer months to even make contact with one of Cullen's men and another two months to persuade the man to introduce him to the general. He had memorized the manifesto Cullen had written and using it and the information he already had on Cullen, Sawyer had conned his way into the inner circle. Right where he wanted to be.

What his superior at the bureau had ordered him to do— only this morning via his cell phone—might well jeopardize nine months of undercover work. But what choice did he have? He had to follow orders, didn't he? Besides, a fourteen-year-old boy's life might well depend on his actions.

Maggie hadn't been on a horse in years. Not since she'd been a teenager and used to visit Aunt Sue and Uncle Jim on their farm. But the only way to reach Cullen's fort was by horseback or on foot, unless you could helicopter in the way the Dundee squad was going to do. But then Cullen wasn't keeping an eye on Ellen's agents the way he was them. Miles back, Joe and Egan had told her that someone was watching them, remaining a safe distance behind. They had surmised that one of Cullen's men had been in Minerva and had been following them.

Joe had found a fairly clear trail and they had followed it for several miles, winding slowly but surely higher and higher up the mountain. Lush ponderosa pines grew in profusion. Thick grass blanketed the ground like carpet in some areas, and towering boulders hovered around them from time to time. When the trail ran out, Joe made a new path, ever mindful of not only their safety, but the safety of the animals they rode. Maggie could tell quite easily that Joe had an affinity with the horses.

At sunset, they stopped to rest for a bit, and refilled their canteens with cool, clean water from a mountain spring. She heard Joe and Egan talking in hushed tones as they checked the map again. Then Joe came over to her and took her hand in his.

"I will see you in the morning, Maggie."

"Are you leaving us already?" she asked, not wanting to see him go. Not wanting to be alone with Egan.

"I need to meet up with the others before nightfall," he told her. "You and Egan don't have much farther to go before you make camp. Whoever's following us needs to know that you and Egan are going the rest of the way alone. Doing it this way substantiates our story that Egan hired me as a guide."

"What if he follows you?" Maggie squeezed Joe's hand.

"I don't think he will, but if he does, I can easily lose him or I can— Anyway, we figure his orders were to stick with Egan and you."

Maggie realized that Joe had been about to say *or I can kill him.* How had her life come to this? she wondered. Climbing a mountain in Arizona, trying to reach a madman's fortress, joining forces with a highly trained squad of professionals who were all capable of killing. In the most horrible nightmare imaginable, she would never have dreamed that her son would be kidnapped, the pawn in some sick game of revenge.

You know how this all happened, a taunting inner voice said. *Fifteen years ago, you fell in love with a man you barely knew. You gave yourself to him, body and soul, and he left you pregnant with his child. But he didn't bother to tell you that by simply existing, your son would be in unspeakable danger.*

Maggie bid farewell to Joe, then she and Egan remounted and, leading the packhorse behind them, resumed their journey upward and onward—straight to hell.

Chapter 6

When the sun set in a blaze of color over the western slopes, the temperatures began dropping almost immediately. Egan dug into their supplies for their jackets before continuing the journey. He had hoped to be within five miles of Cullen's mountaintop fort before they would be forced to stop for the night, but he now realized that eight miles would be as close as they could get. It would soon be dark and he had to set up camp and get Maggie settled. Thank God Maggie was in good physical condition and had experience as an amateur hiker, otherwise this trip would have been far more difficult for her, and thus for him.

Tonight might well be the last night of his life. He knew that fact only too well. Tomorrow he would meet the enemy, accept the challenge and fight a battle that had been in the making for twenty-eight years. But his life didn't matter. He had no qualms about dying to save his son or in laying down his life to keep Maggie safe.

Sweet Maggie. The bravest woman he'd ever known. A

lesser woman, when confronted with similar circumstances, would have already broken under the strain. Oh, she had cracked a few times, splintered apart slightly, but she had somehow managed to hold herself together. She was being strong for Bent.

There were so many things he wanted to say to Maggie, so many things he needed to tell her. Tonight might be his last opportunity. Right before he had departed, Joe Ornelas had given Egan some advice.

Tell Maggie the truth. Tell her everything. She has a right to know.

Maggie did have a right to know, not only about the secret plans to rescue Bent, but about his backup plan and the inevitability of his own death. If anything went wrong, there was no way Cullen would allow him to live. Of course, Egan had no intention of giving up without the fight of his life, but if it came down to a choice between saving Bent's life and his coming out of this alive, there would be no question of which he would choose.

Twenty minutes later, with the fading sunlight almost gone, Egan selected a small, secluded clearing surrounded by towering trees. From the looks of the site, he figured that sometime in the past few months, someone—members of Cullen's Ultimate Survivalists group perhaps?—had used the spot. The clearing was man-made. Already the brush was beginning to reclaim the area. A stone circle that had once encompassed a campfire remained intact.

"We'll camp here," Egan told Maggie. "There's not much light left, so this will have to do."

She nodded agreement, then followed him when he dismounted. "Are we still being followed?" she whispered.

"I don't think so. I'm pretty sure that once he saw Joe leaving, he headed out, back to the fort, to report to Cullen."

Egan slid the rifle from its leather sheath and propped it against a nearby pine, then removed the saddles from his and Maggie's horses and dumped their gear on the ground.

"We'll set the horses free in the morning," he said. "We'll have to make the last eight miles or so on foot because most of it is a steep climb straight up and the horses will be of no use to us."

Again she nodded before falling into step beside Egan, as he strode toward the packhorse.

"Why don't you sit down over there—" he pointed to a small boulder protruding out of the ground "—and rest, while I get the tent set up."

"Why don't I help you instead?"

Egan snapped around to look at her. When he saw the determined set of her jaw and the fierceness in her eyes, he smiled. "Okay. Why don't you help me?"

Together they set up the two-person tent without any trouble. Three aluminum poles crisscrossed into a four-pole junction that suspended the canopy. The rainfly attached to the pole with snaps and the tent came equipped with extra-long stake-out loops.

"I'll leave the rifle with you," he told her. "If I remember correctly, you know how to handle a rifle, don't you?"

"Yes, I know how, but I haven't handled one in years. I used to go skeet shooting with Daddy and Bentley."

While Maggie spread out their featherweight sleeping bags inside the tent, Egan went in search of firewood. By the time he returned with enough wood to build a decent fire, Maggie had placed a blanket on the ground and sat cross-legged, staring up at the starry sky.

He hesitated at the edge of the clearing and watched her, instinctively realizing that she was praying. Pleading with God. Making a bargain with *the* higher power. Sending out positive thoughts into the vast universe. The serenity that encompassed her swept over him without warning, as if subconsciously she was sharing her hope with him. In that one instant, Egan dared to believe that the impossible was possible. Tomorrow he would save Bent, keep Maggie unharmed and escape with his life.

When he dumped the firewood and kindling twigs into the rock circle, Maggie tilted up her head and glanced at him. "Do you want something to eat or drink?" she asked. "We seem to have a week's supply of rations."

"Nothing for me." Kneeling, he arranged the pieces of dead tree limbs and the handful of sticks into a proper stack, then removed a lighter from his pocket and used it to ignite the dry kindling that would catch the logs afire and leave a warm, glowing fire.

"It's a beautiful night," Maggie said, her gaze returning to the heavens.

Egan sat beside her and looked up at the black sky littered with tiny, sparkling stars and a huge three-quarter moon. "Maggie, there are some things you need to know."

"Hmm-mmm." She continued staring up at the night sky. "About tomorrow?"

"About Grant Cullen. About the Dundee squad's secret weapon. About tomorrow…and about me."

He felt her stir beside him and when he turned to face her, she scooted far enough away from him that there was no chance their bodies would accidentally touch. But then she looked directly at him. Her gaze bold. Strong. Daring him.

He recognized the fear in her eyes and knew she was bracing herself for whatever he would tell her. For just an instant he seriously thought of letting the moment pass, of glossing over the facts in order to protect her. But he owed her nothing less than the truth. By not being completely honest with Maggie, the only person he'd be protecting would be himself.

"I thought you had already told me everything about Grant Cullen," she said. "Is there more?"

"Not about the past…about our past history. But there is more about the man himself. Who and what he is now."

"Oh."

Her lips formed a perfect oval. Moonlight glimmered in her hair, burnishing the rich mahogany with dark red highlights. A reflection of the campfire's flames danced in her brown eyes. Attracted to her beauty, tempted by the aura of unaffected sensuality that was a part of the woman, Egan's body reacted on a purely physical level.

"Cullen has been a mercenary most of his life," Egan said.

"Like you."

"Yeah, like me," he admitted. "But regardless of what I did, I always lived by my own moral code. Cullen has no morals. He amassed a fortune over the years by taking on jobs no one else would take. That's how he could afford to buy so much land and build his fort here in Arizona."

"Why would he want a fort?" Maggie asked.

"To house his army and rule his little kingdom." Egan settled his open palms over his knees. "Cullen heads up a group he refers to as the Ultimate Survivalists. Our government suspects Cullen's little band of merry men are responsible for several bombings over the past few years that have resulted in numerous deaths."

"My God!"

"What I'm about to tell you is strictly confidential."

Maggie nodded, understanding.

"About six months ago, an FBI agent went undercover and joined the Ultimate Survivalists. Recently he's become one of Cullen's bodyguards."

"The secret weapon!" Maggie said. "An inside man."

"Yeah, something like that." Egan flexed his shoulder muscles, trying to relax them. Tension coiled inside him like a rattler preparing to attack. "Before dawn, this federal agent will unlock a secret passageway that leads up into Cullen's fort. The Dundee squad will be inside and already in place when you and I arrive."

"Why would this FBI agent help us? And how did you know about this undercover man? I don't understand any of this. How have y'all been communicating with him?"

"Cellular phones that use a scrambling security frequency is our means of communication. We know about the inside man because the Dundee Agency has some contacts, at pretty high levels, within all the government agencies. You need to remember that seventy-five percent of our agents are either former government agents or were members of various elite military groups."

"Then why aren't government agents handling this raid?"

"They're involved," Egan said. "They've been waiting for a reason to storm Cullen's fort and clean out that vipers nest. We've made a bargain with them—they allow us to get Bent out safely and we let them use Bent's kidnapping as their reason to attack the Ultimate Survivalists."

"Now, let me get this straight—the Dundee Agency is working with the government, using Bent's kidnapping and our rescue attempt as a means to destroy Grant Cullen. Is that right?"

Even before she shot up off the blanket and her cold stare pierced daggers into him, it wasn't difficult for Egan to see that Maggie was angry. No, more than angry. She was furious.

"How could you, Egan? How could you! Our son's life is at stake, and you've turned this rescue into an all-out war with Grant Cullen.'' Enraged, she stomped away from the campfire.

Ah, hell, he'd done it now, Egan thought. This is what happens when you're totally honest with a woman. They misinterpret, they misunderstand and they overreact.

''Maggie!'' He jumped up and followed her.

The closer he got to her, the faster she ran, until he had no choice—for her safety—but to chase her and tackle her down to the ground. She fought him at first, but when he pinned her hands over her head and trapped her body between his spread legs, she ceased struggling and stared up into his face. Moonlight glistened off her tears. Egan's gut clenched tightly. Dammit! He had hurt Maggie again. It was as if everything he said and everything he did caused her pain.

''Will you listen to me?'' he pleaded.

''Do I have a choice?'' Her chest rose and fell in undulating rhythm as she panted, her breath quick and ragged.

''This whole deal is one of 'you scratch our back, we scratch yours.' We need them and they need us.''

''Don't you lie to me, Egan Cassidy. Not when it concerns my son's life.''

''You may not believe me, but I've never lied to you, Maggie. And I'm not lying now. Without help, our chances of rescuing Bent wouldn't be good. The truth of the matter is that Cullen plans to kill Bent and you and then me. And I figure he intends to make my agony last as long as possible—maybe for days.''

''I—I'm not sure I understand.''

Egan felt the fury inside Maggie's tense body begin to subside, ever so slowly. ''Cullen wants to torture Bent—'' Egan pressed his cheek to Maggie's when she gasped ''—and you. He probably intends to rape you and make me watch.'' Egan pulled Maggie up into a sitting position, his bent knees on either side of her, and wrapped her in his arms. "That's what kind of man we're dealing with."

Maggie sat there on the ground, enfolded in Egan's embrace and didn't say a word as she trembled uncontrollably.

"I'm using whatever means necessary to prevent any harm from coming to you or Bent. And if that meant blackmailing the president, I'd do it." Egan lifted Maggie to her feet. "This ground is cold, honey. Come on, let's get back to the fire."

She walked unsteadily at his side, supported by his tight grip around her waist. They returned to the blanket and sat together, Egan holding her close.

"By joining forces with the FBI, I'm not putting Bent in more danger," Egan explained. "What we're doing is giving us a better chance of saving him. That's the only reason I agreed to the arrangement."

"What's going to happen in the morning, when you and I arrive at the fort?" With the rage completely drained from her, Maggie's voice returned to a calm, controlled tone.

"The plan is for the Dundee agents and the government boys to take Cullen's little army off guard, once you and I are inside to distract Cullen. He'll be expecting an attack only from the outside, so the element of surprise will be on our side."

"How can you predict what will happen?" she asked. "Something could go wrong. Bent could be caught in the middle of—"

Egan tightened his hold on Maggie. "Trust me to make sure Bent is safe. I promise you that my top priority is to get the two of you out of Cullen's clutches and make sure he's never a threat to either of you again."

"But—"

Egan pressed his index finger over her lips, silencing her. Ah, Maggie. Maggie, my love. Always so inquisitive, so headstrong and determined. A lady who knew her own mind and wouldn't be pacified by half-truths.

"There is nothing I won't do to save Bent's life," Egan promised, then clasped her face with his hands, leaned forward and kissed her forehead. "I'll do whatever is necessary." Grasping her hands, he urged her to her feet. "We have a big day tomorrow. Why don't you get some rest, even if you can't sleep?"

"You're right. I am tired." Without saying another word or giving him a backward glance, Maggie stood, walked away from him and crawled inside the tent.

Egan sat alone on the blanket. Nocturnal animal sounds echoed in the stillness. An owl's eerily mournful hoots. A predatory cat's distant cry. Insects sang their unique songs, blending together in an arthropodan serenade. With the forest all around him and the dark heavens above, Egan felt encompassed by nature. He had been alone most of his life, but he had never felt as lonely as he did at this precise moment. Maggie had withdrawn from him, leaving an emptiness inside him that he couldn't explain.

If this was his last night on earth, he didn't want to spend it alone. He needed human comfort. A kind word. A gentle touch. The feel of a loving woman in his arms. If he went to Maggie, if he asked for solace, would she turn him away?

Maggie removed her boots and set them aside, then unzipped her sleeping bag and slid her legs inside the folds. Trying to relax, she closed her eyes and listened to the rhythm of her heart as she breathed in and out. In and out.

Rest, she told herself. Rest. You have to be at your physical and mental best in the morning. Tomorrow is the single most important day of your life. By day's end tomorrow, you and Bent will be home in Alabama. And this nightmare will be behind you.

But what about Egan? a concerned inner voice asked.

Yes, what about Egan? Egan, Bent's father. Egan, the man she had once loved with mindless passion. Egan, the person who would risk anything—including his own life—to save their son.

Maggie's eyelids flew open. Her heartbeat accelerated. With trembling fingers, she unzipped her sleeping bag and scrambled from its confinement.

Oh, dear God! It can't be true. It can't be.

With a blinding moment of gut-wrenching insight, Maggie realized a horrifying truth. Egan had every intention of sacrificing his life to save Bent. Despite a surprise attack from the Dundee squad, Egan couldn't be certain that Cullen wouldn't have time to strike, wouldn't have time to kill Bent. Now she understood Egan's backup plan—the one he hadn't mentioned.

"Oh, Egan!" she cried.

With adrenaline rushing through her body, she raced out of the tent in search of Egan. She halted, momentarily hesitating when she saw him standing only a few feet away, his gaze fixed on the sky. Armed with the truth—the deadly reality of what tomorrow might bring—Maggie faced her feelings honestly, for the first time in many years. Despite the fact that he had rejected her, left her pregnant and never returned, she still had deep feelings for Egan Cassidy. And she still wanted him in a way she'd never wanted another man. She knew her feelings weren't logical—hell, they never had been where Egan was concerned. But love wasn't supposed to make sense, was it? At least not the wild, all-consuming type of love that she and Egan had shared.

Tomorrow could bring death to Egan. And to her. For each of them were equally prepared to sacrifice themselves for their child. Tonight might well be their last night together.

In her sock feet, Maggie flew toward Egan, her heart beating erratically. Her mind filled with thoughts of one final shared intimacy. Her body yearning to celebrate life, to grasp the pleasure and savor it for as long as possible.

"Egan!"

Turning when she called his name, Egan moved toward her, his arms open to catch her. She flung herself at him. Her arms circled his waist, clinging to him, hugging him, whimpering his name. Grasping her shoulders, he shook her gently.

"What's wrong, Maggie? What is it?"

She looked up at him, tears pooling in her eyes, her mouth open on a gasping sigh. "I know," she said. "I know."

Forking his fingers through her hair, which hung loosely around her shoulders, Egan clutched the back of her head with his open palm. "What do you know?"

Tears trickled down her cheeks, around her nose and over her lips. "I know what you're planning to do, and I love you for being willing to…to…"

He understood then that she had figured out his backup plan, if it came to a choice between letting Cullen kill Bent and in dying himself. "Maggie…I—"

He swept his hands down her arms and then up to cup her face and stare into her eyes. Her expression spoke volumes. All her emotions showed plainly on her face. Compassion and passion. Fear. Gratitude. Hope and hopelessness. And love. God, was it possible that Maggie still cared about him?

"Once this is all over, I won't ever let anything or anyone hurt you again, Maggie. Not even me. I swear!"

She nodded her understanding, her face wet with tears. "Make love to me tonight. Now."

While there's still time. Before we walk straight into hell tomorrow, knowing one or both of us may die. Neither of them verbally expressed what they both thought, what each of them silently acknowledged.

Egan shut his eyes. Tremors racked his body. Like a precious gift from heaven, her invitation touched his heart and opened up the emotions he had kept buried for fifteen long, lonely years. Maggie was the only woman he had ever allowed himself to truly care about, but he had ended things with her abruptly, thinking that by doing so he was protecting her.

His kiss took her breath away. Tender passion. Barely contained hunger, tempered by loving consideration. She opened herself to him, taking pleasure in the taste and smell of him. In the sound of his ragged breath. The feel of his hard body beneath her fingertips. The rasp of his beard and mustache against her skin.

The whole world faded into oblivion, ceasing to exist. Only she and Egan and the compulsion to come together as one existed in their private universe. A man. A woman. And a primeval instinct that thousands of years of civilization had left unchanged.

With his mouth clinging, his teeth nipping, Egan swung Maggie up into his arms and headed toward their tent. She draped her arm around his neck, giving herself to him, surrendering to the desperate need that rode them both so relentlessly.

Inside the tent, closed off from the outside elements, warm and secure, Egan and Maggie knelt on their knees and faced each other. Only the light from a gas lantern illuminated the cosy interior as Egan reached out and slid Maggie's jacket from her shoulders and down her arms.

She shucked off the lightweight coat, letting it drop to her side before she responded by removing Egan's jacket.

Her fingers shook when she undid the first button on his heavy cotton shirt. She hadn't been with a man since her divorce from Gil. Her sexual experience was limited to two men. Everything she knew about passion and mindless pleasure, she had learned from Egan. The anticipation of experiencing once again the earth-shattering loving she had known only with Egan filled Maggie with longing. She practically ripped his shirt from his body, leaving his broad chest bare. He was older, his chest hair dusted with gray, but his body appeared as toned and hard as it had been fifteen years ago.

Egan unbuttoned Maggie's shirt and tossed it aside, leaving only her bra standing between him and the sight of her breasts. He pressed the center front catch of her bra and the plastic mechanism popped open. Dropping his palms over her shoulders, he hooked each index finger under the straps and glided the bit of satin down her arms.

"My body isn't the same as it was when I was twenty-three," she said. "I'm thirty-eight now and I've carried and given birth to a child."

"My child."

Maggie shivered, even before his hands cupped and lifted her breasts. His touch ignited shards of tingling awareness within the very core of her femininity.

"You're more beautiful now," he said, his voice a rugged moan as his thumbs raked over her pebble-hard nipples.

"So—so are you."

It was the passion talking and they both knew it. They saw each other through a rosy haze of lust and longing. And a need to make these last sweet moments together as perfect as possible. Now was not the time for brutal honesty or harsh reality.

Egan dragged her up against him, crushing her breasts against his chest, rubbing their bodies together as they sighed and moaned with the pleasure of flesh on flesh. Holding her to him, his sex throbbing, his heartbeat roaring in his ears, he consumed her mouth. She clung to him, returning in equal measure the intensity of his kiss. As their tongues dueled, he tumbled her onto her open sleeping bag and came down over her, grinding his arousal into her mound.

Sighing with pleasure, she lifted her hips and thrust upward. "I want you so."

Lifting himself onto his knees, straddling her hips, Egan worked furiously to unsnap and unzip her jeans. He slid his hands beneath her, grasped the waistband and dragged her jeans down her hips and legs. After pulling them over her feet, he threw them to his side and concentrated on the white lace panties that hid her lush red curls from his view.

Maggie unbuckled Egan's belt and slid it through the loops on his jeans, then undid the snap and zipper. Not waiting to remove his pants, she slipped her hand inside and caressed the hardness covered by his briefs. Egan groaned deep in his throat, then covered her hand with his and urged her to continue fondling him.

Rising just enough to be able to kiss his chest, Maggie began a sensual assault that soon had Egan begging her to stop. He grabbed her by the back of the neck and pulled her marauding lips and seductive tongue away from his body.

"I can't take much more of this, Maggie, my love."

She smiled at him, savoring the triumph of unnerving him completely. "Want me to stop?"

"Yeah. Maybe in a hundred years."

He held her at bay until he could get rid of his boots and jeans. Then when nothing stood between them except her panties and his briefs, he placed her hand back where it had been and put his in the corresponding spot on her body. As he began to rub, so did she. And when he inched his fingers inside the leg-band of her panties, she inserted her fingers beneath the leg-band of his briefs. Her fingers curled around his erection. His fingers parted her moist feminine folds and sought her throbbing kernel.

After petting her until she wriggled and moaned, Egan urged her panties down her hips. Maggie maneuvered her legs so that he could remove her underwear. He inserted two fingers up and into her. She gasped when he invaded her, the sensation electrifying as he added the strumming of his thumb over her pulsating nub.

She yanked on the waistband of his briefs, tugging them downward by slow degrees. The minute he helped her remove them, she circled him with her hand. Pumping rhythmically, her soft hand stiffened his sex to the rock-hard stage.

Lowering his head, Egan captured one tight nipple in his mouth and suckled her greedily. And all the while his talented fingers worked their magic between her legs. Within minutes her body clenched his fingers and her nub swelled. She squirmed against his hand, seeking fulfillment. He gave her what she wanted, increasing the tempo and pressure until she cried out and shuddered with release. While the aftershocks of her climax rippled over her nerve endings, Egan shoved her onto her back and plunged into her. Deeply. Completely.

Maggie draped her arms over his shoulders, wrapped her legs around his hips and sought his mouth with hers. His kisses were wet and wild, a frenzy of tongue and lips and teeth. She met him thrust for pounding thrust. Giving and taking. Loving and being loved.

And just as his pace doubled until he was jackhammering

into her, Maggie reached the pinnacle a second time. Fireworks exploded inside her body, sending her soaring. Her completion ignited his. His body tensed. Then with several quick, stabbing jabs, delving deeply, he jetted his release into her receptive body.

The animal roar that he uttered echoed inside the small tent. Maggie covered his face with kisses and wept with a joy she hadn't known since the last time Egan had loved her.

Egan eased his big body to her side and wrapped her in his arms. He kissed her forehead. Her eyelids. Her nose. And then her lips.

"Thank you," he said, his voice only a whisper.

"Oh, Egan. Don't thank me," she snuggled against him as close as she could get. "I wanted you every bit as much as you wanted me."

"It's always been that way between us, hasn't it? So much hunger and passion."

And love, she thought. *Heaven help me, I've always loved you!*

Chapter 7

The heavy metal door creaked as Sawyer eased it open. He made a quick check around and behind him to make sure no one else had heard. He'd been a hundred percent sure that no one saw him enter the stairwell that led to the subterranean vault, two levels below the fort. But it always paid to be extra careful, especially when so many people's lives depended on it.

Grant Cullen had planned this escape hatch as a means to freedom, the tunnel leading a quarter of a mile away and opening in the forest. He had installed the underground passage, just in case he ever needed it. Cullen might have other alternate ways to escape the fortress, but this was the only one Sawyer had learned of during his time with the Ultimate Survivalists. The general's paranoia kept him ever diligent. Always on the lookout for enemies, real and imagined.

In a whispered voice, Sawyer called, "All clear."

The first to appear, stepping out of the tunnel, was a

small guy, no taller than five-six. But the minute the Dundee agent's face and body came into full view, Sawyer realized this was no *he* but a *she*.

"I'm Denby," she said, then moved aside to allow room for her men to enter.

For just a minute Sawyer couldn't take his eyes off Ellen Denby. He'd heard about her, of course. Who hadn't? The gorgeous, hard-as-nails CEO of the nation's top private security and investigation agency. The black BDU she wore did nothing to disguise the lush contours of her very feminine shape. Sawyer swallowed. Damn, she was a looker. When she caught him staring at her, she gave him an eat-dirt-and-die look.

Clearing his throat, Sawyer switched his attention to the four big men, all wearing SWAT BDUs. Their weapons of choice—MP5 submachine guns and AK-47 rifles.

"Our pilot is with the chopper," Ellen said. "As soon as we get the kid, Ornelas and Whitelaw will take him out of here. Once the boy is safely on board, the rest of us will have ten minutes—tops—to clear out of this hellhole. What happens to Cullen and his followers after that is up to you G-men."

"What about Cassidy and the boy's mother?" Sawyer asked.

"The plans are for the mother to go with the boy. Cassidy will be on his own. He's going after Cullen, if we don't get him first."

Morning came too soon. Reality reappeared with the dawn. As daylight slowly spread across the eastern horizon, Egan enveloped Maggie in his arms and held her. His face was buried against her breasts. Her chin rested on the top of his head. They had made love again only moments ago.

Slow, sweet, desperate love. Each knowing what lay ahead of them.

"We need to get going soon," he told her. "It's nearly eight miles on foot to reach Cullen's fort."

"I'll do my best not to slow us down," she said. "I walk three or four days a week, most of the time. And I can usually make four miles in less than an hour."

"We'll move at your pace. The trek will tire us some, but we don't need to be totally exhausted when we get there."

Maggie speared her fingers through Egan's salt-and-pepper hair, grasped his head and titled it backward so that she could see his face. "If we—" She cleared her throat. "If we all three come out of this alive—Bent and you and me—I want you to get to know your son. He's a wonderful boy. And he's so much like you."

Egan eased up into a sitting position, bringing Maggie with him. "I want the opportunity to get to know Bent, but how do you think he'll feel about me? After all these years, he probably believes I don't give a damn about him."

"What you're doing today proves that theory wrong, doesn't it? He's a smart boy. He'll know." Maggie brushed her lips over Egan's. A gentle kiss. "No matter what happens, I'm glad we had this time together."

He caressed her cheek. "Me, too, Maggie, my love. Me, too."

Maggie cherished the hope that the rescue attempt would come off without any problems. She would not allow herself to even think about the worst-case scenario—that she and Egan and Bent could all die. She clung to the dream of a happily ever after for the three of them. But that was all it was—a dream. And probably a foolish one at that. There was a good chance that even if Bent and she made it out alive, Egan wouldn't. And if he did somehow survive, that didn't mean he'd become a part of their lives on a permanent basis. How would Bent react to a father he'd never known, a man he refused to discuss with her? And would it be possible for the three of them to actually become a family? Or would the anger and pain from the past and the sheer terror of Bent's kidnapping form a wedge that would forever keep them apart?

Maggie sought Egan's lips, longing for one final kiss. She had never been in love with anyone else, not even Gil. Egan had been the true love of her life, and after being with him again last night, she realized that there would never be anyone else for her. But sometimes love wasn't enough. Not unless the bond was equally strong for both partners. How did Egan truly feel about her? He hadn't told her that he loved her. Not in the past. Not in the present.

Within half an hour, they had dressed, eaten and taken down the tent. Morning sunshine spread quickly, lighting the sky and illuminating the forest thicket that surrounded them. Egan stashed their equipment behind a boulder, freed their horses and held out his hand to Maggie.

"Ready?"

She nodded.

"No matter what happens, concentrate on only one thing—saving Bent. Don't even think about me." He grabbed her shoulders. "Do you understand?"

"Yes, I understand."

When he noted the stricken expression on her face, he ran his hands up and down her arms, then released her. "This isn't a suicide mission for me. I have every intention of coming out alive. But I'm prepared to die, if that's what it takes."

The look in her eyes said it all and said it far more eloquently than words could have. Egan had never wanted

to live as badly as he did now. Now that he knew Maggie
still cared. Now that he knew he had a son.

"Let's go," he told her.

"You lead. I'll follow."

Today was the day he had been waiting for all these
years. The day Egan Cassidy would suffer the torment of
the damned. Grant's head ached slightly. He had consumed
a little too much wine last night. But why not? He'd had
every reason to celebrate. Later today, he would celebrate
even more. And Egan would be present for the event! Ah,
the games he would play with them. The fun he would
have. He would keep most of his soldiers on guard, preparing for the inevitable attack. But he could spare a dozen
or so to witness the game playing. He would take more
pleasure in the proceedings if he had an audience present.
An audience of devoted followers.

A smile curved Grant's lips as he thought about making
both father and son watch while he enjoyed himself with
Maggie. Egan's Maggie. The mother of his son.

He had no intention of killing his captives quickly or
painlessly. The joy would be in their suffering. The real
pleasure would come from listening to their pitiful cries for
mercy.

Even in his most vivid fantasies, revenge had never been
this incredibly perfect. He'd never dared hope that out there
somewhere Egan had loved a woman and fathered a child.

Grant laughed, the sound echoing in the stillness of his
bedchamber. *Good things come to those who wait,* he
thought.

He rose from the bed, naked and aroused.

After the first four miles, Maggie and Egan took a five-
minute break. Hiking up a mountainside took more stamina

than a fast-paced walk in the park, but Maggie had held her own. He was proud of her. A Southern lady through and through, with breeding, education and a keen intelligence, she impressed him even more now than she had fifteen years ago.

He had never fallen so hard, so fast, as he had for the twenty-three-year-old Maggie. She had represented the unobtainable. She was everything he'd ever wanted—and more. He'd had no right to take her, but when she'd come to him willingly, happily, offering him her heart and her body, he had been unable to refuse her. Not fifteen years ago. Not last night.

There had never been another woman—before or after Maggie—who had meant as much to him. No one else had been unforgettable. Only Maggie had remained a part of him, a memory he hadn't been able to erase. All those old feelings had resurfaced last night. That gut-wrenching hunger. That animalistic need to mate. That emotional yearning. He wanted her now, more than ever. And deserved her even less.

"Thirsty?" Egan asked.

"Yes," she replied.

He uncapped the canteen and they shared the tepid water. With weak smiles and looks of understanding exchanged, they resumed their journey. Three and a half miles later, Grant Cullen's towering rock and wood fortress appeared before them, like a giant monster emerging from the bowels of the earth.

Maggie skidded to a halt when they were within ten yards of the massive entrance gates. She grabbed Egan's hand. "I'm scared."

He squeezed her hand. "I know. So am I."

Hand-in-hand, they approached the gates. As if by magic, the nine-foot-high metal gates swung open and a six-man guard quickly surrounded them. The men wore tan uniforms, the insignia of the Ultimate Survivalists organization attached to their jacket sleeves and emblazoned just above the bill of the their caps: a crossed black rifle and a red sword, on a field of white.

A stocky young man, apparently the officer in charge, issued orders for the *guests* to be searched. Egan tensed at the thought of one of these militant idiots touching Maggie, but he held his tongue and his temper. When Maggie's gaze caught his, he nodded, signaling her not to protest.

First they were asked to remove their jackets, which the soldiers searched and then returned. The searches were thorough, but quick. And despite the flush that stained Maggie's cheeks, she appeared unaffected. With her head held high and her backbone stiff, she remained silent.

"The general is expecting you," the young officer said. "I'm Colonel Sherman. If you'll come this way, please."

"Where is my son?" Maggie demanded.

Without looking directly at Maggie, Colonel Sherman said, "I'll bring your son to you when the general requests his presence in the grand hall."

Egan gave Maggie a nod and the two of them fell into step with their captors. When they entered the compound, Egan noted the flurry of activity. He counted two and a half dozen soldiers preparing for battle. Expecting and thus preparing for an attack from the outside. Apparently Cullen had figured that Egan wouldn't come alone. But what Cullen hadn't counted on was a federal agent named Sawyer MacNamara.

Sherman led Maggie and Egan into a massive round room filled with benches. A large dais had been placed in the center, directly beneath a circular skylight. What was this place? Egan wondered. A meeting hall? A place of worship? An enormous, intricately carved throne sat in the middle of the podium. Of course, this was the hub of the fortress, the *grand hall* Sawyer had mentioned as the place where Cullen would bring Bent for the showdown.

Egan's stomach knotted as realization dawned. This was Cullen's throne room, where he held court. This was the place he had chosen to come face-to-face with his longtime enemy. Cullen would want an audience to watch while he brought Egan to his knees—figuratively and literally. That meant part of his little army would be summoned to the grand hall to act as witnesses. While the feds kept Cullen's troops busy with their frontal attack, the Dundee agents could concentrate on this area.

The thought of bowing and scraping to that bastard sickened Egan, but he would do whatever he had to do. He had to make sure everything was timed perfectly, even if it meant waiting and enduring some humiliation. Nothing could go wrong. Absolutely nothing. Bent's life depended upon precise action.

The man who had introduced himself as Colonel Sherman motioned to one of the front benches. "Sit here and wait."

"I want to know where Bent is! Where is my son and how is he?" Maggie glared viciously at the colonel.

"Your son is quite safe, Ms. Douglas," Sherman said. "He's unharmed."

"Where's Cullen?" Egan asked.

"I'm here, Cassidy." The voice came from the doorway.

Egan and Maggie whirled around just in time to see the general make his grand entrance. Wearing an ostentatious uniform, as gaudy as any movie star dictator, Grant Cullen marched into the arena. Flanked by an honor guard carrying rifles, the madman smiled fiendishly, as he saluted Egan.

Time had taken a toll on Cullen, but Egan suspected the evil within him had aged the man far more than the passing years. Although his hair was gray and his face heavily wrinkled, his body seemed to still be hard and thickly muscled.

"My old comrade, we meet again," Cullen said, then with a wave of his hand dismissed his guard. They fell away from him, but remained in two separate lines of three, awaiting his next command. He leaned over and whispered something to Colonel Sherman, who clicked his heels, saluted and left the room.

Boys, Egan thought. A bunch of boy soldiers. Not a one in the lot over twenty-five. Easily brainwashed youths, seeking a charismatic leader. Well, they'd found one in Cullen. But they had also signed their own death warrants by following a devil doomed to his own particular hell.

"We're here, as you requested," Egan said. "Maggie and I. Now, we want you to hold up your end of the bargain and release Bent."

"Ah, yes, Bentley Tyson Douglas...a fine young man. Reminds me a great deal of you, Cassidy. He's got your grit. You'd be proud of him. He pretty much told me to go to hell."

Maggie shoved her fist against her mouth in an effort to mask her frightened gasp. In his peripheral vision, Egan caught a glimpse of the terror in Maggie's eyes. Don't unravel now, he wanted to tell her. That's what Cullen wants. He will feed on our fear and our anger.

"No need to worry, Ms. Douglas," Cullen said, his smile widening. "I haven't harmed a hair on your son's head, despite the fact that he hasn't appreciated my hospitality. Bent has been under the watchful eye of my most valued soldier, Colonel Sherman."

"Where is Bent?" Maggie asked.

"I've sent for him," Cullen told her. "You'll see him shortly. Until then, please be seated. Both of you."

Egan took the suggestion as a cordial command. Grasping Maggie's arm, he pulled her down beside him on the front pew. "So, what now?"

"We wait." Cullen climbed the three steps up onto the dais and took his place on the majestic throne. "And while we wait, we can either talk over old times or we can discuss the present. Which do you prefer?"

"I prefer not to talk to you at all," Egan said. "I prefer that you allow Maggie and Bent to go free and that I stay here for the two of us to settle this between ourselves."

Cullen's boisterous laughter echoed off the walls. "So, you haven't lost your sense of humor. Not yet." His gaze settled on Maggie. His lips twisted into a vicious smirk. "But you will. You will. You didn't trust me to keep my word any more than I trusted you to keep yours."

"Are you saying that you aren't going to let Bent and Maggie go free?" Egan asked, knowing the answer only too well, but playing the game by Cullen's rules.

"And are you telling me that there isn't a group of agents on their way here, prepared to attack my fortress? Want to tell me when they're arriving? This morning? This afternoon?"

Maggie shuffled at his side. Without looking at her, he dropped his hand to the bench between them, palm open and down, in a *stay calm* gesture. Then he focused his attention on Cullen. "You said for us to come alone. With Bent's life at stake, would I lie to you?"

"Yeah, sure you would. And I told you that I'd let the boy and his mother go free, didn't I? Looks like we're both a couple of liars."

Marching through two double-wide doorways, uniformed soldiers began assembling. Egan scanned the room, counting bodies. Two dozen, give or take. Thirty-some-odd men in the outer courtyard preparing for an attack and half that number congregating for Cullen's upcoming stage show.

All in all, possibly fifty men. A small army, but an army all the same. Personally trained by Cullen, a shrewd professional. Soldiers equipped with up-to-date weapons. But from what the feds had found out about this operation, Egan's guess was that half the troops were green recruits, still being trained. And if he knew Cullen—and he did—the trained soldiers were the ones preparing for attack and the unseasoned ones were right here in the grand hall.

Good. That meant the Dundee squad might be outnumbered, but they would be dealing with amateurs. The odds in their favor just improved.

"Well, there's the young man of the hour." Cullen grinned as he held out his hand in a gesture to draw everyone's attention to the middle aisle.

"Bent!" Maggie came halfway to her feet.

Egan jerked her back down and gave her a disapproving frown. Tears gathered in the corners of her eyes as she twisted her head just enough to catch a glimpse, over Egan's shoulder, of her son.

Egan inclined his head slightly, in order to take his first look at Maggie's child. The boy was no longer a boy, but a young man. Tall, lean and handsome. A bit gangly in the way most fourteen-year-old boys are. Thick black hair, the color Egan's own hair had been before the gray set in. And dark gray eyes. Cassidy eyes. Like Egan's and Egan's father's. Looking at Bent was like looking into a mirror and seeing himself at that age. Except his son was better looking, having inherited a touch of glamour from Maggie that softened his features just a bit.

Bent walked down the aisle, head high, shoulders squared. He was probably scared out of his mind, but he didn't show it. *Never let them see you sweat, son!*

Egan's heart filled with pride at the sight of the child Maggie had given him. And he ached with a fear akin to none he'd ever known. He had already decided that he would gladly forfeit his life to save Bent's, and seeing his son only reinforced that resolve a thousand times over.

"Would you like to hug your son, Ms. Douglas?" Cullen asked. "And talk to him for a few minutes? Before we proceed with more important matters."

Maggie glanced at Egan, who nodded. "Yes," she said. "I'd very much like to hug my son."

Colonel Sherman walked Bent up the steps and onto the dais, halting him a good eight feet to Cullen's left.

Cullen motioned to Maggie. "Come up here."

Maggie stood on unsteady legs, trying to keep her composure and not allow Grant Cullen the satisfaction of seeing her fall apart. After taking a deep breath and saying a quick, silent prayer, she hurried up onto the dais. The moment she reached Bent, she wrapped her arms around him and hugged him fiercely.

She wanted to never let him go. If only she could pick him up and hold him, the way she'd done when he was a little boy. If only she could carry him out of this prison and flee with him to safety. This tall, proud young man was her baby. If anything happened to him, she wouldn't want to go on living.

"Are you all right?" she asked, her voice low.

"I'm fine."

"Some men are going to rescue you," Maggie whispered. "They're friends of your father's. When they arrive, go with them and do whatever they tell you to do."

Cullen snapped his fingers. "Enough! Say your goodbyes."

"Mama?" Bent looked to Maggie for an explanation.

"I love you," she said.

"I love you, too, Mama."

Colonel Sherman grabbed Bent's arm and hauled him

over to one of two poles that ran from the floor to the ceiling on each side of the dais. As if preparing Bent for a firing squad execution, Sherman draped Bent's hands behind the pole and secured them with rope. Then he wrapped a length of rope around the boy's chest and looped it together behind the post.

"What are you doing?" Maggie cried.

"Bring Ms. Douglas to me," Cullen ordered.

When Sherman grabbed her, she struggled at first, but when her gaze met Egan's, she stopped fighting and went with the young colonel. He shoved her down at Cullen's feet, then pulled a dog collar and leash from the pocket of his jacket. After attaching the collar to Maggie's neck, he handed the leash to Cullen.

Egan balled his hands into tight fists. Every protective instinct he possessed ordered him to attack. But now was not the time. Not yet. He glanced casually at his watch. Thirteen minutes. He had to keep Maggie and Bent alive for thirteen more minutes. And if he'd guessed correctly about Cullen's intentions, his old enemy had planned the next couple of hours to consist of only pregame preparations. Setting the stage for the big show.

But once the feds attacked, Cullen would immediately step things up and put the deadly game into high gear. He no doubt believed his army could hold off an attack, mainly due to the almost impenetrable location of his mountainside fort and due even more to his own illogical, cocky self-assurance. The man thought he was invincible. He had probably planned for endless hours of torture, perhaps even days, despite the fact that he was well aware of an imminent attack.

Cullen stood, jerked on Maggie's leash and yanked her to her feet. "Have you ever played Russian roulette, Ms. Douglas?"

"No." Maggie gulped the word, as emotion lodged in her throat.

She had promised Egan that she could handle this, that she could be strong and brave. That she wouldn't break. He had promised her that he would save Bent. She had to hold on to that promise. She had to believe that he could fulfill his pledge to save their child.

"Well, we're going to play a little game of it now," Cullen told her, then motioned for a young soldier, who rose out of the audience and came forward to do his master's bidding.

Cullen snapped his fingers and Sherman produced a revolver, which he handed to the young soldier. "This could all be over quickly, without any suffering. I'm willing to let fate be the judge of whether we end this now or we enjoy ourselves for a few more hours."

Maggie held her breath. What was this madman going to do? she wondered. *God, help us!*

"Hold the gun to your temple," Cullen ordered the soldier, who obeyed without question. "Now, pull the trigger."

Maggie gasped. The soldier did as he'd been told. A distinct click reverberated in the hushed stillness of the arena. Cullen snatched the weapon from the boy's hand, then patted him on the back. "Well done."

Cullen dragged Maggie with him as he headed toward Egan. He held the gun to Egan's temple, a wicked smile on his lips. Maggie trembled from head to toe. She closed her eyes and pleaded to God to intervene. *Another loud click.* Breathing a sigh of relief, she slumped her shoulders and said a quick prayer of thanks.

How much longer until the attack? a frightened voice within Maggie's mind demanded. Cullen's games had only just begun and already she was on the verge of hysteria.

The Dundee agents were supposed to already be inside the fortress and federal agents were supposed to be on their way here. What were they waiting for? *Help us, now!*

Cullen's laughter echoed inside Maggie's head. When he drew in the chain leash, bringing her closer and closer to him, she cringed. Holding the gun to her temple, he leaned over and kissed her cheek. Her instincts told her to scratch his eyes out, to kick and claw. But she did nothing. Her breathing grew ragged when she felt the cold steel of the gun barrel against her skin.

"I hope there isn't a bullet with your name on it, Maggie. I do have such delicious plans for you."

"Wait!" Egan yelled.

Cullen's lazy glance in Egan's direction chilled Maggie to the bone.

"Wait for what?" Cullen asked.

"I'll take Maggie's turn," Egan said.

"Do you hear that?" Cullen rubbed the tip of the gun barrel around in circles on Maggie's temple. "Isn't that gallant? What do you say, Maggie, do you want Egan to take your turn?"

"No, I—" Maggie said.

"Yes, dammit, yes!" Egan said.

"Well, we have quite a quandary, don't we?" Cullen's self-satisfied smile etched his face with deep laugh lines. He snapped his fingers. "I have the perfect solution. We'll let Bent take his mother's turn."

"No!" Maggie and Egan screamed in unison.

Egan checked his watch. Five minutes. Five freaking minutes! The moment the attack began, Cullen would assume he had everything under control. He'd probably be in no hurry to dismiss his audience, but if he allowed his military training to rule his actions, he'd order these soldiers to join their comrades on the front line. But whether the Dundee squad had to face a handful of Cullen's men or an even two dozen, they knew what had to be done.

Egan had to play for time. And he had to get Maggie away from Cullen before the Dundee squad made their move. Once Cullen realized what was happening, he'd kill Maggie instantly and go for Bent next.

"Such devoted parents," Cullen said snidely. "Aren't you a lucky boy."

Cullen hauled Maggie with him across the dais to where Bent stood shackled to the pole. When he laid the gun against Bent's cheek, Maggie keened loudly. Cullen smiled at her. "*Tsk-tsk.* Mustn't get so upset. After all the odds are in his favor. There really is only one bullet in this gun."

"I'll take my turn," Maggie pleaded. "And I'll take Bent's turn. Please let me take my son's turn!"

"You're too eager," Cullen told her. "Besides, using the boy will make this so much more painful for Cassidy. He'll not only die a thousand deaths waiting for the sound of the gun to fire, but he'll be in agony watching you suffer."

"You're a monster!" Maggie lunged at Cullen, knocking him off balance enough so that he lost his tight grip on the revolver.

Colonel Sherman jumped to the rescue, snatching the gun off the floor the minute it landed. Cullen jerked Maggie's leash, pulling her close, then pressed his nose against hers. "I like spirit in a woman. It makes the conquest all the sweeter."

"Leave my mother alone!" Bent yelled.

"Ah, the protective son heard from." Cullen handed Maggie's leash to Sherman and took the gun from him. "Walk Maggie over to stand by her lover. They can watch together."

The young colonel dragged Maggie off the dais so

quickly that she almost lost her footing, but she somehow managed to remain on her feet. The moment Sherman shoved her up against Egan, she gritted her teeth and whispered to Egan, "Do something!"

Egan checked his watch. One minute and counting.

"Hang on, Maggie. Hang on," he said, his voice a low rumble.

Cullen held the revolver to Bent's temple. "Any last words?"

"Yeah," Bent said. "Go to hell!"

My baby. My baby. Oh, Bent! The silent cries shrieked from Maggie's heart.

A barrage of artillery bombarded the fortress. A loud explosion shook the very foundation of Cullen's hideaway. Egan suspected that Cullen's private helicopter had just gone up in smoke. The boy soldiers in the audience mumbled loudly as they jumped to their feet. Egan grasped one of Maggie's trembling hands.

Cullen eased the gun away from Bent's head and smiled at Egan.

"By the time they blast their way into here, you'll all be dead and I'll be long gone."

"You seem awfully sure," Egan shouted over the roar of nearby artillery fire.

"I am," Cullen said, then turned to Colonel Sherman. "Take all but half a dozen men. They'll be needed out there—" Cullen inclined his head toward the doorway. "Report back to me when you've assessed the situation."

"Yes, sir!"

Sherman followed orders, leaving behind six soldiers, who spread out around the room, their rifles ready.

"If Cassidy makes a move, shoot him," Cullen said, then motioned to Maggie. "Come here."

Maggie didn't budge.

"You can buy some time for yourself, as well as your son and Egan, if you cooperate," he told her. "I had hoped we'd have more time, but I won't need more than a few minutes to—"

"Don't you touch her!" Bent cried. "Don't you dare—"

"Shut up!" Cullen slapped Bent with the back of his hand.

Maggie moaned when she saw the trickle of blood oozing from Bent's bursted lip.

Cullen stomped off the dais, heading straight toward Maggie. She stood frozen to the spot, waiting, counting the seconds. Before he was halfway to her, the doors flew open and five black-clad commandos stormed the inner sanctum. Taken off guard, the boy soldiers didn't react immediately. Cullen yelled for them to fire.

Egan shoved Maggie to the floor and quickly covered her body with his as bullets whizzed overhead.

"Kill the boy!" Cullen shouted.

"No!" Maggie screamed.

Chapter 8

Egan held Maggie down, knowing that if he let her go, she would run headlong into the middle of the gunfire between Cullen's soldiers and the Dundee squad. Her maternal instincts had shifted into overdrive. Her only thoughts were of protecting her child. But her panic could get her killed and interfere with Bent's rescue. Egan had no choice but to subdue her. She struggled to free herself, crying, begging him to help Bent before it was too late.

"Joe and Hunter will take care of Bent," he told her, praying he could get through to her in her panicked state of mind. "He's their first priority." How did he make her understand that Bent's best chance of survival rested in the hands of the two Dundee agents and that neither he nor she could get to Bent in time?

Maggie trembled, shudders racking her body. Egan grabbed her and rolled them under the nearest bench. Hot metal zoomed all around them as the sound of repetitive shooting became deafening. After endless moments of intense warfare, a deadly silence prevailed.

"Cassidy!" a loud female voice shouted.

"Stay put," Egan told Maggie, then scooted out from under the bench just enough to see Ellen Denby scanning the room, while Wolfe and Jack Parker kept her covered. Egan lifted his arm and signaled to Ellen.

The moment Ellen noted his location, she held out a handgun and with effortless ease tossed the Glock to Egan. He caught the weapon in midair. After quickly checking the magazine, he chambered a round.

"We've got Bent!" Joe Ornelas shouted.

"Get him out of here!" Ellen ordered.

Egan caught a glimpse of Bent, flanked by Joe Ornelas and Hunter Whitelaw, as they took him out of immediate harm's way.

Maggie grasped Egan's shirtfront. "Bent's safe?"

Maggie's teardrops hit his hand—the hand that held the 9-mm. "Yeah, honey, Bent's safe." He didn't bother qualifying his statement, explaining that the squad had to get Bent out of the fortress before he would be truly safe. Or that the only way to obtain Bent's safety one hundred percent now and in the future was to eliminate Cullen permanently.

"Room's cleared," Ellen said. "Let's get moving while we can."

"We have to get out of here," Egan told Maggie. "I'm going to remove this damn dog collar from your neck—" he unsnapped the catch "—and then we're going to ease out from underneath this bench and make a run for the doors on the right. Stay with me. Understand?"

"Yes," she managed to reply, her voice shaky as Egan removed the collar and tossed it aside.

When Egan and Maggie reached the hallway, Ellen

Denby, an MP5 in her hands, motioned for them to wait. Three Survivalists charged up the hallway, shooting repeatedly, as if they thought firepower alone could protect them. Bullets splintered wood and sent shards of concrete flying. Overconfident as only the young and inexperienced could be, they walked right into the ambush. The threesome wouldn't know what hit them, Egan thought.

From their vantage points on either side of the curved corridor, Parker aimed his AK-47 and Wolfe did the same. The blasts reverberated down the hallway as they took out all three of Cullen's soldiers. Parker waved an all clear. Ellen nodded to Egan, who clutched Maggie's arm and shoved her into motion. Guiding her around the dead bodies, Egan urged Maggie forward, as Ellen covered them from the rear.

While they hurried down the corridor, ever mindful of the unknown waiting around each turn, Egan felt proud of Maggie. Not only was she keeping pace with them, but once she'd known Bent was safe, she had kept her composure during the maelstrom of battle. Maggie didn't possess Ellen's training, expertise or hard-ass attitude, but in her own way she was every bit as brave and strong.

"Where's Cullen?" Egan asked.

"Two seconds after we showed up and he realized he couldn't shoot at Bent without risking his own life, he made a hasty exit out a back entrance of the throne room," Ellen said.

"Think he'll try the escape tunnel?" Parker asked.

"Don't think so." Egan's breathing remained even as he raced along the hallway. "My bet is he hasn't figured out exactly what happened. Until he does, he'll keep fighting."

Occasionally checking the rear for any sign of the enemy, Ellen kept pace with the others. Suddenly Wolfe stopped and dropped. As he did, a bullet zinged over him, piercing the wall at the exact level his head had been a millisecond before. Just as the lone shooter came into view, Wolfe took him out with one fatal head shot.

"Time's a-wasting, boys and girls," Parker said, his Texas accent decidedly distinctive at the moment. "Once Joe and Hunter have Bent aboard the chopper, O'Brien will wait exactly ten minutes—if he can—and then they're gone and so is our transportation out of Cullen's private little hell."

"We'll make it," Ellen said. "We're nearly to the stairs. Too bad we can't take a chance on the elevator, but we don't dare risk getting caught with nowhere to run."

Within minutes, the five of them were in the stairwell headed to the subterranean level. But they had two flights to descend before reaching their goal. Their stomping boots clanged the metal steps as they scurried ever downward. The stairwell remained clear all the way to the third level. Apparently Cullen hadn't yet figured out how the Dundee squad had gained access to his fortress, Egan thought. But it was only a matter of time before he put two and two together and realized he had a traitor in his midst—someone who had allowed the intruders entrance through the secret tunnel.

Every good commando knew that you had to get in, do your job and get the hell out before the enemy knew what had hit them. Egan grunted. Maybe, just maybe they were going to make it out alive—all of them.

When they reached the vault, deep within the mountain, Parker and Wolfe took the lead, followed by Egan and Maggie. Ellen brought up the rear. Things are going too good, Egan decided. There hadn't been a hitch in the operation. Bent was probably already aboard the chopper and within minutes they would be joining him. The feds were keeping Cullen's troops busy. But where exactly was Cullen? Egan's gut instincts told him that that wily bastard would have a few tricks up his sleeve, even after a surprise attack. But what sort of tricks? And when would he strike?

As they emerged from the tunnel, the bright daylight momentarily blinded them, but within seconds Egan's eyesight returned. In the distance he could hear the roar of the chopper's motor and as he scanned the area, he noted the whirlwind effect blowing through the trees and shrubs. They congregated just outside the tunnel—Egan, Maggie, Wolfe, Parker and Ellen.

"What are we waiting for?" Parker asked. "Let's get the hell out of here."

"Take Maggie with you," Egan told Ellen.

Maggie balked. "What do you mean—"

"I have to find Cullen," Egan said. "Go with Ellen."

"You can't stay here!" Maggie grasped Egan's shirt-front. "I'm not leaving you here. You're coming with us!"

Just as Egan started to shove Maggie away, Wolfe let out an earsplitting warrior's yell, warning them of danger. A good twenty-five feet above them, perched on an overhang, Winn Sherman manned a machine gun. Grant Cullen stood at his side.

No time to think, only to react. Egan dragged Maggie with him as he headed for the closest cover behind a massive boulder near the heavily wooded area to the south. Ellen and Parker dropped and rolled toward Wolfe, who had already made a mad dash and a leap into a gully at the edge of a pathway leading to the chopper. Wolfe, Parker and Denby aimed their weapons.

Rapid machine-gun fire peppered the ground, snapped off spindly tree limbs and chipped off chunks from the boulder. Egan surveyed the situation quickly and realized he and Maggie were cut off from escape, trapped between the wilderness and the fortress.

The three Dundee agents returned fire, but were at a great disadvantage. Egan realized that the smartest thing for them to do was get to the chopper as fast as possible. He had wanted Maggie to go with them, but it didn't look as if that was possible now. After checking the time, Egan realized that O'Brien would be taking off in two minutes, with or without the others.

Get your men aboard that chopper, Denby! Egan's mind issued the order. Ellen would take care of things on her end, and it would be up to Egan to handle things here. He knew that he and Maggie had only one chance to survive.

While the machine gun riddled the boulder, Egan grasped Maggie's chin. She stared at him, a look of sheer terror in her eyes. "We can't make it to the chopper," he told her. "And I won't risk your life letting you stay here until I can eliminate Cullen."

"You were going to stay here and kill him, weren't you, even if it meant dying yourself?"

"Plans have changed," he said. "Eliminating Cullen will have to wait. Right now, getting you to safety is far more important."

The whine of the chopper's engine reached an earsplitting roar as the motors revved. The aircraft lifted, hovering above them. A force of strong air whipped over the towering trees and the resonance of the helicopter's rotating blades hummed noisily. A steady stream of gunfire blasted from the machine gun nest, preventing the chopper from getting anywhere near Egan and Maggie. They were, for all intents and purposes, cut off from any hope of a rescue.

Within minutes the chopper disappeared over the mountain ridge. Egan glanced up at the overhang where Sherman had manned the machine gun. Sunlight glinted off the powerful weapon, but no shooter was in sight. That probably meant Sherman and Cullen had realized Egan and Maggie

hadn't escaped with the squad and were preparing to searc
for them.

"We have to get moving," Egan told Maggie. "There"
a good chance they'll be following us, so we're going t
have to move fast and keep going as long as possible."

She nodded, her head bobbing repeatedly, fear widenin
her eyes. They crawled away from the boulder and into th
nearby brush, then Egan jerked her up behind a stand o
tall ponderosa pines. He checked the area all around then
North. South. East. And west.

"We can't go down the mountain the way we came in
so there's no hope of getting to our supplies. Cullen know
the route we took coming here," Egan explained. "And
don't think there's a chance we could get through to th
feds, without getting caught in the cross fire and this battl
could go on until nightfall. Maybe longer. Cullen will com
after us. Our only choice is to find our way back to civi
lization and contact Ellen." Gazing into Maggie's eyes h
saw weariness, uncertainty and understanding. And a fea
she could not hide. "I won't lie to you. It'll be rough going
We don't have a compass or supplies of any kind, including
food and water. If we don't find a town before night, we'l
have no shelter."

"What other choice do we have?" she asked.

"The only other choices we have are to risk getting
gunned down by either Cullen's soldiers or being acciden
tally shot by the feds if we cross over into the war zone.'
Egan took a deep breath. "Or we can give ourselves t
Cullen."

Maggie shook her head. "Tell me how Cullen and Sher
man got away, if the feds have the fortress surrounded?"

"Undoubtedly he had more than one escape hatch."

"He left his men there to fight and die, didn't he?"

"Yeah. That's exactly what he did. I just hope those poo

stupid boys don't fight to the death. While they're giving their lives for the Ultimate Survivalists cause, their glorious leader will be tracking you and me.''

"He and Sherman will have rifles, maybe even submachine guns, won't they?"

"I have this pistol." He showed her the Glock. "I've got seventeen rounds and I don't intend to waste one shot. Now, come on. Let's get going. Our goal is to stay at least one step ahead of them and if we're lucky, we'll lose them."

Egan knew the odds, but he was willing to accept those fifty-fifty odds and bet he and Maggie could come out of this the winners. Just the fact that Bent was safe put them ahead in the game already.

He might not know this country as well as Cullen did, but he had survived in the wilderness more than once and he'd put his skills up against Cullen's any day of the week. He had to make sure to cover his tracks, to take the unexpected path, to do the illogical. Cullen was the type of man who would become easily frustrated if confused. And Egan meant to confuse the hell out of the son of a bitch!

"Why did you go off and leave them?" Bent Douglas demanded in a tone that reminded Ellen of Egan Cassidy's ferocious growl. "How could you have—"

Hunter Whitelaw laid his bear-paw of a hand on Bent's shoulder. "There's no way they could have made it to the chopper from where they were. Not without being shot down by that machine gun. We couldn't get to them and they couldn't get to us."

"Our orders were to take you away and keep you safe, no matter what else went down," Ellen said.

"Whose orders?" Bent asked.

"Your father's," Ellen replied.

Bent searched Ellen's face. "Who are you people and what does Egan Cassidy have to do with what happened to me? That man, that General Cullen, knew my father, didn't he? He was using me as bait to bring Egan Cassidy to him."

"Cassidy is a former mercenary," Ellen said. "He worked freelance for the CIA several years before he retired. A couple of years ago, he came to work for us. The Dundee Private Security and Investigation Agency in Atlanta. There's been bad blood between Grant Cullen and your father for a long time, but I'll let Egan explain the details to you."

"Then you believe he and my mother will be all right?"

Hunter squeezed Bent's shoulder. Ellen wished she could tell the boy what he wanted to hear and for just a moment she considered lying to him. But she owed Egan's son the truth, even if she did choose to put a positive spin on it.

"I believe that if any man can find a way out of that situation and bring your mother back to you, then Egan Cassidy can."

"Isn't there anything you can do?" Bent asked. "Can't you go back and help them?"

"There's no way to know for sure where they went," Ellen said. "That's a big mountain down there."

"Then what are you going to do?" Bent glared at Ellen.

"I'm going to take you to Flagstaff and wait there for Egan to contact us. Ornelas and Whitelaw—" she nodded first toward one and then toward the other "—are going to be your personal bodyguards."

"Why do I need bodyguards if the man who kidnapped me is still back at the fort?"

"Because Cullen heads up a group called the Ultimate Survivalists and we have no idea how far-reaching this group is or if Cullen has issued orders to harm you." Ellen hated being brutally honest, but these circumstances called for nothing less. Bent wasn't a child. He was a young man of fourteen. He would be safer armed with the knowledge that his life might still be in danger.

What a freaking mess to be in, Ellen thought. If Cassidy didn't make it through, if he and Maggie didn't survive, then the Dundee agents would have an orphan on their hands. And if Cassidy didn't take care of Cullen, Bent's life would remain in danger. There was only one solution to this problem.

Grant Cullen had to die. And Egan Cassidy had to live.

Winn Sherman loaded a backpack onto the young soldier, then draped a rifle over his shoulder. "We're ready, sir."

"The men have their orders," Cullen said. "They'll hold the fort as long as possible to give us time to escape and then they'll surrender."

"We'd better get going," Sherman suggested. "Cassidy and the woman already have an hour's head start."

"Not to worry." Cullen grinned as he petted the submachine gun he held, then knelt to caress MacArthur and Patton. "Where can they go except down the mountain? If we don't catch them on the way down, we'll catch them at the bottom. This game isn't over until I win. And that can't happen until Cassidy, his son and his woman are all dead."

Maggie and Egan had been hiking at a hard, steady pace for over three and a half hours, a grueling journey to put as much distance as possible between them and their pursuers. Egan had used every method he knew to throw their searchers off track, including choosing a destination on the far side of the mountain that would prolong their descent. He hoped Cullen would assume he would choose the quickest and easiest way.

Egan had rushed Maggie, forcing her into an uncomfortable pace, wanting them to reach water for two reasons. First, they were both hot, tired and thirsty. One of the greatest dangers to survival was dehydration. And second, despite his best efforts, it was possible that Cullen might pick up their trail. But if they could follow a streambed for several miles, they could improve their odds of escaping completely.

"Listen!" Egan shouted. "Do you hear it?"

"A waterfall?" Maggie asked.

"And where there's a waterfall in these mountains, there's usually a streambed. Come on. Follow me."

Maggie's lungs burned, her calf muscles quivered and her back ached. She wanted nothing more than to lie down and rest. And never get up again. But instead, she tagged after Egan like an obedient puppy. Doing her best to keep up, she made her way behind Egan through a narrow passage that led them down into a steep gorge. Towering walls of jagged rock closed in around them, waiting to rip and tear their clothes and skin. Gravel slipped beneath their feet, often showering in a rockslide to the bottom of the gorge.

When Egan reached level ground, he grasped Maggie's hand and led her into a box canyon, deep within the mountain. Sheer walls of stone rose up a good two hundred feet. Three-fourths in the middle of the granite wall, a spray of pummeling water spouted forth and jetted in a twelve-foot fall to the pond, which created a meandering stream that disappeared around the bend.

"Just a little farther and we can take a longer rest," Egan told her. "But we can stop here for a few minutes."

Maggie dropped to her knees, not caring that the rocky terrain of the streambed ate into her jeans. Cupping her hands, she swooped up cool, crystal-clear water and brought it to her lips. Nothing had ever tasted as sweet. After drinking several handfuls, she lifted another and splashed the water in her face.

Egan drank his fill from the stream, then doused his head into the creek. Rising up onto his feet, he waited for Maggie to stand, and when she didn't, he grabbed her arm and jerked her up beside him.

"I think we're safe from Cullen. At least temporarily. He'll have a damn hard time finding us." Egan swiped flyaway strands of Maggie's hair from her face. A warm flush brightened her cheeks a shade darker than the sunburn on her nose and forehead. "You've got the beginning of a sunburn." He tapped the tip of her nose.

"It's this darn peaches-and-cream complexion of mine," she said, a faint smile curving the corners of her mouth.

"Sorry we don't have anything you can use to protect that beautiful skin of yours." He caressed her cheek. "But I'm afraid we have more immediate and essential problems to concern us."

"I assume you mean other than escaping from Cullen."

"Shelter," he told her. "Come night, we'll need a safe place to sleep."

"What about food?"

"If necessary, we could live for weeks without food, but only days without water."

"Anything else I should worry about?" she asked.

"Let me do the worrying for both of us." When she frowned, her forehead wrinkling and her eyes narrowing into a don't-try-to-placate-me glare, Egan gave her a gentle shove. "Let's get moving. We'll rest farther upstream. I promise."

Knowing that her child was safe, Maggie could face anything that came her way. And she had no doubts that she was in good hands with Egan. Nodding agreement, her frown turned into a halfhearted smile.

"That's my Maggie."

She had no idea where they were. All she knew was that they hadn't reached civilization and hadn't seen any sign of human life all day. Egan had backtracked and zigzagged and by his own admission, taken them miles out of their way, all in an effort to throw Cullen off track. Once Egan had felt reasonably certain they had circumvented Cullen's search, they took frequent rest stops, for which Maggie was eternally grateful.

The sun sank low on the western horizon, melting into a rotund crescent pool of golden orange. The terrain spread across the rocky ground to a dense stand of pine and spruce trees. A lichen that Egan had told her was called "Old Man's Beard" dangled from the branches of many of the spruce trees. Farther along the mountainside, white aspens grew in profusion and New Mexican locust flowers hovered around their trunks.

Night was fast approaching and they had yet to find shelter. The last rays of sunlight shot across the horizon, creating a red and purple hued display in the sky. The temperature had already begun to drop. Maggie shivered.

"Even when we stop for the night, we can't risk a fire," Egan said. "I'm sorry."

"What are we going to do, huddle under a tree?"

"Maybe. But I keep hoping we'll run across a cave."

"Yeah, sure." Maggie's stomach growled. "And while you're hoping, hope for a bowl of chili and some corn bread."

"What's the matter, didn't you like the nuts and berries I found for us?" he asked teasingly.

"I know we won't starve without food for quite some

time, but subsisting on sour berries and bitter nuts that even a squirrel wouldn't touch could definitely affect my normally sunny disposition.''

''Then tomorrow I'll see if I can't find you more edible fare.''

''How about bacon and eggs?'' Maggie sighed. ''I suppose I should be more concerned about where we're spending the night than about what we'll have for breakfast.''

Perhaps she should consider it odd that they could joke at a time like this, but somehow, with Egan and her, the jovial comradery seemed perfectly natural. After all, not only was their son safe with the Dundee agents, but they themselves had escaped death more than once today. Despite the threat of Cullen's pursuit, she felt lucky. Lucky to be alive and lucky to be with Egan. She knew, in her heart, that if anyone could get them to safety, he could.

But once Egan reunited her with Bent, what would happen then? an inner voice asked. But she knew the answer. He would hunt down Cullen, face his worst enemy and destroy him. Or be destroyed!

''I think I've found an economy suite for us.'' Egan clutched Maggie's shoulders and maneuvered her around to stand in front of him. ''Take a look. It doesn't provide the security and total privacy of a cave, but it allows us a great view of the stars.''

At the foot of a rocky embankment littered with brush and wildflowers, Maggie spotted Egan's discovery—an odd-shaped boulder, with an overhanging lip curved like the letter *C*. It wasn't a cave, she thought, but it was the next best thing.

''I'm sorry that I haven't been able to find a better place for us to spend the night, but the overhang will provide a modicum of shelter and the jagged cliff wall surrounding it will add to the feel of privacy.''

"Looks like Motel Heaven to me." Maggie offered him a weary, but appreciative smile. "How do we get down there?"

"We climb down," he said.

"I was afraid that's what you'd say."

"Not wimping out on me at this late stage are you, Maggie mine?"

"You lead, I'll follow," she repeated the words that had now become a litany.

"Just what I wanted to hear." Egan flashed her a brilliant smile. "A woman who knows how to take orders."

"We'll head back to Minerva," Cullen said. "There's not much daylight left, so call and have someone meet us before dark."

"Yes, sir," Colonel Sherman said.

Winn Sherman instantly obeyed the general. He made a quick phone call, while young Lieutenant Shatz handed Cullen a canteen of water. Cullen drank his fill, then motioned to Shatz. The lieutenant removed a bowl from his backpack and filled it with water from his own canteen. Cullen led his rottweilers to the tepid liquid and then handed their reins to Shatz.

"Where the hell is he?" Cullen fumed. "He's led us on a merry chase, but if Cassidy thinks he's outsmarted me, he'd better think again. He may have gotten away this time. But our organization has eyes and ears everywhere in this part of the state. Once he shows up, we'll take care of him." Cullen stroked the submachine gun in his hand.

Winn would follow General Cullen to hell and back for the cause. But tracking down Egan Cassidy and Maggie Douglas had nothing to do with the Ultimate Survivalists. This was a personal vendetta in which the general had involved his soldiers. Winn couldn't stop thinking about the men back at the fort. All those who had died and all those who would be arrested. A bunch of fine young men—boys he had helped train. But he didn't dare question Grant Cullen's authority.

The general had promised that once Cassidy and his woman were eliminated, he would regroup and recruit new soldiers. The cause would rise from the ashes more powerful and more glorious than ever.

That's all that mattered to Winn. The Ultimate Survivalists. So when the time came, he would be at his master's side, to hunt down and kill Egan Cassidy.

Chapter 9

The oddly shaped boulder curved over them like a canopy, giving them some protection from the elements. Even though the breeze that rustled through the treetops didn't touch them, the falling temperature chilled them. Egan finished the mattress of branches, moss and leaves he had built, row after row, to cover the cold ground.

"Lie down," he told Maggie. "And turn toward the boulder."

With exhaustion claiming her body and mind, Maggie gladly complied with his command. Although the cushion beneath her lacked the comfort of her bed at home, Maggie's weary body appreciated the luxury of simply lying down and relaxing. The aromatic evergreen boughs filled the night air with their fresh, woodsy scent.

Egan lifted the small branches he had stripped from nearby spruce trees and dragged them with him as he eased down beside Maggie, his chest to her back. He removed the pistol he'd worn secured by his belt and set it within his reach. Once in place, their bodies lying spoon fashion, he rearranged the branches, covering Maggie and himself from ankles to shoulders as he completed their survival bed.

"Is your back exposed?" Maggie asked. "Are you cold?"

"I'm fine, honey. How about you?"

"I never thought a bed of sticks and leaves would feel so heavenly. Or smell so good." Her soft sigh transformed into a deep yawn. "I don't think there's a muscle in my body that isn't aching. Even my hair aches."

He nuzzled her hair, then kissed her head. "Your hair smells like sunshine."

A tiny giggle hung in her throat. "I can't decide if that was a sweet thing for you to say or just downright silly."

"I'd prefer for you to think it was romantic."

"It was," she told him. "But then you always were a romantic. Always said just the right words, always did just the right thing. Inside that warrior's body, you have the heart and soul of a poet."

Egan chuckled. "You think so, do you?"

"I know so."

A languid silence, a soul-felt weariness equal to the debility of their bodies, shrouded them. Long-ago memories invaded their thoughts. A week out of time, when they had been lovers. Tender words spoken in the quiet moments after lovemaking. Earthy, erotic phrases whispered in the heat of passion. Gentle strokes. Flesh against flesh. A joining of hearts and bodies. And souls.

A child, created in those sweet, unforgettable moments when nothing and no one had existed except the two of them.

Egan splayed his hand across her belly. "I wish I could have been with you when you were carrying Bent."

Maggie placed her hand over his. "I wanted you there with me. I needed you." She shuddered ever so slightly.

"Can you ever forgive me for what I did? And for putting you and Bent at risk? I never intended to hurt you. I would rather have died than to have harmed you in any way."

She snuggled against him, loving the feel of his big body draped around her, warming her, protecting her. "Our romance...our love affair was as much my doing as yours."

"But you weren't the one harboring deadly secrets," he said. "I was the one who had no right to become emotionally involved, to chance creating a child. I knew I couldn't fall in love and marry and have children. Cullen was always breathing down my neck. Just waiting for the opportunity to use a woman—or a child—against me."

"Oh, Egan." Maggie gulped down the tears that threatened her. "How terribly unfair life has been to you. And all because you exposed that monster for what he was...for what he still is."

"Don't think about Cullen." Egan lifted his head enough so that he could kiss her cheek. Her jaw. The spot below her ear. "I'll make sure he's never a threat to you or Bent again."

Maggie understood what Egan was telling her, that he would have to face his enemy and destroy him. The gentle side of Maggie's nature abhorred the thought of Egan killing another human being. But the protective, maternal instincts that were equally a part of her nature wanted Grant Cullen dead.

"Do you think someone will explain the situation to Bent?" Maggie asked. "He must be awfully confused. I hope—" her voice cracked with emotion. "I know he's fourteen, but he's still just a little boy in so many ways."

"Ellen will give him an explanation," Egan said. "Probably the condensed version, but enough so that he won't wonder why Cullen kidnapped him. And she'll assure him that I'll get you safely back to him.'' Egan caressed Maggie's belly, his hand moving in wide circles from waist to thighs. ''Tell me about my son. Please.''

Maggie breathed deeply, then exhaled on a long, slow sigh. ''You saw him today. Don't you think he resembles you a great deal?''

''He's my spitting image,'' Egan agreed. ''Except he's prettier than I ever was. Got that from you. That natural glamour.''

''He inherited your adventurous streak. Sometimes his fearlessness scares me to death. You know what a cautious person I am.'' Except when it came to loving Egan, she thought. Then she was totally reckless and took enormous risks. In the past. But what about now? She had given him her body, freely, lovingly, last night. But could she truly take a life-altering chance and give her heart to this man? Was he capable of living a normal life? Without danger and excitement? Without adventure and risk?

''He's a good kid, though, isn't he?'' Egan asked.

''Oh, yes. Bent is a really good kid. He's kind and considerate and loving. And he's always been my little man.'' Tears gathered in Maggie's eyes. ''I suppose he somehow felt that he had to take care of me because his father wasn't... Even when I was married to Gil, Bent looked out for me. If Gil and I ever argued, Bent was always ready to come to my defense.''

''If it hadn't been for me...if I hadn't shown up in your life, you'd have married Gil and lived happily ever after.'' Egan clutched Maggie to him, a purely possessive gesture. ''And Bent would have been his son, not mine. I really screwed things up for you, didn't I?''

Maggie wriggled around, reversing her position and

shedding several shielding branches in the process, until she lay facing Egan. The glimmering moonlight cast shadows across their bodies and allowed her to see the dark silhouette of Egan's face. She burrowed her head against the side of his neck and wrapped her arm around his waist.

"I don't know how my life would have turned out if you'd never been a part of it," she said, her soft voice laced with emotion. "But no one, least of all Gil, could have given me a son half as wonderful as Bent."

"Ah, Maggie. Sweet Maggie mine."

His lips sought and found hers in the darkness. Tender passion.

A soothing balm to Egan's wounded soul. An unspoken confession from Maggie's heart. When the kiss ended, they held each other, seeking warmth and comfort.

"Bent was a big baby. Nine pounds and ten ounces. And twenty-two inches long," Maggie said. "And man did he have an appetite." She laughed. "He still has a ravenous appetite. I can't fill him up. We can finish dinner and within two hours, he's back in the kitchen fixing himself a couple of sandwiches and getting another helping of dessert."

"He's a big boy. Close to six feet. Right?"

"Right. And he's healthy and intelligent and good at sports. Baseball and softball are his favorites. You should see his collection of baseball cards. If we traded them in, we could afford to send him to college from the proceeds."

"What's he interested in doing with his life? I mean, when he finishes high school?"

"Well, his future plans change on a fairly regular basis. One month his plans are to get a baseball scholarship and eventually play in the major leagues. Then another month, he talks about being a psychiatrist and helping people like his uncle Bentley. Several times he's mentioned he might like a military career, but when he sees that his talking about being a professional soldier upsets me, he changes the subject.''

"When this is all over...when Cullen is no longer a threat—'' Egan paused. His voice lowered and softened. ''I know I don't deserve it, but I'd very much like the opportunity to get to know my son, to be a part of his life.''

Maggie's heartbeat accelerated. Did she want Egan in her life on a permanent basis? Could they build a relationship on passion? Or on their shared parenthood? Egan was asking to be a part of Bent's life, not a part of hers, she reminded herself. But didn't the one include the other?

"I won't try to keep you and Bent apart,'' she said. "Now that you are aware of his existence, whatever relationship you form with Bent will be up to you and him.''

"Does he hate me? If you've told him that I deserted you when you were pregnant, then he must—''

"He doesn't hate you. But he doesn't know you.'' Maggie reverted to her original position, turning her back on Egan. "You'll have to earn his trust and his friendship.''

"You don't have any objections?''

"Why should I? You *are* his father.''

Egan laid his hand over Maggie's waist and pulled her body closer until they were once again nestled snugly together. "Thank you,'' he whispered.

Swirling mists surrounded Maggie, like mountaintop fog, thick and damp and grayish white. Egan was with her, his big, hard body hovering over her, his lips seeking, his sex probing. The ecstasy of their joining splintered through her body, sending waves of pleasure into every fiber of her being.

Suddenly Egan was gone and she was alone. So alone. Her hand settled over her swollen belly. No, not alone. Egan had left her with his child. The man she loved was

*lost to her forever, but she had his baby, growing inside
her. Safe. Secure.*

*And then Bent lay in his mother's arm, tiny and sweet-
smelling, as only infants can be. She held him to her breast
and his eager little mouth latched on greedily. If only Egan
were here. If only he could see his son. Egan! her heart
cried. Please, come back.*

*From out of nowhere Grant Cullen appeared and
wrenched Bent from Maggie's arms. He kicked her aside
when she tried to fight him. He held Bent by the back of
his little cotton pajamas and dangled him over the edge of
a fiery precipice. She begged and pleaded and bargained
with the inhuman devil, but all he did was laugh at her.
Shrill, maniacal screeches.*

*Maggie tried to move, tried to reach out for Bent, but
she found herself bound and gagged, rendered helpless to
defend her baby.*

Egan! Help us, Egan! Help us!

*But Egan was not there. He wasn't going to come to their
aid. He wasn't going to save Bent.*

*Cullen released his hold on Bent and his round, little
body began a headlong fall into the volcanic depths.*

No! Maggie screamed. Egan!

She woke with a start, Egan hovering over her, shaking
her gently. She stared up at his dark silhouette and for one
brief moment was lost between the nightmare and reality.

"Maggie, honey, what's wrong? You were screaming
and saying my name."

She sat up and scooted away from him, then gulped
down air as she tried to take control of her wild thoughts
and frazzled nerves. "Dream," she said. "No, not a dream.
A nightmare. Bent was…Bent was a baby and Cullen took
him from me and—"

Egan laid two fingers over Maggie's lips, silencing her.

''It's all over. Bent is safe. Cullen will never get near him again.''

''Oh, Egan, I kept calling for you. I needed you. We needed you and you weren't there. You didn't help us. Bent…Bent—'' Maggie sucked in quick, harsh breaths. ''Cullen threw Bent into a fiery hole. My baby. My baby! And you weren't there. Where were you, Egan? Why didn't you help us?''

Shedding the blanket of branches, Egan reached out for Maggie. She fought him as he jerked her into his arms, but he held her, allowing her to struggle and cry and vent her anger. She fought like a madwoman until she exhausted herself and fell limply against Egan. He encompassed her within his embrace and stroked her back tenderly.

Maggie lifted her arms, twining them around Egan's neck. ''You didn't come back.'' Clinging to him, she sobbed quietly.

Egan's heart ached with a desperate need to console Maggie, but he knew only too well that he was powerless to ease her pain. All he could do was hold her, protect her and continue reassuring her. She had lived through hell, through a mother's darkest, most twisted and evil nightmare. What had he expected, that Bent's kidnapping would leave no scars on her kind, gentle soul?

Losing track of time, he held Maggie until she finally fell asleep in his arms. He wriggled around, easing Maggie along with him, until he could lean against the rock wall of the boulder. As she slept soundly, he prayed her sleep would remain undisturbed.

Her dream—her nightmare—had revealed her heart's fears, her repressed memories. But he understood the depth of her hatred and anger—both directed at him. Fifteen years ago when he had left her, he had thought he was doing the right thing. He had truly believed he was protecting her.

But he hadn't known about the child. God, how she must have hated him for leaving her pregnant! How long had she waited for him to return? How many years had she spent expecting him to come back to her and claim his son?

You didn't come back. Her accusatory words echoed inside his head. She had waited for years. And when she'd given up hope, she had married Gil. He realized now what he'd done to Maggie and why, even if she loved him, she would never be able to forgive him.

He had left her without giving her the true reason and by doing so had given her false hopes. And by not telling her about the threat Grant Cullen posed, he had put both Maggie's life and their son's life in danger.

Oh, Maggie, my love, you didn't deserve the hand fate dealt you. You deserve a better man, one who has never broken your heart and shattered your life.

I will never hurt you again. I promise.

Maggie awoke slowly, leisurely, stretching out on the survival bed. As her mind begin to clear, she remembered where she was. She searched the bed for any sign of her companion. He wasn't there!

"Egan!"

Remnants of her nightmare remained clearly in her mind, as did her furious struggle with Egan when he'd tried to calm her. What had she said to him? Try to remember, Maggie. Try to remember!

Egan approached the boulder, his hands filled with edible berries and nuts. "Were you calling for me? I'd gone out to collect our breakfast."

He knelt in front of her and held out his harvest. "If we could build a fire, I'd catch some fish. But to be on the safe side—"

"Do you think Cullen is still following us?"

"Maybe. I don't think so, but we can't afford to take any chances."

"How much longer will we be wandering in the wilderness? Shouldn't we be close to finding a town by now?"

"Hold out your hands," he instructed. "Let's eat and then we can wash up in the stream and—"

"How much longer?" Her exasperated expression added strength to her demand.

"I should have you back in civilization by nightfall."

She held out her hands. He dumped half the nuts and berries into her open palms. Their gazes met and locked. Maggie's eyes questioned him, but he wasn't quite sure what she was asking.

"Unless I've read my directions wrong, going by the sun and the growth signs of the trees and the location of the stars last night, we can head that way—" he indicated with his index finger "—this morning and be reasonably sure we're going northwest. If we don't run into any trouble, and don't take too many rest stops—"

"What sort of trouble?"

"I wasn't referring to Cullen," he told her, then picked out several berries and popped them into his mouth.

"Egan, about last night...about my nightmare—"

"You don't have to explain," he said. "Having a crazy, mixed-up dream about Bent being in danger from Cullen was perfectly normal, after what happened at the fort. And wanting to beat the hell out of me was just as normal. After all, I'm the reason Bent was kidnapped and you and he were almost killed."

"I'm sorry about the way I reacted." She wanted to reach out and touch him, to tell him that she didn't blame him. She knew he had saved her life and Bent's.

"My feud with Cullen put our son's life in danger. That

was my fault. You have nothing to be sorry about. I'm the one with all the regrets, the one who's at fault.''

"You saved us."

"I saved you from a danger that I had created." He rose to his feet, turned his back to her and stomped toward the stand of evergreens.

What was he thinking? Maggie wondered. How did he truly feel about her? About his son? He had done what any honorable man would have done—whatever was necessary to protect his child and that child's mother. He'd made it perfectly clear that he wanted a relationship with Bent, but that didn't necessarily mean she was included, did it? She had fooled herself once, when she'd been younger and much more naive about men and about love. She had thought because Egan had made love to her that he loved her and would want her to be his wife. She wouldn't make that mistake again. She could not allow herself to assume anything when it came to Egan Cassidy's emotions.

Hurriedly Maggie picked out the berries, held them in one hand and tossed the nuts to the ground. Filling her mouth with the sour fruit, she munched and then swallowed. Nourishment was nourishment, she told herself. She certainly wasn't going to starve to death.

She rose to her feet, then brushed green spruce needles from her clothes. "I need to...er...to...you know." She cleared her throat. "Then I'll be ready to leave."

"Yeah, sure. Go ahead. I'll wait here for you and then we'll head toward the stream. We can clean up, drink our fill and then be on our way."

She didn't like this tension between them, but how could she defuse it? Her nightmare had somehow created a wall between them—an invisible barrier formed from her anger and fear and his guilt and regret.

Maggie scurried into the wooded area to relieve herself,

then returned hurriedly and placed a smile on her face as she approached Egan. All she could do now was reach out to him with warmth and pleasantness. But would he accept her cordiality, after she had furiously attacked him last night?

"Ready," she said.

Without a smile, he inclined his head and gestured for her to follow him. Her heart ached. She wanted to beg him not to shut her out this way, not to close down his emotions and pretend he didn't care. *Maybe he doesn't care,* an inner voice nagged. *Maybe he'll be glad to see the last of you. No, you're wrong! He does care. He does.*

Egan purposefully slowed his gait, allowing Maggie to keep pace. He had pushed her yesterday, out of necessity, but today he could go easy on her. If Cullen hadn't caught up with them by now, the odds were that he'd given up and was at this very minute plotting a way to find them before they left Arizona.

But surely Cullen knew that he would come after him, that since he had kidnapped Bent, there would be no place he could hide. And Egan had no intention of sending Maggie and Bent home. Not until Cullen was no longer a threat to them. He'd find a safe place for them. A secret sanctuary. And once Cullen had been eliminated, he would take Maggie and her son home where they could resume their normal life. And if Bent wanted him to be a part of that life, he would do everything within his power to build a relationship with the boy. But he would make no demands on Maggie, no requests. He would never do anything to hurt her— not ever again.

He couldn't bear to think about the way she had cried out for him, the way she'd said, *you didn't come back.* She had suffered enough at his hands. Asking for forgiveness would never be enough. He couldn't give her back those lost years of waiting and hoping for a man who hadn't returned. He couldn't undo the past. But he could protect her now—protect her from him.

Ellen Denby punched the End button on her cellular phone and slid the phone into her vest pocket. "That was Sawyer MacNamara. The siege at Cullen's fort is over. Thirty-five Ultimate Survivalists surrendered this morning, but Grant Cullen and Winn Sherman weren't among the captured."

"So, Cullen's escaped," Hunter Whitelaw said.

"Bastard's tracking Egan." Joe Ornelas slammed his big fist down on the table, rattling their breakfast dishes.

"Maybe," Ellen said, casting a glance at Bent Douglas, who lay on the sofa in their Flagstaff hotel suite, his hands crossed under his head. He hadn't moved a muscle, but she sensed that he was listening to every word they said. "If Egan hasn't shown up by tonight, we'll see if we can't get a search party organized. Maybe the feds can spare MacNamara and he can arrange for a few local boys to help out."

"Do y'all think something has happened to my mother and...er...Mr. Cassidy?" Bent asked.

"Not really," Ellen assured him. "I'd lay odds that Cassidy will show up by nightfall. He's taken his own sweet time coming down off the mountain because he's been outfoxing Cullen."

"But if they don't contact you by—"

Bent's question ended abruptly when Ellen's cellular phone rang again. Both Dundee agents, as well as Bent, focused their attention on Ellen, each holding their breath, waiting for word on Egan and Maggie.

"Denby here." Ellen's eyes narrowed. Her forehead wrinkled. "Damn. Yeah, sure thing, Sam. I'll leave Wolfe with Joe and Hunter until things are settled here. Jack and Matt and I will take the Dundee jet back to Atlanta ASAP.'' Ellen returned her cell phone to her vest pocket.

''What's going on?'' Hunter asked.

''A new case that demands my personal attention,'' Ellen explained. ''Joe, you and Hunter will continue to act as Bent's personal bodyguards, until…well, until Egan tells you otherwise. When our man Cassidy is no longer AWOL and has figured out how he plans to proceed, I can spare Wolfe for a few more days. He's told me that he wants to help Egan track down Cullen.''

Grant Cullen, wearing a silk robe, emerged from the bathroom and hailed Lieutenant Shatz with a wave of his hand. ''You may bring in my breakfast now.''

''Yes, sir.''

The young man hurried out of the bedroom and returned within minutes, carrying a silver tray. After placing the tray on the small table in front of the windows, he removed the domed lid to reveal a plate of pork chops and scrambled eggs. Steam rose from a cup of black coffee at the side of the plate.

Cullen tightened the silk cord belt around his waist, eased out a chair and sat down at the table. ''Is Colonel Sherman back yet?''

''Yes, sir, he returned about five minutes ago.''

''Ask him to come in, please. I want a full report.''

''Yes, sir.''

Winn Sherman, dressed in civilian attire, marched into his superior's bedroom, halted in front of him, clicked his heels and saluted.

''What did you find out?'' Cullen speared one pork chop with his knife, then sliced it into small pieces.

"The soldiers at the fort surrendered this morning and were taken into custody."

"Did you make arrangements for lawyers?" Cullen placed a piece of meat in his mouth and chewed.

"Yes, sir. And I made some phone calls, to certain loyal supporters and have found out that Cassidy's fellow Dundee agents are staying in Flagstaff. Apparently Cassidy and Ms. Douglas haven't shown up, yet."

"That means they're still in the mountains." Cullen lifted his coffee cup. "No doubt he thinks he's outsmarted me. But I'm the smart one. Tucked away here in my little house in Minerva, where the citizenry will keep my whereabouts a secret, I can rest and make plans for our next confrontation."

"What if Cassidy takes the woman and boy back to Alabama?"

"If that happens, we'll follow. In a few days. But knowing Cassidy as I do, I'm sure he'll send them somewhere he thinks is safe and then he'll try to track me down. I'll just have to make sure I get to him before he gets to me."

Chapter 10

Towering cottonwoods dotted the landscape, blending in with the junipers, pines and blackjack oaks. Enormous saguaros, their fat, prickly arms reaching skyward, grew throughout the thick brush. Clusters of prickly pear cactuses pushed up through the rocky ground. During Egan and Maggie's journey down a winding track along the mountain wall, dark storm clouds gathered overhead, blocking out the sun and forecasting rain. The wind picked up, swaying treetops and whistling around craggy boulders.

When Egan changed directions, heading up a rock-studded path, Maggie balked. "Where are you going?"

"In case it's slipped your notice, the bottom is fixing to fall out," he said, casting his gaze at the swirling gray clouds. "We need to find some kind of shelter before we get caught in a downpour."

"And just where do you think we'll find any shelter out here in the middle of nowhere?" She planted her hands on her hips and glared at him.

"If I'm not mistaken, this weed-infested path could lead to an abandoned mine or a ghost town or maybe just a couple of old shacks. From the Arizona maps I studied and the data I read, there are numerous places throughout the mountains in this state that were left to the elements when mines played out."

As her gaze lingered on the gloomy sky, Maggie noted two buzzards hovering high above them. An uneasy shudder racked her body. "I'd settle for a damp cave right now."

"Yeah, so would I. I don't relish the idea of our being swept away in a spring rain." He motioned for her to follow him.

As if to encourage Maggie's cooperation, a clap of thunder boomed in the distance. She gasped and jumped simultaneously. "I'm coming. I'm coming."

As the intervals between thunder claps and lightning flashes shortened, Egan's search for shelter escalated. He placed Maggie in front of him, knowing that he had to let her set the pace or he would force her into an unmerciful march. The farther they climbed, the wider the pathway. Egan became convinced that this had once been a road. And roads always led somewhere, didn't they?

Maggie's unnerving screech halted Egan immediately. "What's wrong?" He jerked the Glock from where he'd stuffed it under his belt and rushed to her side just in time to see a coyote dash across the road. "Good God, woman, you scared me to death over a coyote?"

"I'm sorry," she said sarcastically. "But the thing startled me. It just came out of nowhere."

"And now it's gone. So there's nothing to be afraid of." He returned the pistol to its nest at his back, then reached over and patted Maggie on the shoulder. "I didn't mean to snap at you."

"And I didn't mean to overreact. I guess we can both be forgiven for being nervous and on edge."

Tiny droplets splattered onto Maggie and Egan and pitted the dirt pathway at their feet. Egan grabbed Maggie's hand.

"Come on, honey. We'd better head into the woods. The tree branches should provide some protection. At least it's better than nothing."

Within minutes the feisty wind increased, picking up dead leaves and scattered debris and sending them whirling around in the air. Thunder drummed. Lightning crackled. And a heavy downpour soaked the earth.

Egan and Maggie ran into a wooded area, just off the road. Breathless, their bodies dripping with moisture, they stopped beneath a large sheltering grove of trees. Egan gently shoved Maggie back against the trunk of a cottonwood and shielded her body with his.

Their breaths mingled as he pressed his forehead to hers. She closed her eyes and listened. Listened to the rain. Listened to her thumping heartbeat. With his chest pushing against her damp breasts, her already peaked nipples responded by tightening even more and tingling with awareness. How could she possibly be sexually aroused at a time like this? she wondered. Wet, tired and on the run. *With Egan.* His presence alone excited her. Now as much as it had in the past. The aura of strength and danger that surrounded him possessed aphrodisiacal powers.

Maggie's lips parted on an indrawn breath. Aligning their lower bodies so that his erection nestled between the apex of her thighs, Egan covered her mouth with his. Hot and wet and wild, they shared a kiss that left them both breathless and yearning for more.

"I can hardly take you here and now!" he said, his words a harsh curse. "What is it about you, Maggie mine, that makes me lose my head whenever I'm around you?"

She didn't respond. There were no words to describe the way she felt or explain the unexplainable. The chemistry between them couldn't be denied. A look. A touch. A kiss. An explosion of the senses.

As the rain seeped between the branches, dripping down onto Egan's head and back, reality momentarily returned. His gaze searched past Maggie, through the trees and beyond the grove. At first he thought his imagination was playing tricks on him. He blinked a couple of times. But what he'd thought might be a mirage was still there. About a hundred yards above the wooded area, a stone building with a rusted roof awaited them.

"Let's go." Egan dragged Maggie out from under the canopy of trees.

As the rain pelted her relentlessly, Maggie swiped the moisture from her face. "Where are we going?" Has he lost his mind? she wondered.

"Look straight ahead," he told her.

"It's a house!" she cried.

"It's a shack," he corrected. "But even if the roof is leaking, it'll provide better shelter for us."

By the time they reached the small rock building, they were soaked to the skin. Maggie barely had time to notice the crumbling rock wall that jutted out from either side of the abandoned hovel before Egan shoved open the creaking wooden door and propelled her into the dark, dank belly of the one-room dump. Signifying countless years of neglect, strong mustiness and a faint malodorous scent assailed her senses. Bending over double as she fought to catch her breath, droplets cascaded off her body and puddled around her feet. When Egan pushed the door closed, the rusted hinges squealed and the bottom edge of the door scraped along the dirt floor.

With her breathing returning to normal and her eyesight

adjusting to the dim interior, lit only from daylight passing through two small, high windows, Maggie took note of her surroundings. Several cobweb-draped bottles perched in one windowsill. A dust-coated wooden table and chairs, along with an ancient wood-burning stove, created a kitchen nook on one side of the room, while a simple metal bed, without a mattress, and a rickety wooden chest provided what had once been the sleeping quarters. Tiny streams of rain leaked through holes in the old tin roof, pitter-pattering onto the rusted iron bedstead, dripping down on the center of the table and boring little pools into the packed-dirt floor. Maggie's nose crinkled when she saw the dried pellets littering the floor here and there, reminders of non-human inhabitants.

"Be it ever so humble," Egan said.

"I think humble is an overestimation."

He shook his head, shooting a shower of raindrops all round him. "At least we're out of the rain."

"More or less." Maggie eyed the numerous areas where the leaking roof allowed the rain inside the house.

Egan pulled out a chair from the table and sat, then crossed one leg over the other and proceeded to remove his boots. "Better than a cave, don't you think?"

"Much," she agreed, then slumped down in the chair opposite him and mimicked his actions. After taking off her boots and wet socks, she rubbed her aching feet. "I've got blisters on the bottom of my feet."

"Are they bad?" He removed the pistol, laid it on the table and immediately scooted his chair around the table and grabbed both of Maggie's feet.

"What are you doing?"

"I'd think it's obvious. I'm seeing for myself how bad your blisters are."

When she tried to jerk her feet out of his grasp, his big

hands circled her ankles and placed her feet in his lap. Egan grinned at her. She tried to frown, but instead the corners of her mouth lifted into a hint of a smile.

He studied the tiny blister on the underside of her right foot, then inspected the larger blister on the pad of her left foot. As she watched, he pulled one foot between his legs, setting the heel directly against his sex. After lifting her other leg up so that her foot was even with his chest, he ran caressing fingers over, under and around, being careful to avoid the blister.

"What—" she cleared her throat "—what are you doing?"

"Inspecting your blisters."

"Oh."

He lifted his gaze from her long, slender feet to her big, brown eyes. "If I could build a fire, our clothes would dry faster and we'd dry out faster, too."

"But you can't build a fire," she said.

"There's more than one kind of fire." Egan slid his hand beneath the hem of Maggie's jeans, his touch tender and seductive as he petted her ankle. And all the while he maintained eye contact with her.

"Is there…more than one kind of fire?" She sucked in a deep, unsteady breath, knowing that if he continued touching her, she would soon be begging him to make love to her.

Her twitching toes patted against his erection. His wicked grin widened as his eyes lowered to her breasts. Her clearly outlined nipples strained against the wet material of her chambray shirt.

"Oh, yes, there is most definitely more than one kind of fire," he said.

Egan lifted her right leg and then her left, placing them on either side of his hips. Immediately he reached over and auled her out of her chair and onto his lap. As her bottom ettled onto his thighs and her mound softened against his rection, her toes grazed the dirt floor as she straddled him.

"Every time I touch you, a fire ignites inside me. Intantaneous combustion," he said. "Something beyond my ontrol. Believe me, sweet Maggie, I can't help responding o you the way I do."

"I know." She wrapped her arms around him and laid er head on his shoulder. With her lips brushing his neck, ne whimpered, "It's the same with me. I can't stop myself rom wanting you. Only you. I've never felt this way with nyone else."

He lifted her head from his shoulder and cupped her chin etween his thumb and index finger. "And I have never elt this way with anyone else."

When his lips touched hers, her feminine core squeezed ght as tingling sparks of desire radiated upward and outard through her body. Alive with sensations, she reponded to every stimulus. The taste of his tongue mating vith hers. The feel of his beard and mustache gently cratching her skin. The smell of his purely masculine cent.

Egan ended the kiss, leaving them both breathless, roused and aching. He buried his face against her breasts nd nuzzled her. His mouth sought and found a beaded ipple, covered it and suckled her through the wet cloth of er shirt. Maggie keened deep in her throat, tossing back er hair, which glistened with raindrops, as Egan slid his and beneath the waistband and down inside her jeans and anties. He caressed her hip. Her warm, wet lips traveled ver his neck and up to his ear. She nibbled on his earlobe.

Egan grasped her bottom with one hand and clutched the ack of her neck with the other. Lust wound tightly inside

him, hardening his sex and urging him to take what h
wanted.

"Stop me now, Maggie, or there will be no turnin
back."

She responded by unbuttoning his shirt and exposing hi
chest. The moment she ran her fingers through his ches
hair, he unbelted, unsnapped and unzipped her jeans i
rapid succession. Standing, Maggie allowed him to remov
her jeans and panties. He cupped her buttocks and nuzzle
her belly, then hurriedly undid the fly of his jeans and free
his sex.

Maggie trembled with longing, her body aching for re
lease. She glanced down at him for just a second before h
impaled her, dragging her down and onto his shaft. Tha
momentary glimpse of him, big and hard and ready, excite
every feminine instinct within her.

Hot and wet and swollen with desire, her sheath sur
rounded him tightly. He held her in place for a hear
pounding minute, letting her body adjust to his. And the
he lifted her hips, almost removing his sex from within he
before burying himself deeply with one surging thrust.

Her voice crying out with the pleasure of their joinin
echoed in the hushed stillness of the deserted cabin. Outsid
the rain continued drenching the earth. Lightning crackle
across the sky and thunder shook the broken windowpane

Once he had taken her completely, he removed he
jacket. Then he unbuttoned her shirt, spread it apart an
unhooked her bra. With the utmost tenderness, he attacke
first one breast and then the other. When his mouth tugge
on her nipple, powerful, titillating fissions exploded insid
her.

With his mouth at her breast, he placed his hands unde
her bottom, lifting her. "Ride me," he demanded, as hi
fingers bit into her naked hips.

She quickly set the rhythm, beginning with a slow, seductive dance. In and out. Up and down. Leisurely enjoying each stroke. As tension coiled tighter and tighter, Maggie accelerated the pace.

"That's it," Egan mouthed the words against her breast. "Harder and faster!"

With a frenzied desire pushing her, Maggie gave herself over to the primitive needs of her body and of his. Egan took control, clutching her hips and pumping into her with deep, hard lunges that soon had her moaning with pleasure. Her release hit her with the force of a raging storm. She shuddered when an overwhelming climax claimed her. Egan accelerated his thrusts to a frantic tempo. He came apart, unraveling at the speed of light as he jetted into her, all the while deep groans erupted from his throat.

While aftershocks rippled along their nerve endings and Maggie's body quivered with supersensitivity to his touch, they clung to each other, their breaths labored, their skin sticky with perspiration.

His sex remained inside her. He didn't want to disengage his body from hers. At this moment she was still a part of him. When he stroked her back with his fingertips, she shuddered. Oh, how he loved the fact that she was so easily aroused and that even after fulfillment, she could be receptive to renewed passion. At his age, once was usually more than enough to satisfy him—with any other woman. But with Maggie, once would never be enough.

She was his only as long as she needed him. Once the threat of Grant Cullen's existence was removed, Egan would have to let her go. She deserved to have her sane and sensible life in Alabama restored. It was what she wanted—what he wanted for her. But until that time came, he intended to store up as many perfect memories as possible. Enough to last the rest of his life.

Maggie rubbed her smooth cheek against his beard-rough cheek. "Listen. It's still raining. We could be stuck here for hours."

"So we could." Egan lifted her up and off his lap, disengaging their connection. When she stood on wobbly legs, he reached out to steady her.

Maggie possessed a woman's body. Lush, full, rounded. Egan's gaze traveled the length of her form, from wild, mahogany hair hanging in damp curling strands across her back and over her shoulders to the dark, fiery triangle at the apex of her legs. And oh, those legs. Those long, luscious legs. Remembering the way she had mounted him, straddling him as they made love, his sex twitched with renewed vigor.

"Wish that bed had a mattress," he said. "I feel like taking a long nap."

She stared pointedly at his unzipped jeans. "Are you sure you feel like taking a nap? From where I'm standing, it looks like you might have something else in mind besides sleeping."

"Nah," he teased her. "That's just wishful thinking on your part. Remember, honey, I'm an old man, and you just wore me out."

"Did I indeed?"

Maggie inched backward, far enough so that he couldn't touch her without getting up out of the chair. Then she removed her open shirt and unhooked bra and tossed them onto the table. Naked, humming with sexual energy and hungry for dessert to follow the banquet she had shared with Egan only minutes earlier, Maggie stretched her arms over her head and lifted her hair atop her head. Closing her eyes, she let her hair tumble slowly, seductively, through her fingers, parting it in the back and tossing it forward so that the strands rested on the rise of her breasts.

Egan licked his lips, then swallowed hard. Maggie was as much in the grips of this madness as he, as completely controlled by the sexual urges of her body as he was dominated by his. Only once before had he allowed passion to overrule every rational thought—a never-to-be-forgotten week with Maggie. Fifteen years ago.

He had used protection then, every time, except the first time, when they'd both been wild with need. But now, he had made love to Maggie for the second time—without a condom. What if she became pregnant again?

Some selfish demon inside him hoped for that impossible dream. If Maggie were pregnant with his child…

"It's getting hot in here," Maggie said, as she rubbed the sweat from her neck with the palm of her hand, her fingers coming to rest inches above the indention between her full breasts.

She was tempting him, playing the seductress. Years ago, she had been like this—a spirited, hungry wanton, insatiable in her desire for him. She evoked every protective, possessive, primevally male instinct within him. All that was feminine about her summoned all that was masculine about him.

"We could go outside and cool off in the rain," he suggested and laughed when he noted the surprised look on her face.

"Cool water might douse that fire I see beginning to burn in you." She glanced meaningfully at his semierect sex.

Egan rose to his feet, shucked off his jacket and shirt, stripped out of his jeans and nodded his head toward the back door. "Why don't we find out?"

He grabbed her hand as he walked past her. She followed him across the room, knowing at that precise moment she would follow this man anywhere. The door creaked and groaned as he forced it open. A cool mist blew into the interior, spraying their naked bodies. Without a word of warning, Egan tugged Maggie up against him and then pulled her through the door and out onto the back porch. Rain splattered down over them, washing through the partially dilapidated tin roof.

"Oh!" Maggie gulped as rainwater cooled her heated body.

"Are you still hot?" he asked, rubbing his chest against her breasts, teasing her.

"My skin is just warm now, but inside, I'm still hot."

"How hot are you, Maggie, my love?"

With his arm around her waist, he led her off the porch and out into the yard. A four-foot stone fence, crumbled to the ground in several sections, encircled what had once been a private spot. Tiny, pink wild roses wove up and around the wall nearest the house. Ankle-high weeds dotted the rocky earth. Like two children, carefree and happy, they danced in the rain, their bodies drenched, their desires escalating.

Maggie watched Egan, a man like no other. Entranced by the essence of his masculinity, she couldn't take her eyes off him. Tall and lean, every ounce of muscle superbly toned. Coated with moisture, his graying chest hair curled into tight rings, as did the darker hair that dusted his arms and legs. His sex, still aroused, beckoned her touch. Unable to resist the temptation, she reached out and ran a fingertip over the smooth, bulbous head, which reacted with a hefty jerk. When she circled him with her hand, he groaned. When she set her hand into motion, every muscle in his big body tensed.

"You're killing me, honey." He grabbed her hand to stop its movement.

"That wasn't my intention." She released him, but

nched her hand up and over his belly, around his waist and back down to palm one tight buttock.

Manacling the wrist of her other hand, he hauled her up against him. She gasped when their wet bodies collided. "What was your intention?" he asked.

She rubbed herself against him, pressing the intimate parts of their bodies together. "Being out here is like stepping under a giant shower, isn't it?"

Egan laughed. "If you want me primed and ready for action again, then we'd better get out of this rain."

She pulled away from him and raced toward the porch. When Egan caught her, he whirled her around and instantly shoved her gently up against the exterior wall of the house. She reached out, intending to put her arms around his neck and draw him into her embrace. But he escaped her clutches by dropping to his knees. The moment he buried his face against her belly and wrapped his arms around her hips, Maggie quivered like a willow in the wind.

His lips dotted kisses from waist to thigh, then nuzzled her damp, red curls. As his hand slid between her legs, she braced herself by planting one hand on his shoulder. She threaded the fingers of her other hand through his hair and gripped his head. His fingers probed, delved and stroked. Maggie's body tightened around those caressing fingers. After he had urged her thighs farther apart and had prepared her with his fingertips, he held her legs separated enough to allow his mouth to take charge.

Smoldering hot sensations blazed up from her depths, spreading quickly through her body, setting her afire. Maggie's knees liquefied and began to give way, spreading her legs even farther apart. While Egan slid one big hand behind her to cup her bottom and support her, his other hand reached up to encompass her left breast.

Pleasure almost too intense to bear claimed her, shatter-

ing her composure and tossing her headlong into fulfill
ment. Before the last convulsion racked Maggie's body,
Egan lifted her just enough to accommodate a quick, hard
thrust, embedding himself to the hilt. Her legs curled
around his hips. Her buttocks pressed against the smooth,
wet surface of the stone wall.

They mated there on the porch, their hunger for each
other without bounds. Giving and taking in equal amounts,
they shared a mutual gratification. And when Egan roared
as fulfillment drained every ounce of strength from his
body, Maggie toppled over the edge, spiraling out of con
trol.

She slid her legs down his hips, placed her feet on the
floor and slumped against him. Keeping her wedged be
tween his body and the wall, Egan dipped his head and
found her lips.

"If I lived a thousand years, I could never get enough
of you," he murmured, then kissed her with the conviction
of his words.

Chapter 11

Tinkling raindrops dripped off the edge of the tin roof. Afternoon sunshine glutted the interior with abundant illumination, washing over the dingy walls and floor, reflecting off the metal bedstead and revealing the shabbiness of their rock house refuge. Maggie pulled on her socks, their cool dampness soothing to her blisters. After lifting one of her boots from the floor, she glanced sideways toward the open front door. Egan waited in the doorway, his back to her, his wide shoulders almost touching either side of the rotting wooden frame.

Maggie supposed she could lie to herself about what had happened between them. She could blame Egan. She could pretend that he had seduced her. But what good would lying to herself do? None! The truth of the matter was that she had wanted Egan. She always had and probably always would. Before meeting him fifteen years ago, she had laughed at the thought that loving someone could become

a *fever in your blood*. But that's exactly what her feelings
for Egan were. A fever in her blood. An incurable fever.

What had happened between them—what always happened between them—was by mutual consent. But accepting that fact didn't help Maggie much right now. She found
it easy enough to lose her head, to throw caution to the
wind and become a wild woman in Egan's arms. But the
difficult part came afterward. Once their insatiable hunger
had been temporarily fed and she was thinking straight
That's when doubt and fear and a hint of regret came into
play.

Why was it that with Gil, a man who had loved her
made a commitment to her and even adopted her child, she
had never been able to feel such mindless passion? Somehow with Egan, a temporary lover who had never made her
any promises beyond the moment, she had found an incomparable ecstasy.

"Are you about ready?" Egan asked, glancing back over
his shoulder.

She looked away, down at her feet, deliberately avoiding
prolonged eye contact. "Yes. Just a couple of minutes
more." Hurriedly she slipped into her boots. After tying
the laces, she stood, brushed her hands down the sides of
her damp jeans and headed for the front door.

Suddenly in her peripheral vision, Maggie noticed something moving across the floor only a few inches from her
feet. Silently gliding. Slithering. Then she heard the deadly
rattle. A snake! A rattlesnake! The minute her mind reg-
istered the danger, Maggie let out a bloodcurdling scream
Instinctive fear. A totally emotional reaction.

Instantly Egan reached for the pistol, whirled around and
saw the stricken look on Maggie's face. His gaze followed
her line of vision down to where the rattler curled, prepar-

ing to attack. He aimed the 9-mm and with one precisely aimed shot blew the reptile in two.

As the gunshot echoed in Maggie's ears, she rushed toward Egan. He hauled her up to his side and walked her out of the cabin and into the sunlight. Slightly breathless, her heart hammering madly, Maggie gazed into Egan's eyes. And there it was—that protective, possessive, caring look that told her she was his woman. He had always stared at her that way, since the first moment he saw her.

"I'm sorry I screamed," she said. "I know I overreacted again. I could have just told you the snake was there, without getting hysterical."

"It's okay." He stroked her back, letting his hand linger between her shoulder blades. "After what you've been through the past couple of days, you deserved at least one good scream."

"I suppose I did." A nervous giggle caught in her throat.

His fingertips inched their way upward and wound around the back of her neck. "Do we need to talk about what happened?"

"With the snake?" *Don't be a ninny,* an inner voice scolded. *You know he's not referring to the incident with the snake.*

"Maggie… I don't want to hurt you. Not ever again. I never meant for my actions to cause you harm in the past."

"You didn't make me any promises back then and you haven't made me any now." *But I want you to,* she silently pleaded. *I want you to promise to love me and be with me the rest of our lives.*

"You might not believe this, but I'm usually very much in control of myself and my actions. Except with you. I can't seem to keep my hands off you."

The giggle trapped inside her escaped, tittering from her throat. "You're taking the blame for something that is equally my fault. If what happened between us today ends up causing me any pain or creating any problems in my life, then I'll deal with it.''

"Alone? The way you dealt with Bent?" He caressed her neck.

"Bent wasn't a problem. He was a blessing." Maggie pulled away from Egan. "I've regretted many things in my life, but having Bent isn't one of them."

"I should have been there for you...and for my son." Egan stuffed his hands into the front pockets of his jeans in an effort not to grab Maggie and kiss the breath out of her. "Do you think it's too late for me to form some sort of relationship with Bent?"

Maggie sighed deeply. "I honestly don't know. Ten years ago, you definitely could have formed a bond with him. Even five years ago. But he isn't a child anymore. He's very much his own man. I'd like nothing better than for him to accept you as his father and for the two of you... All I know is that I'll encourage him to give you a chance."

"That's more than I deserve from you, after—"

She pressed an index finger over his lips, silencing him. "How about you get me back to civilization so we can see our son? I'm going to hug him so hard he'll turn beet red with embarrassment. But I don't care."

Egan cupped his hand over hers, kissed her finger and clasped her hand in his. "Let's head out." He led her away from the hut that had protected them from the rainstorm and toward the overgrown, winding pathway down the mountain. "As soon as we get to a phone, I'll contact Joe and Hunter and have them bring Bent to you as quickly as possible."

"And then we'll all go home to Alabama," she said.

Egan squeezed her hand, then halted abruptly. "Eventually."

"What do you mean—eventually?"

He released her hand and looked her square in the eye. "Until I find Cullen and eliminate him, you and Bent won't be safe back in Alabama. I plan to send you somewhere safe, someplace that Cullen knows nothing about. Joe and Hunter will stay with y'all until—"

"Until you either kill Cullen or he kills you!" Maggie whirled around and walked several feet away from Egan. With her arms crossed over her chest, she sucked in air, trying desperately not to cry.

"Maggie."

When he came up behind her and placed his hands on her shoulders, she shrugged off his embrace and refused to face him. "Don't tell me that there isn't a possibility that he'll kill you and not the other way around. And don't try to explain that this is something you have to do, that you can't leave it to the FBI to track him down and arrest him."

Egan allowed his hands to hover over her shoulders for a second or two before balling them into tight fists. "You and Bent will never be safe as long as Cullen is alive. If I thought his vendetta against me would end if he were arrested and sent to prison, then, yes, maybe I'd leave him to the authorities. But that's not the way this thing is going to play out. Not when your life and Bent's are at risk."

Maggie eased around slowly and brought her gaze up from the pathway at her feet to make direct eye contact with Egan. "I really don't have a choice, do I? I'll have to do as you ask. Bent and I both will." She took a tentative step toward Egan, but stopped herself before she reached him. "You don't think you have a choice either, do you?"

"No, honey, I don't. Not when it's either go after Cullen or allow him to come after us."

"And when Cullen has been…eliminated?" she asked.

"Then you and Bent can go home."

"And you?"

"Me? I'll come for a visit and see if my son is willing to let me be a part of his life." *And you, Maggie, my love, will you let me be a part of your life, too? Could we ever move beyond the past? Could you ever forget the kind of life I've lived and forgive me of all my sins?*

Two and a half hours later, the afternoon sun low on the western horizon, Egan and Maggie entered the outskirts of Stonyford, Arizona. Population 1,895. A *has-been* little town that appeared to have been around since the late nineteenth century. Although a few vehicles meandered up and down Main Street and across Medicine Bow Avenue, the only other paved street, most of the downtown area seemed deserted.

"Bet there's no chance this place has a hotel," Maggie said. "I doubt there's even a pay telephone available."

"Wrong on both counts," Egan corrected, his gaze focused up Main Street to the intersection with the town's lone traffic light. "That sign reads Stonyford Hotel—" He nodded to the right. "And over there—" he nodded left "—at that service station, is a pay phone."

"Will wonders never cease."

Maggie's legs ached and the blisters on her feet were now raw and burning. Despite sharing a rain bath with Egan earlier that afternoon, she felt grimy after two days in the wilderness.

"The sign painted on the front window of the hotel says Café." As if on cue, Egan's stomach growled. "Hope that place is still in business."

"Call Joe and Hunter first," Maggie said. "Then we can check out the hotel and café."

When they passed the barber shop, an elderly, white-haired cowboy, boots on his feet and a Stetson on his head, emerged. "Howdy, folks. You two look lost. Do you need some help?"

"As a matter of fact, we do," Egan said. "My wife and I—" he smiled at Maggie "—got lost up in the mountains and we need to contact some friends to come pick us up."

The grizzly old man pursed his thin lips. "Hmph! I don't understand you young folks hiking off into the mountains without a guide. There's bears and snakes and coyotes in the hills. And some of the roughest wilderness in this here United States." He looked Maggie up and down. "If I had me a wife like her, I'd keep her home and not drag her all over God's green earth."

"Believe me, Mr....er...Mr....?" Maggie bestowed her most endearing smile on the old man.

"Butram, ma'am. Ed Butram." He quickly removed his Stetson, lifted his shoulders and stood a good inch taller.

"Well, Mr. Butram, believe me when I tell you that this is my last trip into the mountains." Maggie laid her hand on Ed's arm. "Our son is staying with friends in Flagstaff and I know he's terribly worried about us. We need to call him as soon as possible to let him know we're all right."

"After we use that pay phone—" Egan inclined his head in the direction of the service station "—we were planning to check out the hotel and café."

"Can't use the phone over at Hamm's," Ed told them.

"Why not?" Maggie asked.

"Been out of order for the past two years." Ed chuckled. "Didn't nobody ever use it anyway. But the hotel has a phone you can use."

"Then the hotel is open?" Egan asked.

"What about the café?" Maggie's stomach rumbled.

"Why don't you two come along with me," Ed suggested as he stepped off the sidewalk and into the street. "Me and my sister, Corrie, own the hotel. Don't get many customers, so we closed off most of the rooms. But we keep a few cleaned and aired-out.''

"May we use the phone?'' Egan asked. "We'll reimburse you when our friends arrive with some money.''

"Of course you can use the phone.'' Ed motioned for them to follow him. "I'm afraid the café closed five years ago, but I'll get Corrie to rustle you up something while you call your boy.''

"This is so nice of you, Mr. Butram.'' Maggie kept in step with their host. When she glanced over her shoulder at Egan, who stayed a few feet behind, she noticed him surveying the town, as if he were searching for something—or someone. Did he honestly think Grant Cullen might be lurking around the corner?

"My pleasure, Mrs....'' Ed laughed. "Don't think you mentioned your name.''

"Smith,'' Egan said.

"Jones,'' Maggie said.

Ed stopped, scratched his head and gave Maggie a puzzled look. "Which is it, Smith or Jones?''

"Both,'' Maggie told him. "My maiden name, which I retained after my marriage, is Jones. And my husband is Mr. Smith.'' Maggie's tense glare warned Egan to just go along with her explanation.

"What a darn fool thing for a woman to do,'' Ed said, then grumbled incoherently to himself. He gave Egan a sharp, disapproving look. "Son, if I was you, I'd make this gal use my name.'' When the thought struck him, Ed cursed. "I'll be damned. What name does your boy use?''

"Smith,'' Maggie and Egan said in unison.

Ed smiled, seemingly satisfied with their answer. "Come along and make your phone call. I'll see if I can get Corrie away from that fool talk show she watches on TV every afternoon. Maybe you two could go on that show and tell folks why you go by two different last names after being married...how long did you say you'd been married?''

"Fifteen years," Maggie said as they followed Ed into the hotel foyer.

The entry had all the charm of an old lodge, with animal heads mounted on the wall and wooden beams crisscrossing the ceiling. Fresh paint hadn't touched the tan walls in years. Wear and tear had removed whatever veneer the hardwood floors might once have possessed.

"Phone's in there." Ed motioned toward an open doorway to a room that Maggie guessed served as the hotel office. "Just make yourselves at home and I'll go tell Corrie that we got guests."

"Thank you." Maggie kept smiling until Ed disappeared down the long, dimly lit hallway, then she swerved around and followed Egan. "Wait up, will you?"

Catching up with Egan just as he lifted the telephone receiver, she grabbed his hand. "Will it be safe to bring Bent here?"

Egan nodded. "Bent will be as safe here as in Flagstaff. As long as Cullen is alive you're both in danger, no matter where you are. Bent will have Joe, Hunter and Wolfe with him on the trip and once he's here, he'll have four of us protecting him."

"Five," she corrected. "Don't forget that I'd die to protect him, just as you would."

When a keening series of peeps reminded Egan that he still held the telephone receiver in his hand, he returned it to the base. "Look, Maggie, I know how much you want to see Bent and the risk is minimal in bringing him here, since Cullen has no idea where we are. We're getting out of here first thing in the morning to take you and Bent somewhere for safekeeping until..."

"Where are we going?"

"Somewhere close by, if possible. I'm counting on Joe knowing a safe place, maybe even on the Navajo reservation. If that's the case, then we'll be heading east anyway and it's best for the guys to bring Bent to us since we're already farther west than Flagstaff."

"I'll be so glad when this is all over and we're safe. All of us."

"Yeah, honey, me, too." He caressed her cheek. "Now, do you want to talk to your son?"

"Most definitely."

Waiting impatiently while he dialed, she patted her foot on the floor. When Egan glanced down at her dancing foot, she held it still and offered him an okay-I'm-nervous-so-shoot-me look.

"Joe? Yeah, Egan here. Maggie and I are safe and sound in some wide-place-in-the-road town called Stonyford, at the town's only hotel. Right on Main Street."

"Tell him I want to talk to Bent." Maggie tugged on Egan's arm.

"Maggie's anxious to talk to her son, but first I need to discuss something with Ellen."

As Egan eased his hip down on the edge of the desk, Maggie noted the frown on his face and wondered what was wrong.

"Okay. Let me talk to Wolfe then."

"Where's Ellen?" Maggie asked.

"She had to go back to Atlanta. An emergency," he explained.

"When can I—"

"Yeah, Wolfe, I'm going to need a safe place for Maggie and Bent to stay while I tend to business. And I'll want Joe and Hunter to remain with them for as long as it takes."

Maggie waited and waited while Egan's discussion continued. She listened halfheartedly, wishing he'd finish his business and let her talk to Bent. Finally she heard Egan say, "Put Bent on the phone."

He handed her the receiver, which she grabbed. "Hello, Bent?"

"Hi, Mama. Are you all right?"

"I'm fine, now that I hear your voice. Are you all right, sweetie?"

"I'm okay. Just worried about you. But now that I know you're safe and we can go home, everything will be all right, won't it?"

"Listen, Bent." Maggie hesitated, took a calming breath and started again. "We can't go home. Not right away."

"Why not?"

"The man who kidnapped you hasn't been caught and as long as he's free, he poses a danger to you and me."

"Because that General Cullen hates Egan Cassidy. All of this is his fault. My being kidnapped and our almost getting killed."

"Bent, sweetheart, this isn't Egan's fault."

"Yes, it is, and you know it! Don't try to defend him."

"All right. I won't. We don't need to settle this right now. Just cooperate with Mr. Ornelas and Mr. Whitelaw because whatever they do, it's for your safety."

"I understand. I'm not some dumb kid."

"I know you're not, sweetie. Now, listen, the Dundee agents are going to bring you here…to me. Tonight."

"Will I have to see *him?*"

She knew he was referring to Egan. "Yes, Bent, you will." She hadn't expected so much hostility from Bent, focused entirely on Egan. Although they had seldom discussed his father, Maggie wondered if all these years Bent had harbored hatred for a man he didn't even know. If he did, was it her fault?

"Well, don't expect me to be glad about it," Bent said. "He nearly got us both killed."

"I love you," she told her son, changing the subject. "I can hardly wait to see you."

"Yeah, me, too, Mama."

"See you very soon."

Maggie handed the receiver back to Egan. He eased it down on the cradle and glanced at Maggie.

"I take it that my son is none too happy with me right now." Egan rose to his feet. "I suppose expecting him to understand was wishful thinking on my part."

Maggie curled her fingers over Egan's forearm. "You can win him over. It may take time and a great deal of effort on your part, but Bent needs a father. He needs you. And whether he knows it or not, he wants you in his life."

"I'd like to believe that." Egan covered Maggie's hand with his. "But knowing that you and he are safe and that Cullen can never threaten either of you again, will be enough for me. I don't have the right to expect anything more."

"Oh, Egan, that's not—"

Ed poked his head around the door. "Got grub in the kitchen waiting on you, Corrie warmed up some chicken stew in the microwave and sliced some chocolate cake. I put on a fresh pot of coffee, too."

"Oh, Mr. Butram, that sounds wonderful." Maggie slipped her hand from beneath Egan's.

"After you eat, I'll show you upstairs to your room," Ed said. "Just one bathroom on the second floor is in operating order, but there's a big ol' tub and the shower works just fine."

"I don't suppose there's a chance you might find us some clean clothes?" Egan asked.

Ed inspected Egan's and Maggie's soiled, tattered attire.

''Corrie's shorter and rounder than you—'' he eyed Maggie ''—but I reckon you can tighten the belt on a pair of her jeans.'' Ed surveyed Egan from head to toe. ''Now, you big fellow, pose a problem. Wouldn't none of my clothes fit you.'' He snapped his fingers as an idea struck him. ''My nephew, Preston, is about your size. I think he might've left some things here. He comes for a visit a couple of times a year. I'll check with Corrie.''

''We can't thank you...and Corrie...enough for you hospitality.'' Maggie patted Ed on the arm. ''We spoke with our son and our friends. They'll be coming here sometime tonight. Do you have a couple of more rooms available?''

''Sure thing, little lady.''

Maggie studied herself in the tall, narrow mirror attached to the back of the bathroom door. Corrie's jeans weren't a bad fit, only one size too large and the legs were a bit short. And where the plump, large-breasted Corrie would have filled out the blue chambray shirt, Maggie wore it like a minitent. But for once in her life, she really didn't care how she looked. She was clean, well-fed and she and Bent were safe. Within an hour or less, she'd see her son, be able to touch him and hold him and reassure herself that he was all right.

After slipping into Corrie's socks and putting on her own dirty boots, Maggie gathered up the damp towels and her filthy clothes. Ed had told her to just place the items in the wicker basket outside the bathroom door, so she followed instructions and dumped them on top of Egan's discarded apparel. He had come upstairs first to bathe, while she'd helped Corrie clean up the supper dishes.

Maggie opened the door to *their* bedroom. Egan lay stretched out atop the jacquard-style coverlet on the four-poster tester bed. His boots rested by the nightstand and his pistol lay on top, beside the lamp. Corrie's son's jeans fit Egan snugly, outlining the shape of his long, lean legs. The borrowed plaid shirt hung open from collar to hem, exposing his chest.

"When Bent arrives, you'll have to move to another bedroom." Maggie hovered in the doorway.

"I take it that our son wouldn't approve of our sharing a room." Egan smiled halfheartedly. "No problem. I'll share with Wolfe."

Maggie entered the room, but steered clear of the bed. She knew only too well that a partially undressed Egan might prove to be too much temptation. "Where do you suppose Joe and Hunter will take us in the morning?"

"You can be sure that it will be somewhere they can keep you and Bent safe." With his palms cupping the back of his head, which rested on two pillows, Egan gazed up at the ceiling. "Is Bent going to stir up a fuss about not getting to go home right away?"

Maggie sat in one of two overstuffed armchairs that flanked the double windows overlooking Main Street. The floral print material was slightly discolored and worn on the arms, but the thick padding afforded her a comfortable seat.

"He isn't pleased, but he'll cooperate. Bent's stubborn and sometimes headstrong, but he's very smart. He'll understand that staying in hiding is necessary."

"They should get here soon." Egan glanced quickly in Maggie's direction, then returned his gaze to the ceiling. "Should I make an effort to talk to Bent tonight or should I let it wait until—"

"Talk to him tonight." Maggie rubbed her neck and shoulders.

"What should I say to him?"

"Tell him the truth about what happened between you

and Grant Cullen. The first step in forming a relationship with Bent will be making him understand that his kidnapping and the danger we're in now isn't your fault.''

"But it is my fault." Egan sat up, pivoted slowly and scooted to the edge of the bed.

"It isn't! You're blaming yourself for something that is Grant Cullen's doing. You have no control over his actions. You never did.''

"I could have told you about Cullen fifteen years ago."

"Yes, you could have," she agreed. "And I could have told you about Bent years ago, too. But you didn't and I didn't. So, if any of this is your fault, it's my fault, too."

"Don't be ridiculous, Maggie. You're completely innocent of—"

"No, I'm not. Bent is the only innocent party. You made a mistake in not telling me about Cullen. And I made a mistake in not telling you about your son. But Cullen is the person who is at fault for ruining your life and putting Bent and me in danger."

Egan rose to his feet, but hesitated before venturing closer to Maggie. "You're the most understanding person I know. You realize that Cullen's pursuit of revenge has ruined my life."

Maggie's gaze locked with Egan's and for one endless moment, time stopped. Unspoken confessions passed between them. Unfulfilled hopes and dreams became a common thought. Heartfelt longing for what had been lost and could never be recaptured united them in mourning.

"Oh, Egan. My poor Egan." Teardrops gathered in her eyes as she held open her arms.

Drawn to her loving kindness, Egan crossed the room and knelt in front of her. She wrapped her arms across his back as he laid his head in her lap. With gentle fingers threading through his hair, she caressed his head.

Outside the last rays of sunlight faded. Dark shadows fell across the room. The sound of a car horn came from somewhere up the street. Egan didn't move. Barely breathed. A tender quiet cocooned them. Maggie had never felt more connected to—more a part of—anyone than she did Egan at that precise moment. Earlier today their bodies had mated, giving and receiving pleasure. And now their hearts joined, sharing sympathy and concern and deep understanding.

"Howdy. This here is Corrie Nesbitt, up in Stonyford. You remember me, Mr. Baker?"

"I'm afraid I don't. How can I help you, Mrs. Nesbitt?"

"Well, you stayed at my hotel when you was covering that story about the Johnson boy who fell down in the mine shaft and—"

"Oh, yes, I remember you now," Travis Baker said.

"You told me then that if anything else interesting ever happened up our way, I was to give you a call."

"Absolutely. I did tell you that, didn't I? Has something interesting happened *up your way?*"

"Is your TV station still paying out a hundred dollars for a news tip?" Corrie asked.

"Yes, ma'am, we sure are."

"All right then, I might have a story for you."

"I'm listening."

"Well, late this afternoon a man and a woman—they call themselves Mr. Smith and Ms. Jones—they come wandering into town looking like death warmed over, if you know what I mean."

"Strangers?" Travis Baker asked.

"Yes sirree. They said they'd been lost up in the mountains and they sure looked it. But I'm telling you, that even though they're both just as nice as they can be, there's more to their story than meets the eye. Might make a great human interest story for your viewers, if they'd tell you the details on camera.''

"Where are they now, this Mr. Smith and Ms. Jones?''

"Upstairs in one of our rooms,'' Corrie said. "They told Ed that they was married and had a son. Some friends is supposed to be bringing the boy and coming here tonight.''

"Mrs. Nesbitt—''

"Call me Corrie.''

"All right, Corrie, do you think these folks are criminals?''

Corrie harrumphed. "I didn't say that. I just figure there might be an interesting story here and I could make myself a hundred dollars.''

"I'll tell you what, if you can keep them there overnight, I'll drive down first thing in the morning with a cameraman and see what Mr. Smith and Ms. Jones have to say for themselves.''

"And you'll bring my money?''

Travis chuckled. "Yes, ma'am. I'll give you the money, if I actually get an interesting story.''

Chapter 12

The Dundee agents arrived in Stonyford around eight-thirty. If the situation hadn't been so dead serious, Egan would have found it amusing. Corrie Nesbitt peeked out from a front window, her large, round eyes bulging with surprise and suspicion when she saw the men emerge from their car. Ed Butram stood just inside the hotel entrance, his arms crossed over his thin chest and a look of concerned curiosity on his weathered face.

Hunter Whitelaw got out of the car first, his big, bearlike body moving with amazing agility for a man so large. He scanned the area, then threw up his hand in greeting to Egan and Maggie, who stood side by side on the walk in front of the hotel. Egan nodded. Maggie smiled weakly.

Joe Ornelas emerged from the other side of the back seat, scanned the area and said something to the driver of the vehicle, David Wolfe.

"Your friend there is an Indian, ain't he?" Ed Butram asked.

"Navajo," Egan replied.

"Thought as much."

Hunter motioned to the other back seat occupant and Bent Douglas appeared. Tall, lean and good-looking. Egan's hands curled into loose fists and his heart swelled with pride at the sight of his son. His son! But the boy hated him. And who could blame him?

With Hunter and Joe flanking Bent, the three of them approached. Maggie ran down the sidewalk and into the street. Bent started to run to her, but was refrained by Hunter's big hand on his shoulder. The minute Maggie reached her son, she flung her arms around him and enveloped him in a smothering hug. Bent wrapped his arms around his mother and returned her fierce hug. Then Maggie grabbed his face between her hands and covered it with kisses.

Tears streamed down her cheeks as she stepped back, grasped Bent's hands and just stood there on the street looking at him. Egan ached with emotion. The love Maggie and Bent shared was a precious thing—something he wasn't a part of.

Don't ask for too much, Egan reminded himself. Maggie is safe. Bent is safe. And he was going to make sure they stayed safe always. He realized that he might never be allowed to become a part of their lives on a permanent basis, but knowing that Cullen could never threaten them again would have to be enough.

Who was he kidding? He wanted more. He wanted it all. Maggie. Bent. A normal life. But what were the odds that it could happen for him? Could Maggie ever truly trust him enough to give him a second chance? And was it possible for his son to forgive him? Would Bent ever allow him to be a real father to him?

Egan stepped aside as Maggie and Bent approached the

hotel, Joe and Hunter guarding them. Maggie paused momentarily as they passed, her gaze locking with Egan's. But Bent looked straight ahead, not even acknowledging Egan's existence.

"Your boy don't seem none too glad to see you," Ed Butram commented, then tossed a chew of tobacco into his mouth and went inside the hotel.

Ed was right about that, Egan thought. His son sure as hell wasn't glad to see him. But how could he blame Bent? After all, the boy had just lived through the most traumatic experience of his life—and he blamed Egan.

Wolfe pulled the car around into the alley, then returned to the hotel entrance, where Egan waited for him.

"Any problems?" Wolfe asked.

Egan stared into the man's eyes—a light, earthy green, a direct contrast to his dark skin. "No problems. Not even a hint of Cullen. Any word on what happened to him?"

"None," Wolfe said. "But then you didn't expect he'd make his location known, did you? He's hidden away somewhere safe and sound, waiting to find out where you are before he makes a move."

"I want Maggie and Bent to be taken someplace safe, somewhere they can be guarded day and night, until I've taken care of Cullen."

Wolfe eased up beside Egan. The man's movements mimicked a sleek panther. Perfectly coordinated. Deadly quiet.

"Ornelas's cousin, J.T. Blackwood, who used to be a Dundee agent, owns a ranch in New Mexico. He plans to take Maggie and Bent there. Either he or Whitelaw will be with them at all times and Blackwood's ranch hands will provide extra protection, as will Blackwood himself. And Maggie won't feel so alone with Blackwood's wife and sister around."

"First thing in the morning, we'll leave," Egan said. "Are you heading back to Atlanta or will you be going to New Mexico first?"

"Neither," Wolfe told him. "I'm going with you."

Egan snapped his head around and glared at Wolfe. "What do you mean you're going with me?"

"We discussed things, before Ellen left, and we decided that apprehending Cullen is a two-man job."

"This isn't a Dundee matter," Egan said. "This is a personal matter and I don't want to involve anyone else. I'll take care of Cullen by myself."

"You need an accomplice. Someone who isn't personally involved. Someone who can think rationally."

Egan chuckled. "You know I'm going to kill the bastard, don't you?"

"If we can bring him in alive—"

"Not an option!"

"The kidnapping charges alone would put him in prison for the rest of his life," Wolfe said. "If we can do this legally, you'd never have to explain to Maggie or to your son why—"

"I doubt my son will ever give me the chance to explain anything. And Maggie already understands."

Wolfe shrugged his wide shoulders. "However you decide to handle this, consider me your shadow until it's finished."

"Who decided that you'd get this assignment?" Egan didn't know David Wolfe very well. He suspected that no one did. Except maybe Sam Dundee, the big boss who had hired him.

"I volunteered."

Wolfe's facial expression didn't alter, but Egan noted a slight change in his eyes. Those damn pale eyes were spooky. Like the eyes of some predatory animal.

"So you enjoy suicide missions, do you?" Egan suspected he'd just learned something about the mysterious David Wolfe. Maybe the man didn't have a death wish, but the prospect of dying certainly didn't worry him.

When Wolfe made no reply, Egan slapped him on the back. The man tensed visibly. Egan let his hand fall away, then turned toward the hotel entrance. "Maggie wants me to talk to Bent tonight. She thinks he'll listen to what I have to say."

"Perhaps he will," Wolfe said. "But if you expect too much, you will be disappointed."

"I don't expect anything," Egan told him, then mumbled to himself, "I don't deserve anything."

Maggie sat beside Bent on the edge of the twin bed in the room Ed had assigned to her son. The old man had seemed to understand that their circumstances weren't normal and didn't question them. But Corrie's nosiness bothered Maggie slightly. The woman was as sweet as she could be and was truly friendly, but she possessed an abundance of curiosity that prompted her to ask too many questions.

Maggie glanced at Joe Ornelas who stood guard at the door. "Mr. Ornelas, would you mind if I had a few minutes alone with my son?"

"No, ma'am. I understand. I'll be right outside the door."

"Thank you."

The minute Joe closed the door behind him, Maggie took Bent's hand in hers and squeezed tightly. She had never realized how much she'd taken life for granted—the normal, everyday events like eating and sleeping and working. After coming so close to losing Bent, she would forever be aware of how quickly the most important things in your life can be taken from you. In the blink of an eye.

"Are you really all right?" she asked.

"Yeah, Mama, I'm really all right."

When Bent smiled at her, she saw Egan's smile. Looking at Bent now, she realized how very much he was his father's son. Not only did Egan deserve a chance to know their child, but Bent deserved a chance to know his father. She had to find a way to convince Bent that Egan was worthy of a second chance.

"I want you to do something for me," Maggie said.

"What?"

"I want you to talk to your father."

Bent jerked his hand from Maggie's grasp, shot up off the bed and paced around the room. "I don't have a father. Gil Douglas might have adopted me and called himself my father, but he was never anything but a temporary stepfather. And Egan Cassidy might have provided the sperm that helped create me, but he isn't my father. He's a stranger who walked out on my mother and never looked back. He's a man whose association with the scum of the earth put your life and mine in danger."

"Grant Cullen is a madman who has ruined Egan's life. He sought revenge against Egan because Egan had once exposed him as the evil man he was—the evil man he still is."

Maggie watched her son pacing, like a trapped animal on the verge of thrusting himself against the unbendable bars of the cage that bound him. Even though Bent had assured her that he was all right, she knew better. A rage that badly needed venting boiled inside her son. He was angry with Egan. With Cullen. And perhaps even with her. How could she help Bent? What could she do to ease his pain?

"Talk to Egan," she said.

"I don't want to talk to him."

"Perhaps you don't want to talk to him, but you need to hear what he has to say." Maggie rose from the bed, walked across the room and placed her hand on her son's shoulder. "Do this for me, Bent. Let Egan explain to you about his relationship with Cullen. I think once you know the truth, you won't blame your father for what happened."

Bent covered Maggie's hand with his own and looked directly into her eyes. "Okay. I'll listen to what he has to say. But only because it's what you want."

"Thank you, darling." She kissed his cheek. "I'll tell Mr. Ornelas to go get Egan and let him know you're ready to see him."

Egan wondered what sort of magic Maggie had performed to persuade their son to talk to him. Whatever means she'd used, he was grateful. But he was nervous. And scared. He didn't kid himself. He knew this might be the only chance he'd ever have with his son. What if he said the wrong thing? What if he misjudged, misstepped, misunderstood? So much was riding on this one conversation. He couldn't blow this opportunity.

God, help me!

Hunter sat in a straight-back chair outside the room. When Egan and Joe approached he nodded. "Maggie's still in there with him."

"He may want her there when we talk," Egan said.

Joe knocked on the door. "I've brought Egan with me."

Within seconds the door swung open. Maggie stood there alone. Then she stepped out into the hallway, leaving the door open behind her. Egan glanced into the room and saw Bent standing at the windows that overlooked the back alley. The boy stood ramrod straight, as if he had an iron bar attached to his spine.

"He's very hostile," Maggie said softly. "He's on the verge of exploding, so if he lashes out at you—"

"If he needs to vent his anger, I'm tough enough to take it." When Egan reached out to touch Maggie, she sidestepped him and he realized that their son's resentment stood between them, a barrier as potentially dangerous to their future together as Grant Cullen's existence was to their lives.

Egan entered the room, but halted just as he crossed the threshold. He glanced over his shoulder and looked at Maggie who waited in the hall. "Aren't you coming in with me?"

"No," she replied. "You and Bent need to be alone for this conversation."

Egan nodded. Maggie closed the door, shutting him inside the room with a young, raging bull, who was ready, willing and able to attack with the least provocation.

"Bent?"

The boy stiffened. "Yes, sir?"

"Your mother said that you've agreed to talk to me."

"I'll listen to whatever you have to say, only because my mother asked me to hear you out."

"Fair enough."

Bent whirled around, his steely gray eyes narrowed, his cheeks flushed and his big, manly hands clenching and unclenching with nervous energy. "Fair? What the hell would you know about fair? Was it fair that you got my mother pregnant and left her? Was it fair that she's had to raise me all by herself? Was it fair that because you've spent your life associating with a bunch of fanatics and lunatics that one of them kidnapped me and put my mother through hell?"

The blast of Bent's venomous anger bombarded Egan, making direct hits to his already overburdened conscience.

Guilt piled upon guilt, weighing him down with regret. "You're right. None of it was fair. Not to you. Not to your mother. And whether you believe it or not, none of it was fair to me, either."

Bent glared at Egan, his gaze surveying his father from head to toe. "Every time Mama looks at me she must see you. If I were her, I'd hate me."

"Maggie loves you more than anything," Egan said.

"I know! My mother is the best. She's a good person who deserved a lot better than you ever gave her."

"Don't you think I know that?" Egan held out his hands, the expression beseeching his son for understanding.

"How could you have taken advantage of her the way you did?"

"Is that what Maggie told you?" Egan asked. "Did she say that I had taken—"

"Gil told me."

"Gil?"

"Yeah, Gil. You know, the guy my mother was engaged to marry when you showed up in her life and screwed up everything." Bent's hands shook; his chin quivered. "If it hadn't been for you, Gil Douglas would have been my real father. They'd have gotten married, had me and they'd still be together. But no, you had to ruin things. Gil told me how you used your friendship with my uncle Bentley to worm your way into Mama's heart—and into her bed!"

"Gil Douglas had no right to tell you anything about my relationship with Maggie. All you've heard is the opinion of a man who hated me because—"

"Because you stole his fiancée right out from under his nose!"

"Because your mother fell in love with me." Egan closed his eyes momentarily as the memory of that last night with Maggie washed over his consciousness. *I love*

ou, Egan. I love you so much. How many times during
e past fifteen years had he heard that sweet voice echoing
side his head?

"But you didn't love her—you used her." Bent sneered
his father, a look of pure contempt on his handsome face.

Admit the truth. Don't lie to your son, Egan's conscience
arned him. "I never meant to hurt Maggie. I didn't mean
use her. You're a little young to understand what hap-
ens between a man and a woman—"

"I know all about sex. You needed a woman, so you
ok advantage of my mother because she was infatuated
ith you."

"It wasn't like that, Bent. I swear to you that Maggie
as never just some woman to me. I cared about her. I still
re. About her and about you."

"Yeah, well, where were you fourteen years ago when
was born? Where was all that caring then?"

Egan took a tentative step in Bent's direction, but halted
mediately when he noticed the stricken look on his son's
ce. The boy was scared to death that Egan might touch
m, but Egan knew better than to tread on thin ice. If he
ven tried to place a hand on Bent's shoulder, the boy was
kely to fly into a panicked rage.

Egan sat down in the only chair in the room, a wingback
at that had definitely seen better days. Once seated, he noted
e slight relaxation in Bent's shoulders.

"When I was eighteen, I got drafted and wound up in
ietnam," Egan said, trying to keep his voice calm and
nemotional. "To make a long story short, I met your uncle
entley when he saved my life. We became friends then
d remained friends as long as he lived. Bentley Tyson
as probably the only real friend I've ever had."

"And you repaid his friendship by getting his little sister
egnant just a few weeks after his funeral."

Bent hovered over Egan, his hands knotted into fists
Egan knew that the boy was itching to hit him.

"If you want to hit me, son, then go ahead and do it.'
Egan lifted his chin and looked up at Bent. "Otherwise
give it a rest until you know the whole story."

Bent fumed. He clenched his jaw, clamped his teeth an•
snorted as his breathing grew fast and hard. Keening, h•
closed his eyes, wheeled around and stomped across th•
room. Egan waited, not saying a word.

With his back still to his father, Bent said, "Go ahead
I'm listening."

"While I was in Nam, I was captured and spent nearl•
a year in a Vietcong POW camp." Egan paused, not want
ing to remember those days and yet never truly able t•
forget. "That's where I met Grant Cullen. I survived. Bu•
most of the men didn't survive…because of Cullen. H•
betrayed his country and his fellow soldiers. He traded in•
formation for favors and he also exposed a planned escap•
that cost a lot of men their lives. So, when I got the chance
I turned him in for what he'd done and a captured Vietcon•
major backed up my story. Cullen's West Point trainin•
and his family's position didn't help him much when th•
truth came out. Cullen's career was over. His wife left hir•
and took their daughter. His father disowned him. And h•
blamed me for all his misfortunes."

"He blamed you for something that was his own fault?"
Bent turned and faced Egan. "He hated you because you'•
told the truth about what he did?"

"He swore that he'd never let me have any peace, tha•
he would watch and wait until the day came when I ha•
something that meant everything to me and then he woul•
take it away."

"But that was how many years ago? Twenty-five•
Thirty? Are you telling me that he's been keeping tabs o•

you all these years, waiting for a chance to hurt you the way he thinks you hurt him?''

Egan nodded. ''I could never allow anyone to be more than a casual part of my life. I couldn't love a woman and get married. I couldn't have any children. I couldn't even spend more than a few days at a time with friends. Anyone who cared about me ran a risk and it wasn't a risk I was willing to let anyone take.''

Bent's shoulders slumped, his whole body relaxing. ''Then why did you get involved with my mother?''

''I didn't mean for it to happen,'' Egan said as he scooted to the edge of the chair. ''But Maggie was…different. She was special. I tried damn hard to resist the way I felt about her, the way I knew she felt about me.'' *But loving her was the sweetest thing I've ever known,* he longed to say, but didn't. *I wanted her as I'd never wanted anything or anyone, before or since. And I still want her, now more than ever.* ''I didn't want to leave her. I swear to you that if I'd thought I had a choice, I'd have stayed with Maggie forever.''

''You left because you didn't want Cullen to know about her, so that he couldn't use her to get to you.''

Egan saw the realization dawn in Bent's eyes. His son knew the truth now. Was he mature enough to accept and understand?

''I should have told Maggie about Cullen.'' Egan dropped his hands between his legs and twined his fingers together as he gazed down at the floor. ''But I had no idea she was pregnant. If I'd known…''

''If you'd known, then what?'' Bent asked eagerly.

''I'd have made damn sure that you and Maggie were safe.''

''How did Cullen find out about us…about me?'' Bent asked.

"A private detective somehow unearthed my credit card records that showed I paid for flowers that were sent to Bentley's grave each year. From there, the detective did a little more digging and discovered that Maggie had a child and that I was listed on his birth certificate as the father."

"And once he found out about me..." Bent walked across the room and stood directly in front of Egan. "I understand. Like Mama said, it wasn't your fault that Cullen kidnapped me. And I guess I owe you my life, don't I?" Bent grunted. "So what happens now? What's to keep Cullen from coming after Mama and me again?"

"Me," Egan said. "I'm what's going to keep him from ever getting anywhere near you and Maggie."

"How are you going to stop him?"

"You don't need to worry about that. All you have to do is cooperate with Joe and Hunter and let them do their job as your and Maggie's bodyguards, until I take care of Cullen."

"You're going to kill him, aren't you?"

Egan didn't know how to respond to Bent's direct question. What would his son say if he admitted that he had no intention of allowing Grant Cullen to live?

"If necessary," Egan admitted and sought his son's eyes for a reaction.

Bent nodded, then glanced away as if he couldn't quite accept the truth. "It won't be the first time that you've killed someone, will it? You were a soldier in Vietnam and then you were a mercenary."

"It wasn't the life I would have willingly chosen. I did what I had to do. Most people have choices. My choices were limited."

"After...after Cullen is *eliminated*," Bent continued, "then Mama and I can go home, back to our normal life. Right?"

"Right."

"What about you?" Bent asked.

"What about me?"

"Will you go back to Atlanta, to your normal life?"

"That depends," Egan said. "On you and your mother."

"Do you really still care about her?" Bent shuffled his eet nervously.

"Yes, I still care."

"What about Mama? Do you think she still cares about ou?"

"You'll have to ask her," Egan said.

"You'd better not ever hurt her again." Bent glowered t his father, his stance boldly aggressive. "She's got me ow and I won't let you or anybody else hurt her."

"I'm glad you love your mother and that you want to rotect her, but you don't have to protect her from me."

"If she doesn't want you to be a part of her life, then hat's fine with me," Bent said. "I don't need you. I'm ractically a man now. What do I need with a father? So vhen Mama and I go home, you'd better just go on back o Atlanta and leave us alone."

"If that's what you and Maggie want, then that's what 'll do."

"If Mama says it's all right for you to come back to 'arsons City with us—for a visit—then that's okay, too. ‡ut only if it's what she wants."

"All right. We're in agreement." Egan held out his and. "We'll leave the decision up to Maggie. We'll both bide by whatever she decides."

Bent stared at his father's hand for several minutes, then ‡luctantly accepted it in a hardy handshake. It took all of ‡gan's willpower not to jerk the boy forward and into his ‡rms. This was his son, his and Maggie's child. And he'd ‡ever held this boy when he'd been a baby, never rocked

him, never cared for him when he'd been sick. Bent ha•
grown into a fine young man without ever having know؛
the love and support of his father. Despite what Maggi•
had said, maybe Bent didn't need him, but Egan knew on•
thing for sure and certain—he needed Bent.

Now that he knew he had a son, there was no way h•
could ever walk away and leave him. More than anything
he wanted a second chance. A chance to make things righ•
with Bent, to try to become a father to his son.

He held Bent's hand in his a little longer than necessary
until finally Bent pulled free and stood there staring ؛
Egan.

"In case I don't get the chance to tell you tomorro\•
before you and Maggie leave, I want you to know that I'r•
proud you're my son and I'm sorry that I haven't bee•
around since you were born."

A fine mist formed over Bent's eyes. He cleared hi•
throat. "I guess we'd better let Mama know that every•
thing's cleared up now and I understand why things hap•
pened the way they did." Bent headed for the door.

"Bent?"

"Yeah?" He glanced over his shoulder.

"Thanks."

Bent nodded, then opened the door and called out to hi•
mother. Maggie came to the door, then glanced back an•
forth from father to son.

"Is everything all right?" she asked.

"Yes," Bent said. "Egan told me all about Grant Culle•
and why he's been trying to find a way to get revenge a•
these years. I understand, so you can stop worrying. I don•
blame Egan for what happened."

Maggie sighed with relief. "Good. I'm glad."

Egan crossed the room, stopped at Maggie's side an•
turned to Bent. "I'll see you both in the morning."

When Egan left the room, Maggie called out to him. She smiled at Bent. "I'll be right back. I need to speak to Egan for just a minute."

"Sure," Bent said. "Just hurry back. Okay?"

Maggie nodded, then rushed out into the hallway to catch Egan. He seemed intent upon escaping, so she ran down the corridor and grabbed his arm.

"I thought everything was all right between you and Bent," she said. "He understands now and he doesn't blame you for what happened with Grant Cullen. Right?"

Egan placed his hand over hers where she gripped his shirt. "Bent is a boy trying very hard to act like a man. He does understand about my relationship with Cullen and he even understands why I left you fifteen years ago." Egan tapped the side of his forehead with his index finger. "He understands with his mind. But in here—" Egan pounded his fist over his heart "—he's a little boy who can't forgive me for hurting his mama and for not being there for you and him all these years."

"Oh, Egan, give him time. Once he gets to know you—"

Egan grabbed Maggie's shoulders. "Is that what you want? Do you really want me to become a part of Bent's life…a part of your life? Our son has made it very clear to me that unless you're willing to give me a second chance, he doesn't want to have a thing to do with me."

"I see. So, you're saying that Bent expects us to come as a package deal. If you take the son, you have to take the mama, too."

"Your son loves you and doesn't want to see you get hurt." Egan eased his hands down Maggie's arms, grasped her wrists and then released her. "So, you think about things while I'm gone. And when I come to the Blackwood Ranch to let you know that y'all are safe from Cullen, you can tell me what the future holds for us."

"Egan, I—"

By placing his index finger over her lips, he silenced her.
"Don't make a rash decision. Take your time. Whateve
you decide will affect all three of us, for the rest of ou
lives."

Chapter 13

With the bedspread wrapped around her, Maggie sat by the windows that overlooked Stonyford's Main Street and watched the predawn sky. She had spent several hours with Bent last night and finally came to the conclusion that despite his lingering resentment of Egan, her son both wanted and needed his father in his life. But before that could happen, Bent and she would have to come to terms not only with the kidnapping, but with how Egan handled putting Grant Cullen out of commission. Permanently.

The world was a violent place—always had been and probably always would be. But living in Parsons City, Alabama, she had been able to shield Bent from a great deal of life's true ugliness. If Egan became a part of their lives, would he be able to leave behind that kill-or-be-killed lifestyle he had led for so many years? Could he survive without the adrenaline rush of danger and excitement on which he'd fed most of his adult life? Even if he were willing to try settling down to a normal life, would he grow bored and eventually leave them?

In her heart, Maggie knew that if Egan's venture into their lives turned out to be only temporary, she and Bent would be better off without him. She had survived when she'd lost Egan the first time, but what would happen if she lost him a second time? And what about Bent? How would having his father desert him, once they had bonded, affect him?

Maggie drew her feet up onto the chair and clutched the edges of the spread where it crossed her chest. A tiny chill trickled along her nerve endings. She had fallen in love with Egan all over again and there was no use denying the truth. Perhaps in the deepest recesses of her heart, she had never stopped loving him. Poor fool that she was! She was doomed to be a one-man woman and there really wasn't anything she could do about it.

Egan wanted her, desired her greatly and couldn't seem to get enough of their lovemaking. But did he love her? Had he ever loved her? *I cared for you,* she remembered him saying. Caring wasn't love. So, would Egan make a commitment to her in order to become a father to Bent? Was he willing to take the package deal, even without loving her?

The door to Maggie's room creaked slightly as it opened ever so slowly. A thin thread of light from the hallway fell across the floor like a pale line of paint. Maggie's senses heightened. Her nerves came to full alert. *You're safe,* she reminded herself. Egan and Wolfe were in the room next to hers. Joe Ornelas slept in the bed beside Bent, just across the hall. And Hunter Whitelaw kept a vigil outside in the corridor.

The moment the door opened farther, she recognized Egan's silhouette. Undoubtedly he was as restless as she, as unable to sleep. They would say goodbye later today and go their separate ways. She and Bent into seclusion. Egan on a quest to find and destroy the threat to their lives. Had Egan been thinking about the possibility that, this time, he wouldn't come back alive? After all, he had survived a lifetime of constant danger. And together they had saved Bent and escaped Cullen's wrath. Did that mean Egan's luck had finally run out? What if instead of him eliminating Cullen, it was the other way around?

"Come in," Maggie said, her voice not much more than a whisper.

Egan walked into the dark room, illuminated only by the moonlight, and quietly closed the door behind him. "I just wanted to check on you. To make sure—"

"You've checked on Bent, too, haven't you?" she asked.

"Yes." Egan stood just inside the doorway, his breathing slow and steady.

"And he was sleeping?"

"Soundly."

"You've come to say goodbye, haven't you?"

"Maggie, I knew you were awake," he admitted. "I've been listening to you stirring around in here for the past hour."

"I've been thinking about us," she told him. "About what might happen to you when you go after Cullen."

Egan didn't move. He simply stood there in the darkness and waited. Maggie knew she would have to make the first move, extend an invitation, before he would come to her. At that very moment he was exerting superhuman control in order to keep his hands off her. She knew this as surely as she knew that in less than an hour the sun would rise in the east. The electrifying chemistry between them radiated an intense energy that drew them together, like a magnet and metal, one incapable of resisting the other.

"I don't want you to worry about me," Egan said, his voice low, as if he didn't want to be overheard. "I know what I'm doing. And I'm not going alone. Wolfe will be with me."

"I'm glad you won't be alone."

"Once this is over...once Cullen is no longer a threat, I'd like to try to find a way to make amends to you and Bent."

Maggie rose from the overstuffed chair, bringing the bedspread up with her as she stood. The edge of the jacquard-style print coverlet dragged behind her as she glided silently across the wooden floor. Transparent gilded moonbeams burnished her hair with gold, deepening the rich red into a dark mahogany. Egan swallowed hard. His body hardened instantly.

He had given himself a dozen good reasons why he should open Maggie's door, but all of the excuses had been lies. The only truth was that he knew they would say goodbye in a few hours and he couldn't bear the thought of not making love to her one final time.

Before she reached Egan, Maggie dropped the spread from around her shoulders. The soft cotton throw cascaded down her hips and legs and pooled around her feet on the floor. She stepped over the puddle of material and came to him, wearing only a pair of slightly oversize panties and an equally oversize, unbuttoned shirt.

Even in the dim light, he could make out the swell of her partially exposed breasts and the long, silky length of her gorgeous legs.

"Are you sure?" he asked, praying that she wouldn't change her mind. Not now. Not when he ached with such a desperate need to be inside her.

"I'm sure." She grasped the front edges of her borrowed

shirt and opened it fully, then slid it off her shoulders, over her arms and down her back.

Egan held his breath.

She let the shirt drop from her fingers and join the coverlet on the floor. With several slow, tormenting steps she made her way to him, then stopped directly in front of him and reached up to touch his bare chest. He let out the breath he'd been holding.

He touched her shoulders, his fingers grazing her skin with the lightness of feathers. Soft, sweet, slow. Tantalizing. Moments ticked by as his tender strokes inflamed her. Touching, but just barely. Across her shoulder, up her neck, over her chin, down her neck and across her other shoulder. Just when she thought she couldn't bear it unless he touched her more intimately, his fingertips glided over and around her breasts, but deliberately avoided her nipples.

Maggie drew in a sharp breath when he finally circled her nipples, but never touched them. Moaning deep in her throat, the sound a muted plea for him to end her torment, Maggie gripped his biceps. Egan lowered his head until his mouth hovered over the center of one breast. He flicked out his tongue and just barely brushed her nipple.

Maggie bit down on her lip to keep from screaming with the pure pleasure of that fleeting touch. As she held him tightly by the arms, he repeated the torture several times and then turned his attention to her other breast.

She rose on tiptoes, tossed back her head and gasped softly. Hurriedly, Egan divested himself of his jeans and then hooked his thumbs under the elastic of Maggie's baggy cotton panties. As soon as they were both naked, he walked her backward and toppled her over and into the center of the bed. He came down over her, straddling her hips. She gazed up at him with such desire in her eyes that he thought he'd lose it right then and there. But he was going to give her pleasure and that meant waiting. Waiting until she was begging him to take her.

He took his sex and began rubbing it against her kernel, tempting and teasing until she bucked her hips up, asking for more. But he continued the movements, slow and maddening, building the tension inside her.

"Oh, please, Egan. Please."

"Not yet."

After agonizing moments of torture, repeatedly petting her body with his, he finally eased the very tip inside her. When she tried to thrust upward to take more, he halted her.

Covering her face and neck with sweet, little pecks, Egan eased in and out a few inches, but he refused her pleas to bury himself inside her. She writhed beneath him, mumbling incoherent phrases. He covered her lips with his and lunged his tongue into her open mouth. She closed her lips around his tongue, trapping him, sucking greedily. The kiss deepened, expanded, becoming a parody of the most intimate of sexual acts.

Maggie grabbed Egan's taut buttocks and brought his body down as she lifted up to meet him. She had taken all the teasing she could endure. She wanted every inch of him. Now!

Egan obliged her—at long last. He thrust into her, deeply, completely. She trapped a scream in her throat. A scream of intense pleasure. And then the mating dance began in earnest. Hard, deep plunges that brought each of them closer and closer to the ultimate climax, to the perfect conclusion.

Maggie's entire body tensed as it reached the moment of fulfillment. One final stroke of Egan's sex and she shattered into a million fragments of quivering pleasure. Her release triggered his and he followed her, headlong, into an earth-shattering completion.

Their bodies damp with perspiration, their breathing ragged, they held each other while the aftershocks rippled through them and strength-robbing satiation claimed them thoroughly.

"General Cullen," Winn Sherman called out as he knocked loudly on Cullen's bedroom door. "Wake up, sir, and turn on your television."

"What the hell!" Cullen roused from sleep, angry for being disturbed, but knowing that Winn wouldn't have bothered him without good reason. He fumbled his fingers across the top of the nightstand, searching for the remote. The moment he found it, he hit the Power button.

"What channel?" Cullen demanded.

Winn called out the channel number. Cullen punched in the number as he sat up in bed. On screen, a pretty-boy reporter with an irritatingly phony smile stood in the middle of a street in some local town nearby. Cullen thought all small towns shared a likeness, especially those out here in the west.

After turning up the sound, he called out to Winn, "What's going on? Why did you want me to see this?"

"May I come in, sir?"

"Get me some coffee first."

"Yes, sir. But listen to what that reporter is saying."

Cullen turned up the sound and listened.

"We're here in Stonyford," the pretty boy said. "We have a report that a man and a woman walked out of the mountains yesterday, after spending days being lost in the wilderness. We're told that Mr. Smith and Ms. Jones are still inside the Stonyford Hotel and will be emerging shortly to speak to us about their harrowing ordeal."

Cullen shot out of bed and grabbed his silk robe. "Well, I'll be damned."

The reporter's name—Travis Baker—flashed across the screen. Travis pointed his handheld microphone toward a plump, elderly woman with a shock of curly gray hair and set of bright blue eyes.

"This is Mrs. Corrie Nesbitt, the proprietor of the hotel, where the couple is staying. What do you know about this Mr. Smith and Ms. Jones?"

"Don't know much," Corrie said. "He's a good-looking man, with a beard and mustache, about forty-five and she's a tall redhead, a few years younger. My brother, Ed Butram, ran across them when they first showed up here after spending a couple of days lost up there in the mountains. They was a couple of sorry-looking folks, I'll tell you. Dirty, hungry and tired."

"Did they share any of the details about their wilderness adventure with you?" Travis asked. "Did they explain how they got lost and what they were doing in the mountains without a guide?"

"Nope. They seem nice enough, but I say there's more to them than meets the eye." Corrie harrumphed loudly. "Three real slick-looking characters showed up here last night with a boy that Mr. Smith and Ms. Jones claim is their son. They all spent the night and are in there right now eating breakfast."

Travis pulled the microphone away from Corrie who had reached out to grab it. "Folks, stay with us. After this message from our sponsors, we will, hopefully, be granted an interview with the mysterious couple Mrs. Nesbitt just told us about."

Winn Sherman entered Cullen's bedroom, a mug of black coffee in his hand. "Here you are, sir."

Cullen muted the sound on the television, took the ceramic mug from Winn and sat on the edge of the bed. "You can run, but you can't hide." Cullen chuckled, then sipped his coffee.

"Do you think Mr. Smith and Ms. Jones are Cassidy and Maggie Douglas?" Winn asked.

"Oh, I'd lay odds that's exactly who they are. Some old nag even described them. A bearded man, about forty-five and a tall, redheaded woman."

"What a stroke of luck."

"Divine intervention," Cullen said. "The Almighty pointing the way for me." He sipped more coffee. "Find out how far Stonyford is from here and round up some good men. There's four of them, not counting the boy and the woman. With a dozen of us, we triple our odds."

"I know where Stonyford is. It's about twenty-five minutes from here, if we take the road around the mountain, and about forty-minutes if we go the main highway."

"As soon as Cassidy finds out that a reporter is on his heels, he'll get out of town as quickly as possible." Cullen placed his mug on the nightstand, then scratched his chin. "He'll figure there's a chance I saw the TV report or that one of my supporters did, so he'll be in a hurry to get his woman and his kid to safety."

"That means he'll probably head for the main highway. I suggest that we try to cut them off while they're still on the back road leading out of Stonyford."

"I agree. We need to set things in motion immediately."

"Yes, sir!" Winn clicked his heels and saluted.

"What the hell is going on out there?" Hunter Whitelaw roared, his deep baritone voice booming as he glanced out the window. "Looks like a TV reporter and a couple of cameramen. And Mrs. Nesbitt is being interviewed."

"Damn! That's all we need," Joe Ornelas said. "How

did they find out about you two?'' He glanced across the room to where Maggie and Egan stood in the corner, talking quietly.

"Knowing Corrie, she probably called that Travis Baker and told him about our wilderness survivors showing up yesterday, hoping she'd collect that hundred dollars they give away for news tips," Ed Butram explained.

"I suggest we head out as soon as possible," Wolfe said. "And preferably by a back entrance."

"I want y'all to take Maggie and Bent and leave immediately," Egan said. "I'll arrange for transportation for myself and—"

Maggie clutched Egan's arm. "No. You said that you weren't going alone, that Wolfe was going with you."

"I'll go with him to find Cullen once you and your son are in safekeeping," Wolfe reassured her, then quickly turned his attention to Ed Butram. "Do you have a car, Mr. Butram?"

"Got an old pickup," he replied.

"Would you be willing to rent or maybe even sell us that truck?" Wolfe asked.

"Ain't worth selling. It's fifteen years old and needs a new coat of paint," Ed said.

"How does it run?" Egan asked.

"Runs just fine. I keep it tuned up. Me and Corrie go into Flagstaff ever now and then."

"How much will you take for it?" Egan asked.

"Whatever you think's a fair amount."

"I'll write you out a check," Wolfe said. "By the way, where is your truck?"

"Out back." Ed hitched his thumb toward the rear of the hotel. "You'll need the registration and the keys."

"What are y'all planning?" Maggie asked when Ed left the room.

"We're planning on getting you and your son to safety," Wolfe said. "I'll contact Sawyer MacNamara and let him know that Cullen might be aware of our location. There's a good chance we'll need some backup."

"You think Cullen will definitely come after us, don't you?" She spoke to Wolfe, but her gaze rested on Egan.

"Better to play it safe than sorry," Hunter commented. "If Cullen's got some Ultimate Survivalists sympathizers, then he could put together a small army to come after us."

"You and Bent will go in the car with Wolfe, Joe and Hunter," Egan said. "I will follow closely behind in Ed Butram's truck, until we reach the Navajo reservation." And if we encounter Cullen and any of his followers, I can hold them off until the others take you and Bent to safety, Egan thought.

"Once we're on the reservation, we'll be able to make sure no one is following us," Joe said. "I'll call ahead and have J.T. bring along some of his ranch hands and meet us."

"What if General Cullen tries to stop us?" Bent's cold glare confronted Egan. "If he knows where we are, he could be on his way here right now."

"Maybe we'll get lucky and that won't happen," Egan said. "But if he does come after us, you can be sure we'll protect you and your mother. That's one of the reasons Wolfe is going to contact the FBI. Believe me, they want Cullen almost as much as I do." Egan laid his hand on Bent's shoulder. "Whatever happens, son, I know you'll watch out for your mother."

"You can count on it," Bent said.

"Do you know how to use a gun, Bent?" Hunter asked.

"No!" Maggie cried. "He doesn't know anything about guns."

"Aim and shoot," Hunter said. "If a target is close

enough, you're bound to hit something. It might become necessary for you and Bent to be armed."

"I'm not sure I could—" Maggie cringed.

"If it meant saving Bent's life, could you?" Egan asked her.

She nodded, then said, "Yes. Yes, I could and would do anything to save Bent."

"You already know how to use a rifle, but just as a precaution, it's probably a good idea to give you and Bent a quick lesson in how to use a handgun," Egan told her.

With his chin held high and his broad shoulders squared, Bent walked straight up to Egan. "Give me a gun and show me how to use it."

While Ed Butram joined his sister on the street, distracting Travis Baker with his version of how he "come upon" Mr. Smith and Ms. Jones yesterday, Stonyford's visitors made their escape. Wolfe had made arrangements with Sawyer MacNamara for federal agents to meet them en route, but Egan couldn't help wishing that they already had backup. Of course, there was no way to know if Cullen had seen the newscast or if someone might have relayed the information to him. But Egan had no doubt that Cullen would learn that he and Maggie had been in Stonyford. He just prayed he could get Maggie and Bent to safety before Cullen caught up with them.

Ed Butram's rusty, dilapidated, old truck chugged along, keeping up with the sleek, black sedan Wolfe maneuvered around the mountain curves. Every instinct Egan possessed sensed danger, but he wasn't sure if his concern for Maggie and their son had somehow altered his usually perfect perception. Did he sense immediate danger simply because he feared for Maggie and Bent?

Ed had told them that if they stayed on the old mountain

road they would eventually connect with a state highway, which would lead them to Interstate 40 and then it would be a straight shot to Gallup.

Once they made it to the interstate, the feds would escort them to the Navajo reservation and block any attempts Cullen might make to overtake them. After Maggie and Bent were safely hidden on the Blackwood Ranch, Egan and Wolfe would be free to pursue Cullen. They weren't bound by the law the way the federal agents were and could use whatever means necessary to stop Cullen—dead in his tracks.

As they descended the mountain, the two-lane road winding ever downward, sometimes at unnervingly steep angles, glimpses of wide valleys came into view. Foxtail grass, yellow-white in the morning sun, grew thickly across the wide vistas near the lake at the foot of the mountain. Dirt trails, cutting off the main road, led into the deep woods. They had passed at least half a dozen of those secluded lanes, and each time they passed one, Egan's heartbeat accelerated. A vehicle could easily hide and wait.

Surely they would reach the state highway soon, Egan thought as he checked his watch. Twenty minutes from Stonyford and so far, they hadn't seen another vehicle on the road. *Let's keep it that way!*

Straight ahead a narrow bridge crossed the East Fork of Pine Wood Creek. A dense stand of evergreens surrounded them, like giant sentinels towering into the sky. Just past the bridge the road turned sharply, concealing whatever lay around the bend. And they had just passed another of those damn little trails that led off into the woods.

The hairs on Egan's neck stood up. A warning chill shivered along his spine. He started to blow the truck's horn to caution Wolfe, but apparently something had forewarned

Wolfe. The sedan slowed to a halt just this side of the bridge.

Egan rolled down the driver's side window and listened. The truck's and the car's engines droned steadily. The only other sound was the hum of nature. A breeze high in the treetops. Leaves rustling. Squirrels chattering. Water flowing. Egan ran his hand over the smooth surface of the rifle Wolfe had given him before their departure, then he removed the pistol from his holster and laid it between his legs. He shifted gears and backed the truck off onto the side of the road. If danger was headed in their direction, he didn't want the truck to stand between the sedan and an escape route.

With a wave of his arm, Egan signaled Wolfe to proceed, knowing full well he didn't have to tell the man to do so with the utmost caution. The minute the sedan drove onto the bridge, a Hummer appeared, maneuvering hurriedly around the bend and into full view.

Egan's heart stopped for one split second before he grabbed the rifle and took aim from the passenger side window. The sedan reversed quickly, sending the vehicle onto the road alongside Egan's truck.

"Head back to Stonyford," Egan yelled. "I'll hold them off here."

The back door of the sedan flew open and Hunter Whitelaw jumped out, rifle in hand. "I'll stay here and help you."

"No!" Egan hollered. "Go with them. Now!"

With only a moment's hesitation, Hunter got back in the sedan and slammed the door. But before Wolfe could turn the car around, shots rang out from across the bridge and several bullets lodged in the car's front tires.

Two sport utility vehicles emerged from one of the half-hidden dirt side roads. Egan immediately recognized the man driving the lead SUV. Grant Cullen, a sickening grin plastered on his face, gunned the vehicle's gas pedal and flew around the Hummer, then came to a screeching halt on the bridge.

Dammit all! A hefty, fear-induced adrenaline rush flooded Egan's body. He'd known this was going to happen. In his gut. He had sensed the inevitability of this moment. He and Cullen face-to-face once again—with Maggie and Bent witnesses to the final showdown.

Chapter 14

Realizing exactly what was happening, Maggie followed Wolfe's orders without question. They had been ambushed by Grant Cullen and a group of his followers. With Joe and Hunter shielding Maggie and Bent with their bodies, they exited the sedan and made a mad dash into the ditch. Egan and Wolfe covered them with a barrage of gunfire that kept the Survivalists occupied.

At least a dozen armed men, not including Cullen and Winn Sherman, poured out of the Hummer and the two sports utility vehicles. A small army in comparison to the four Dundee agents. Fear pumped through Maggie's system as her mind assimilated the situation. This scenic mountain road had suddenly turned into a war zone and she and her son were trapped between the two warring factions. No, that wasn't precisely accurate. She and her son were more than innocent bystanders—they were a part of this battle, their lives at stake because they were important to Egan Cassidy.

Hunter motioned to Egan, who was separated from them by a good twenty-five feet. The two men exchanged some sort of hand signals that Maggie didn't comprehend.

Then Joe Ornelas inched his way over to Maggie. "You and Bent will stay here with Wolfe. I'm going to give you and Bent each weapons, so that if it becomes necessary—"

"I understand," she said, then accepted the 9-mm handgun from Joe.

"Hunter and I are going to make our way around behind them, while Egan and Wolfe keep their attention focused over here," Joe told her.

Hunter handed Bent his pistol, a twin to Joe's weapon, and shoved several extra clips into the pocket of Bent's jacket. "The more firepower the better, to distract Cullen's bunch. You're too far away to actually hit anybody, but they'll know we've got four shooters over here. Think you can do it?"

"Yeah, I can do it," Bent said confidently. "And so can Mama." He glance at Maggie. "Can't you?"

"Yes, of course I can." Maggie's heart lurched with an uneasiness that had nothing to do with the danger surrounding them. There was a look of excitement, of heady anticipation in her son's eyes and that look frightened her more than anything else. She had always known that the adventurous streak ran deep and wide in Bent, but until recently she had been able to curb his danger-seeking tendencies. Now, faced with a life-threatening situation, Bent became his father's son, in every sense of the word.

The gun in Maggie's hand felt alien to her, a weight she would prefer to toss aside. But she knew what she had to do. Joe gave her quick instructions, just as Hunter explained the basics to Bent. And all the while, Egan and Wolfe exchanged gunfire with the Survivalists troops. The noise distracted Maggie, but she tried to blot it out and concentrate on the task at hand.

Lying flat on her belly up against the side of the ditch, she looked across the bridge and immediately saw two men drop to the ground, casualties of Wolfe's expertise. The gunfire intensified when Joe and Hunter disappeared. Bent aimed and fired. Repeatedly. It was as if he'd been born with that gun in his hand, Maggie thought and cringed.

You can do this, she told herself. The first time she fired the weapon, every nerve in her body reacted. Holding back her urge to scream, she fired a second time.

Maggie lost track of the passing minutes as she continued firing the pistol. Her vision focused across the bridge where, one-by-one, the Survivalists began dropping like flies. That's when she realized Joe and Hunter had accomplished their goal. In a flurry of desperate activity, the few remaining troops piled into the Hummer. They're retreating, she thought. That must mean we've won the battle.

The Hummer backed up, turned around and headed in the direction from which it had come. Two lone men remained, one behind the wheel of each SUV. Even at this distance, she recognized Cullen in one vehicle and Colonel Sherman in the other. Within minutes, the two vehicles mimicked the Hummer's withdrawal. Maggie dropped the pistol to the ground. Her hands shook. Her heart raced. Nausea rose in her throat.

The roar of the old truck's engine caught Maggie's immediate attention. Egan! What was he doing? Where was he going? Ed Butram's rust-bucket pickup crossed the bridge, flying around and through the dead and wounded Survivalists.

"Where is he going?" Maggie asked Wolfe.

"Where do you think?"

"After Cullen."

"He can't let Cullen escape," Wolfe said. "You must know that."

Out of nowhere Hunter and Joe appeared. A bright red stain covered Hunter's shoulder.

"You're hurt," Maggie gasped.

"Bullet went straight through," Hunter said. "Looks worse than it is."

"Let's change those tires," Joe said. "So we can get the hell out of here. Egan just might need a little help."

"I'll give you a hand," Bent said and followed Joe around to the sedan's trunk.

"I'll help them," Wolfe told Hunter. "You get in touch with MacNamara and see where our backup is."

While Hunter used his cellular phone, Maggie paced the side of the road, nervous energy turning her into a jittery mess. She didn't know whether to cry, laugh hysterically or simply scream until she was hoarse. How could Egan face Cullen, Winn Sherman and at least four other men alone? He was terribly outnumbered. One against six were suicidal odds. But she understood Egan's reasoning. All that mattered to him was eliminating Cullen. Even if it cost him his own life in the process.

Egan saw Cullen's SUV directly ahead. The dark blue vehicle flew around a deadly curve. Egan floored the old pickup and within minutes caught up to his enemy. Cullen glanced back in the rearview mirror. His gaze wild. His features hard. Egan saw the fear on Cullen's face reflected in the mirror. Neither the Hummer nor the other SUV were within sight. Undoubtedly Sherman and the survivors had only one thing on their minds—escape.

Let them go, Egan thought. All that mattered to him was catching Cullen. And when he did...

With another hairpin curve just ahead, Egan squeezed all

the juice out of the old truck that it had in it, then rammed Cullen's SUV in the rear. Cullen bounded back, switching lanes as they neared the sharp loop. His vehicle skidded off the side of the road, shooting loose gravel in every direction and stirring up a whirlwind of dust.

Egan pulled the pickup alongside the SUV and they began a deadly game, using their vehicles as weapons. Back and forth. Ramming. Crashing. Metal crunching. Rubber burning. Sparks flying.

Cullen got ahead of Egan, the newer vehicle having a slight advantage. But within minutes Egan drew up along side the SUV, this time the truck on the wrong side of the road, near the mountain's edge. Once again, Egan instigated the crunching dance between his truck and the sports utility vehicle Cullen drove.

In a maneuver Egan hadn't been expecting, Cullen slowed down, whipped the SUV sideways and lunged, full-force, into the side of the pickup. Before Egan had a chance to do more than register what had happened, Cullen repeated the process, this time sending the old truck off the road. The back wheels dangled over the precipice, a rocky gorge far below the road. Just as Egan eased across the seat and opened the passenger's side door, Cullen took a shot at him. The bullet barely missed, embedding itself in the seat.

Damn! Egan thought. *I have to get out of this truck before it topples over the side and winds up at the bottom.* He checked to see if there was any space in which to maneuver on the other side. There wasn't. Less than six inches of level ground. The truck creaked and swayed. No choice! It had to be jump now or be swept over the cliff and down into the deep ravine, along with the truck.

Egan grabbed the rifle, flung open the driver's side door and bailed out, bracing himself for the downward lunge.

He rolled over the steep embankment, the huge jagged rocks ripping through his clothes and slicing into the exposed skin of his hands and face. After tumbling a good fifteen feet and losing his rifle in the process, he landed on a smooth boulder sticking out from the side of the mountain.

Every muscle in his body ached and he was pretty sure he had cracked a few ribs. Just as he checked his holster for his gun, he heard the tumbling crash of the old truck and looked up just in time to see it somersaulting past him down into the gorge a good fifty feet below where he rested on the ledge.

No doubt Cullen would be coming for him, so he'd better get on his feet. But that simple task proved more difficult than he'd thought. Pain sliced through his side when he tried to stand. Not only did his ribs hurt like hell, but a piercing ache radiated from his left thigh. When he glanced down, he saw a jagged rock sliver sticking out of his thigh. After casting his gaze upward, checking for Cullen, Egan used both hands to remove the thin slice of rock from his leg. Blood seeped from the wide, deep gash.

Keeping one eye open for Cullen, Egan ripped off a strip of material from the hem of his shirt and used it as a makeshift tourniquet to bind his thigh and slow the flow of blood.

Suddenly a loud boom vibrated the earth. Egan glanced down into the gorge. An explosion ripped through the old truck, shooting flames and swirls of smoke into the sky.

Despite the pain, Egan forced himself to stand and then to move. Just as he took shelter behind a crumbling rock formation, dotted with scrub grass and scraggily brush, Grant Cullen appeared at the top of the ridge. The moment Cullen saw Egan, he took aim and fired. The bullet splintered fragments from the rock formation and ricocheted off, hitting the nearby boulder. Egan got in a couple of shots, both landing just shy of their target.

"Too bad you didn't die, Cassidy," Cullen shouted. "Too bad for you, that is. I'm going to enjoy killing you slowly."

"I don't see it that way," Egan said. "Looks like a fair fight to me. We're both armed."

"Yeah, but I didn't just get banged up the way you did." Cullen's maniacal laughter echoed off the canyon walls.

Egan kept watch, using his pistol sparingly, waiting for Cullen to get within range. He had ten bullets left in this clip and then he'd be out of ammunition. He figured Cullen was equally armed. Maybe Cullen had another clip, but Egan figured it would be back in the SUV. Egan watched and waited as Cullen made his way down off the roadway, using every available rock formation and tree as cover on his descent.

When Cullen hid behind a parallel cluster of rocks, Egan waited for the gun battle to begin. He didn't have long to wait. Cullen fired several times, not even coming close to hitting his target. Egan assumed that Cullen had to be frustrated, wanting so badly to kill him and yet unable to reach him.

What were the odds, Egan wondered, that Cullen's men would return before either the Dundee agents or the FBI arrived? If Cullen's men came back, the chances of him killing Cullen instead of the other way around were slim to none. And if the feds showed up before he'd taken care of Cullen, then they would arrest him and his fate would be in the hands of the justice system. Egan didn't like those odds. For every criminal doing time, there were half a dozen walking around free. They'd gotten off on some technicality or another. He couldn't risk allowing Cullen to live. If he did, Maggie and Bent would never be safe.

"Looks like we're in a Mexican standoff, doesn't it?" Egan called loudly. "What do you say we end this here and now? The better man walks away alive."

"What are you suggesting?" Cullen asked.

"We both throw out our guns and meet face-to-face," Egan replied. "A couple of old soldiers in hand-to-hand combat. That is unless you're afraid I can whip your butt."

"It'd take a tougher son of a bitch than you to whip my butt, Cassidy." Cullen tossed his weapon out onto the steep incline that separated the two rock formations. "Now, you, Cassidy. I trust you to keep your word."

Egan knew there was a possibility that Cullen had another weapon on him, so he'd have to be careful. But it was a chance he had to take. He threw his Glock out on the ground so that Cullen could see it. "Now, who comes out first?"

Cullen emerged from behind the rocks, indeed an old soldier, but one in superb physical condition for his age. Motioning with his hand, he said, "Come on out, Cassidy. Let's find out who the better man is."

Ever cautious, Egan eased out from the protection of the rocks. Prepared to drop and roll if Cullen produced another gun, Egan took several tentative steps forward. Ignoring the pain in his leg and ribs, he faced his opponent.

"You look a little worse for wear, old buddy," Cullen taunted.

"Just a few scratches. Nothing to keep me from ripping you limb from limb."

Motioning again, Cullen grinned. "You want me? Come get me."

The two warriors circled each other, each wary. Suddenly Cullen whipped out a knife from the sheath strapped to his leg, then brandished the shiny blade in Egan's face.

"You didn't honestly think I'll give you an even chance, did you?" Cullen smirked, then lunged toward Egan.

Egan sidestepped the attack, then swerved around and braced himself for the next assault. Cullen recovered quickly and moved in again, jabbing repeatedly as he drew closer and closer. Attack. Avoid. Attack. Avoid. Suddenly Egan lost his balance when he slid across a section of loose gravel. He went down on his wounded knee. The pain spread outward from the cut and raced through his whole body. Cullen took that moment to swoop down, hoping for a kill. Despite great discomfort, Egan whirled sideways, deflecting the direct stab. The knife ripped through his shirt and sliced across his shoulder. Blood seeped through the material, creating a large red oval.

Realizing that now was the time, the exact moment to make his move, when Cullen felt all-powerful, Egan rammed into him, disregarding the threat of the deadly knife. Taken off guard, Cullen bounced backward from the direct blow. Egan wrestled his opponent to the ground and grabbed the hand that held the knife. Struggling fiercely, the two men rolled around on the rocky ground, each battling for supremacy.

Tossing Cullen onto his back, Egan manacled his wrist, then lifted his hand and repeatedly knocked it against the hard earth until Cullen's hand opened and the knife fell out. The two exchanged repeated blows as they tossed and tumbled downward, landing with brutal force on top of the protruding boulder. Their combat intensified. Cullen knocked Egan within an inch of the edge, then dove toward him in an effort to knock him off into the deep gorge.

Just as Cullen thought he was about to land the fatal blow, Egan counteracted with a last-minute maneuver of his own. Cullen cried out when he realized that he and not Egan would be flying through the air in a downward spiral, free-falling to the jagged rocks below. Dropping to his death.

Egan saw the realization on Cullen's face the very second he careened over the edge. Shock. Disbelief. And resignation, as if he were glad the battle was finally over, regardless of the outcome.

Cullen's continuous, bloodcurdling shriek echoed in Egan's ears long after Cullen's body had landed in a broken heap fifty feet below, inside the canyon. Egan stood on the boulder and looked down at death. The death of fear. The death of a wasted life. The final chapter written in blood.

As he made his way up the mountainside, his legs unsteady, Egan heard the approach of a vehicle. Damn! He turned to search for his Glock where it still lay on the ground, a few feet from Cullen's Ruger. Just as he reached for the pistol, he heard Joe Ornelas calling his name.

"Egan? Where the hell are you?"

"Down here!" Egan cried out.

"Where's Cullen?"

"Dead!"

Within minutes, Wolfe and Joe Ornelas made their way down the mountainside. Just as they flanked Egan and lifted his arms, one around each of their shoulders, Egan glanced up to the edge of the roadway. Maggie and Bent stood there together, mother and son side by side. Alive. Unharmed. Free from fear now and forever.

Maggie had insisted that Egan return home to Alabama with Bent and her to recuperate. After an overnight stay in the Flagstaff hospital, Egan had checked himself out, against doctor's orders. Hunter Whitelaw had stayed on several days, until his wound had begun to heal, then he had flown back to Atlanta, just as Joe and Wolfe had done. Once Maggie took charge, Egan had given in and allowed her to boss him around. If truth be told, he kind of liked having Maggie clucking over him like a mother hen. But Bent didn't seem to approve. Not of Egan living in his home nor of his mother giving Egan a great deal of TLC.

Egan had been ensconced on the soft leather sofa in Maggie's den most of the time during the three days since they'd arrived in Parsons City. Bent had returned to school immediately upon their return and the boy avoided Egan in the evenings. Three days of indulgent care and Egan was climbing the walls. He was unaccustomed to lying around doing nothing and being waited on hand and foot.

"Lunch is ready," Maggie called from the doorway.

Egan glanced up to see her standing there, a tray in her hand. "I can come to the table. You don't have to keep treating me as if I were an invalid."

"I know you're not an invalid." She brought the tray to him. "But you're recovering from five broken ribs, a deep cut in your thigh that required twenty stitches and a knife wound on your shoulder that required thirty-five stitches. And you left the hospital before you were supposed to."

"I'm not used to be mollycoddled."

Maggie eased her hand behind his back to help him sit up straight, then she fluffed his pillows and rearranged them for him.

"You're acting worse than Bent does when he gets sick," Maggie scolded. "Why is it that you can't just relax and enjoying letting someone else take care of you?"

Egan inspected his noonday meal. Homemade vegetable soup. A grilled cheese sandwich. And a large slice of Maggie's apple pie. What did he tell her—that he could easily get used to this kind of treatment? That he loved having her fuss over him, but he didn't dare let himself become accustomed to it.

This was a temporary arrangement. A visit with his son

until he was fully recovered. That had been Maggie's reasoning when she'd insisted he come home with them. At the time he'd been too physically weak and too soul-weary to argue with her.

Egan nodded toward the overstuffed, plaid armchair beside the sofa. "Sit down, Maggie. We need to talk."

"About what?" She rubbed her hands together nervously.

"Sit," he said.

She sat on the edge of the chair, placed her hands in her lap and sighed. "I'm sitting. So what do you want to talk about?"

"About you and me and Bent. About my staying here to recuperate."

"You're not leaving!" Maggie shot to her feet.

"Please, sit back down, honey. No, I'm not leaving today or even tomorrow. But you and I know that sooner or later, I'll have to go. Bent has made it perfectly clear that he doesn't want me here. He's not going to give me a chance, no matter how much you and I want him to."

"You've been here three days," she said. "That's hardly enough time. You and Bent are still strangers to each other."

"Do you honestly think that if I stay here a week or a month or even six months, Bent will come around?" Egan rubbed his forehead. "He can't even stand to be in the same room with me. He hasn't said ten words to me since—"

"You are staying here until you're fully recovered. You haven't given Bent an opportunity to get to know you." Maggie eased down and sat on the coffee table in front of the sofa, then reached out and took Egan's hand in hers. "I'm asking you to stay. For your own sake as much as Bent's. You need your son in your life as much as he needs you."

"You actually care about how I feel, don't you? After all I've put you through, you're willing to forgive me and help me win my son's affection. You, Maggie Tyson...Douglas, are one hell of a woman."

"Yes, I know." A soft, delicate smile curved her lips. "Bent will be home early today because he took his last final exam," Maggie explained. "I told him this morning that I expected him to spend the afternoon with us."

"And just what do you have planned?"

"I thought we'd go to the river and take the boat out. We could even stay overnight at our cottage down there. Bent loves the river and you could soak up some fresh air and sunshine."

"Sounds like a nice plan, but what if Bent doesn't want to—"

"He's already promised me."

"What did you do, twist his arm?"

"I asked him to do it as a favor to me," she admitted. "Now, you eat your lunch, while I go pack a few things for our little excursion."

Before Maggie reached the hallway, she heard the back door open.

"Bent?"

"Yeah, Mama, it's me. And wait till you see who I've got with me."

When Maggie entered the kitchen, she stopped dead in her tracks. There beside the refrigerator that Bent had opened searching for a cola stood her ex-husband.

"Hi, Mag," Gil Douglas said.

"What are you doing here?" she asked.

"I called him," Bent said. "I thought if anyone could talk sense to you and make you see what a mistake it is letting that man—" Bent nodded in the direction of the den "—back into your life, it would be Dad."

"Bent, you had no right to involve Gil in our affairs."

"Maggie, the boy is just worried about you," Gil said. "And since when don't I have a right to be concerned about my son?"

"Oh, he's your son, now, is he? Funny thing that you suddenly remember you have a son, just when Bent's biological father comes into his life." Maggie huffed loudly. "You haven't been a father to Bent since our divorce. You weren't even concerned enough about him when he was kidnapped to come here, so why is it that you can take off time from work to drop by and tell me how to run my life?"

"See, I told you that she wouldn't listen to me," Gil said to Bent. "She has a blind spot when it comes to Cassidy. She can't see him for who he is—a hired killer who used her and dumped her. He couldn't care less about her...or about you."

"Mama, listen to him, will you?"

"What I don't understand," Maggie said, "is why you're listening to him."

"Why shouldn't he listen to me?" Gil took a stand there beside Bent, two unlikely allies. "I was around the first time Egan Cassidy stormed into your life and nearly destroyed you. I don't want to see it happen a second time. The first time he wrecked our relationship. This time he'll wreck your relationship with Bent. Is that what you want?"

"How dare you! You have no right—"

"Legally, I'm Bent's father, so that gives me a right."

"I want you to leave," Maggie said. "All you're doing is stirring up trouble. Why, Gil? Have you been waiting fifteen years to pay me back for loving another man more than I could have ever loved you?"

"See?" Gil pointed a finger at Maggie, then glanced at

Bent's stricken face. "I told you that she's still in love with him."

"Damn you, Gil Douglas!" Maggie screamed. "Get out of my house!"

The door leading into the hallway swung open. Egan Cassidy filled the doorway. "I think I heard Maggie ask you to leave."

"It's been a long time, Cassidy," Gil said. "But I see you haven't changed. You just walked in here and took over again, didn't you? Well, you might be able to manipulate Maggie, but you have no power over *my* son. Bent knows what kind of man you are."

"Maybe so," Egan said. "But my guess is that he knows what kind of man you are, too."

"Please, Gil, just go. Now." Maggie looked at her ex-husband pleadingly.

"If Dad goes, I go," Bent said.

"What?" Maggie glared at Bent, shocked by his outburst.

"You heard him, didn't you?" Gil smirked. "Bent wants me to stay, but he wants Cassidy to go. So, what's it going to be, Maggie? Do you choose your son or your lover?"

"Why you slimy, jealous-hearted, backstabbing..." Maggie fumed. Of all the problems she had anticipated in trying to unite Bent and Egan, this one hadn't even entered her mind. During their marriage, Gil had tried to be a father to Bent, but he'd failed miserably. And since their divorce, Gil hadn't really been a part of their lives. But here he was, big as life, playing the role of protective parent.

"You're leaving right this minute." Maggie marched across the kitchen and pointed her index finger right into Gil's face. "And don't you ever come back, without an invitation from me."

"I told you that if Dad leaves, I leave," Bent repeated his threat.

"Pack a bag and meet me in the car," Gil said, then turned to Maggie. "I'll have him call you when we get to Nashville."

"He's not going anywhere with you," Maggie said.

"He's not a child," Gil reminded her. "He has a right to—"

Egan sauntered across the room, heading toward Gil. Gil backed out of the kitchen and onto the screened-in porch. Egan went after him. Bent followed both men outside, as did Maggie.

"I'll wait in the car for you, Bent," Gil said.

"Bent won't be going with you." Egan's voice possessed a dangerous undertone. "So, there's no point in your waiting for him."

When Bent flew past Maggie, heading toward Gil, Egan reached out and clamped his big hand down on Bent's shoulder. "You can leave with this man and break your mother's heart. Is that what you want?"

"I want to get away from you!" Bent shouted.

"You can run away from me, if that's really what you want to do, but nothing is going to change the fact that Gil Douglas isn't your father. I am. Like it or not, you are my son, not his. You look like me. You talk like me. You even walk like me."

"I don't want to be your son. Do you hear me?" Bent jerked out of Egan's hold. "You don't love my mother and you don't love me. You never wanted to be a part of our lives. You weren't here for us when we needed you. And when you finally showed up, it was only because some lunatic who hated you had kidnapped me!"

"Oh, Bent," Maggie cried. "I thought you understood

why Egan left me, why he stayed away. It wasn't because
he wanted to.''

"You say that I don't love your mother or you," Egan
said. "You're wrong on both counts. I loved your mother
That's the reason I left her. I didn't have the right to love
her. And you...Bent...son...you have no idea what you
mean to me or how much I love you.''

Tears welled up in Bent's eyes. "I don't believe you.''

"What do I have to do to prove it to you?" Egan asked

Bent's chin trembled. "I told you that I don't believe
you. There's nothing you can do to prove it to me.''

"Why don't you stick around and give me a chance'
That's all I want. That's all your mother is asking of us—
of you and me. That we give ourselves a chance to get to
know each other. Do you think she's asking for too much?'

"Bent, don't listen to him.'' Gil Douglas glanced anx-
iously back and forth from Bent to Egan. "You know you
can't trust him.''

"Maybe you're right," Bent said. "Maybe I can't trus
him. But I know one thing for sure and that's that the one
person who really loves me is Mama. Not you, Gil.'' Ben
glared at his adoptive father, then he focused his hard gaze
on Egan. "And not you, either." He turned to Maggie. "
won't leave, Mama. I shouldn't have called Gil and go
him involved in our problems. I acted like a stupid kid. I
really am sorry.''

Maggie opened her arms and Bent ran to her. Egan
marched toward Gil Douglas, who made a hasty retreat to
the driveway. Egan followed, catching up with Gil just as
he opened his car door.

Egan grasped Gil's shoulder and whirled Gil around to
face him. "I believe in giving a man fair warning. You stay
in Nashville and take care of your woman and your child
That woman—'' Egan nodded at the house ''—is mine

She always has been and she always will be. And that boy is my son. Mine. Not yours.''

''You have no right to either of them. Not after the way you—''

Egan tightened his hold on Gil's shoulder. "I gave up Maggie, and unknowingly gave up my son, to protect them from a monster. But that monster no longer exists and I'm free to claim what's mine. Neither Bent nor Maggie may ever be able to forgive me or allow me to be a permanent part of their lives, but I plan to do everything I can to persuade them that I deserve a second chance!''

Egan released Gil's shoulder and stepped aside. Gil jumped in his car, started the engine and sped out of the driveway. When Egan turned to go back to the house, he saw Maggie and Bent standing at the backyard gate. Waiting. Waiting for him.

Chapter 15

During his two months of recuperation, Egan had taken full advantage of his time with Maggie and Bent. He had realized early on that although Maggie would allow him to have a relationship with Bent no matter what happened between him and her, Egan could never have Maggie without a relationship with Bent. And he wanted them both. Unfortunately winning Bent over had turned out to be a formidable task. His son distrusted him and seemed to be testing him at every turn. But in all fairness, Egan had to admit that Bent was trying. Mostly to pacify Maggie. But Egan would gladly take whatever he could get, whatever Bent was willing to give.

He and Maggie were walking on eggshells around Bent, both of them doing whatever they could to bring the three of them together as a family. Since school was out, they spent every weekend at the river, swimming, boating and soaking up the fresh air and sunshine. During the week they ate breakfast and dinner together and often Egan and Bent went into town at lunch to join Maggie for sandwiches at Rare Finds. And last week they had taken a family vacation to the Gulf Coast, staying at the Grand Hotel in Point Clear.

Egan's relationship with Bent had improved, but they still had a long way to go to ever truly be father and son. Right now they were friendly acquaintances. The situation with Maggie and him was a different matter, but in its own way just as difficult to handle. He wanted to ask Maggie to marry him, but until Bent truly accepted him, marriage was out of the question. And until he and Maggie were in a committed relationship, they could hardly carry on an affair right under their disapproving son's nose. And disapprove he did!

Days went fairly smoothly since Maggie was gone for eight hours. But nights were hell. He was sleeping in the guest bedroom down the hall from Maggie and every time they tried pulling off a midnight tryst, Bent interrupted them. Nothing like having your fourteen-year-old son as a strict chaperone. Egan knew that Maggie was as frustrated as he. The sexual tension between them had just about reached the explosion point.

Egan had taken to writing at night and had just finished a new collection of Nage Styon verses. He would dedicate this book to Maggie and Bent.

Egan lifted the pages from the desk and bound them together with a metal clip. He did all his work in longhand, never using a typewriter or a computer. He had driven into town this morning and made three copies. One to send his editor. One for Maggie and one for Bent.

He carried the copies downstairs with him and placed them on the kitchen counter before he went outside and fired up the grill. He planned to have steaks ready when Maggie came home. He liked taking care of her, doing things that pleased her. By the way she glowed when he

showed her the smallest amount of attention, he'd learned
that it had been a very long time since anyone had made
her feel special. If given the chance, Egan wanted to spend
the rest of his life making Maggie feel like the most special
woman in the world. And that's exactly what she was—to
him and to Bent.

"Hey, you got time for a little one-on-one?" Bent
bounced the basketball on the driveway, then tossed it into
the net attached to the garage.

"When did you get home?" Egan smiled at his son.

"Chris dropped me off about ten minutes ago," Bent
said.

"I didn't know Chris was old enough—"

"You're as bad as Mama checking up on me and my
friends." Bent's expression didn't soften, but he spoke the
words in a lighthearted manner. "Chris has his learner's
permit and his big brother was in the car. Satisfied?"

Egan nodded. "Let me get the fire started in the grill,
then I'll shoot hoops with you until it's time to put on the
steaks."

Thirty minutes later, a hot and sweaty father and son took
a break. Bent went into the kitchen and came back with
individual bottles of water. He tossed one to Egan, then sat
opposite him in a wicker chair on the back porch.

"I...er...I was wondering if you might want to play in
a softball game with me Saturday," Bent said, then took a
big swig of water, deliberately avoiding making eye contact.

"I didn't know you were on a team," Egan said.

"This is a special tournament sponsored by Chris's
church." Bent gazed out across the backyard. "It's a char-
ity thing."

"Sure, I'd be happy to play softball with you. But I have

to warn you that I haven't played in years. I'm pretty rusty."

"Ah, that won't matter." Bent shrugged. "All the other dads probably won't be very good anyway. None of them are in as good a shape as you."

For a split second Egan's heart stopped. *All the other dads. All the other dads?* This was the closest Bent had come to recognizing Egan as his father. Did his son even realize what he'd said?

"So, what is it, a combination teens and old men's game?" Egan asked jokingly.

"Yeah, something like that." Bent downed the rest of his water in one long giant swallow, then crushed the empty plastic bottle. He got up, went outside and tossed the bottle into the garbage. "Hey, I think the grill's ready for those steaks."

Egan nodded, then went inside and took the marinated steaks from the refrigerator. When he opened the lid of the grill and laid the steaks on the rack above the smoldering coals, Bent came up beside him.

"That softball tournament…it's a 'Father and Son' thing," Bent admitted. "I thought it would make Mama happy if we did something like that together."

Egan closed the lid on the steaks, then cleared his throat. "Yeah, you're right. I think it would make Maggie happy." Taking a chance, praying that Bent wouldn't reject him, Egan laid his hand on Bent's shoulder. "I have to admit that it makes me happy, too."

Bent grinned. Egan's stomach knotted. This was the first genuine smile his son had given him. And it had taken only two months of diligent work to earn that smile.

Relaxing in her recliner in the den, an unread novel in her hand, Maggie watched her two guys sitting side by side on the sofa. They laughed and shouted and shoved or punched each other occasionally while they watched the Atlanta Braves game on television. Seeing Bent and Egan together this way was the answer to many prayers. After two months of cautious courtesy toward his father, Bent had finally let down the walls around his emotions and was making a real effort to allow Egan into his life.

Now, if only her overprotective son would give her permission to open her arms and her heart to Egan. Until the man she loved had come back into her life, she hadn't been overly concerned about not having had sex in years. But now that Egan had reawakened the sensual woman within her, this self-imposed celibacy was killing her. Every night she lay alone in her bed, thinking about Egan. He slept just down the hall. A one-minute walk. But it might as well have been a thousand miles. Bent had been more observant and disapproving than her own father would have been.

The telephone rang, jarring Maggie from her thoughts. She reached over and picked up the portable phone, then took note of the Caller ID number. Atlanta. The Dundee Agency. Maggie's heartbeat accelerated. Ellen had contacted Egan weekly the first month, but she hadn't phoned in weeks now.

Maggie answered on the third ring. "Hello."

"Maggie, this is Ellen Denby. How are you?"

"We're fine. How about you?"

"Doing okay." Ellen paused. "I hate to bother y'all, but I'm afraid something has come up and we're going to need Egan to make a trip to Chicago."

"Oh, I see."

"Is he around somewhere?"

"Yes. He's right here. He and Bent are watching a baseball game on TV." Maggie held the phone out to Egan, who was looking at her questioningly. "It's Ellen Denby."

Egan got up, reached out and took the phone. "Hi, there. What's up?"

"Remember the Marler case you worked on six months ago?" Ellen sighed. "Well, that case has come to trial. The assistant district attorney says he needs you to testify on Sybil Marler's behalf day after tomorrow and he wants to consult with you beforehand."

"That means I'll have to fly to Chicago in the morning," Egan said. "How about faxing the particulars of the case to my hotel room once I get there. I need to refresh my memory on a few points."

"Just remember that Sybil's husband is out on bail and he made some awfully ugly threats against you."

"I can handle Doyce Marler," Egan said. "The man's a pip-squeak."

"He's a pip-squeak who gets his kicks by beating his wife and kids. A guy like that is capable of killing."

"If anyone gets killed, it won't be me," Egan assured Ellen. "I'd like nothing better than the opportunity to beat the hell out that SOB."

"After your trip to Chicago, will you be coming back to Atlanta?" Ellen asked. "Or do you plan to retire and take up residence in Alabama permanently?"

"Depends," Egan replied. "We've still got things to work out."

"Good luck. Call me when you get to Chicago."

"Thanks. And you'll be hearing from me."

When Egan laid the phone on the coffee table, he noticed that Bent had moved across the room and now stood at Maggie's side. Mother and son stared at him, looks of concern on their faces.

"That was Ellen," Egan said. "I have to fly to Chicago tomorrow to testify in a case I worked on six months ago."

"I thought you weren't going back to work at Dundee's,'' Bent said. ''You told us that you were thinking about retiring. You made us believe that you wanted to stay here with us.''

''I do want to stay here with you and Maggie.'' Egan's stomach tightened with apprehension. ''This trip shouldn't last more than a few days.''

''Isn't there some way you can get out of going?'' Bent asked. ''Can't somebody else testify?''

''I'm afraid not. This was my case and I'm the one with the firsthand information.''

''After Chicago, you'll go back to Atlanta, won't you?'' Bent's face flushed. He curled his hands into tight fists. ''You've had your little family reunion, but things are getting pretty dull around here, aren't they?''

''No, son, that's not true.'' Egan held out his hand in a plea for understanding. ''This is just a quick trip. I'll come right back.''

Bent turned to his mother. ''You told me that if I gave him a chance, that if I'd let him be a father to me, he wouldn't leave us. Well, it looks like you were wrong. Again!''

''Bentley Tyson Douglas!'' Maggie glowered at her son. ''You're acting like a child. You're being totally unreasonable. Egan isn't leaving us for good.'' She turned to Egan. ''Tell him! Make him understand.''

''Yeah, Egan, make me understand.'' Bent walked over to his father and looked him square in the eye.

''Do you honestly think that I'd walk away from you and your mother and not come back?''

''Yeah, that's exactly what I think. You did it before, so what's to stop you from doing it again. This trip to Chicago is just an excuse so you can leave without having to explain that the quiet life in Parsons City isn't what you wanted.''

''Bent...son...'' When Egan tried to put his hand on

Bent's shoulder, the boy sidestepped him. "What can I say or do to prove to you that I'm telling you the truth?"

"Don't go to Chicago!"

Egan's shoulders slumped. "I have to go. If I don't testify, a criminal could go free."

"Well, if you leave, don't bother to come back!" Bent yelled. "Ever!"

When Bent stormed out of the den, Egan started to go after him, but Maggie rushed over and grabbed Egan's arm. "Don't. He's not going to listen to you. I know he's acting irrationally, but right now his emotions are in charge. He's convinced himself that you're leaving us and I don't think you'll be able to persuade him otherwise."

Egan grabbed Maggie's shoulder. "You know I'm coming back, don't you?"

Maggie's chin quivered. "Yes, if you tell me that you're coming back to us, then I believe you. But even if you come back, I'm afraid all the progress you've made with Bent these past two months may have been destroyed."

Egan wiped away a lone tear as it trickled down Maggie's cheek. "I'm going to pack and leave tonight." He pulled Maggie into his arms. "But when I come back— and I will be back as soon as I possibly can—I'll fix things with Bent. I promise."

Two hours later, Maggie waited alone at the foot of the stairs as Egan came down with his suitcase in hand. After telling her that he'd be back when *that man* left, Bent had gone for a walk.

Egan set his suitcase by the front door, then lifted Maggie's hand into his and gave her the manuscript pages for his latest volume of poetry. "This is for you. And for Bent."

Maggie glanced down at the title page. *Silence* by Nage Styon. She flipped to the second page and read the dedication. *To the love of my life, Maggie, and to Bent, the wonderful son she gave me.*

"Oh, Egan." Gripping the manuscript tightly, she flung her arms around him and laid her head on his chest. "Thank you."

"You knew, didn't you? You've known all along that I was Nage Styon."

"Yes, I've known ever since I bought the first volume of your poetry. If the name hadn't given you away, then the sentiments of your verses would have. I saw my brother Bentley in every line."

"I left Bent a copy upstairs in his room." Egan kissed Maggie, deeply and passionately, then released her and picked up his suitcase. "I'll be back, Maggie mine. And that's a promise you can take to the bank."

Maggie had been baking for four days. She had frozen cakes and pies and cookies—enough to feed an army for months. Despite what nagging fears remained in her heart, leftovers from the past, she kept telling herself repeatedly that Egan would come back to them. He had called every night, but Bent had refused to speak to him. Their son had been sulking ever since Egan left. If she didn't understand that Bent was acting out of fear and hurt, she would have already given him a tongue-lashing. But she did understand. He had just begun to trust Egan, just barely opened up to his father, when Egan had been called away. Although Bent's reaction might seem irrational to anyone else, she knew why her son had overreacted. He was beginning to love Egan and that love made him vulnerable.

Bent bounded into the kitchen, softball glove in hand. "The game starts in an hour and he's not here. I told you he wouldn't come back."

Maggie wiped her hands off on the towel, removed her

gingham apron and laid it on the counter. "Something must have come up to delay him."

"Why do you keep defending him? Get it through your head, Mama, he's not coming back."

"I don't intend to argue with you." Maggie picked up her bag from the table, hung the straps over her shoulder and then retrieved her car keys from a side pouch. "I'm ready to go."

"Yeah, me, too."

Forty-five minutes later, Maggie sat beside Janice Deweese in the stands at the Parsons City Athletic Park. She had been so sure Egan would keep his promise and make it back to town in time for the game. If he didn't show up, there was no way Bent would ever forgive him.

What if he isn't coming back? an insecure inner voice taunted her. What if Bent's right and Egan has decided that he can't live a quiet, simple life?

"Bent keeps looking around for Egan," Janice said. "He might have told you he doesn't think his father will show up, but he's sure hoping he will."

"I'm hoping he will, too," Maggie admitted. "I keep telling myself that something unavoidable came up."

"But you're having some doubts, aren't you?"

"It's just my insecurity. I know that Egan cares for me and that he wants a life with Bent and me."

"Then why isn't he here?" Janice asked.

"He'll be here. I just know he will." Maggie had to trust her heart, even if that heart had led her astray once before—fifteen years ago. Circumstances were different. Grant Cullen no longer posed a threat. Unlike years ago, Egan had made promises this time. Promises to her and to Bent.

The stands were filled with families. Mothers, brothers and sisters. Grandparents. Aunts and uncles. And groups of fathers and sons comprised the teams. But one father was missing. Bent's father.

She watched Bent as he tossed a ball back and forth with his friend Chris, whose father was present. Suddenly Bent missed the catch. The ball fell to the ground. Bent walked off the field and headed toward the entrance gates. Maggie pivoted slightly and glanced over her shoulder, following her son's journey. That's when she saw Egan. Wearing blue jeans and red T-shirt, identical to Bent's outfit, Egan stood just inside the park entrance.

Maggie's heart leaped into her throat. Tears misted her eyes. Egan laid his hand on his son's shoulder and together they joined the other players on the field. The coach tossed Egan a ball cap. After putting on the cap, he glanced up and scanned the crowd. When he spotted Maggie, he lifted his hand and waved. She stood up, tears streaming down her face, and blew him a kiss.

Egan lifted the sponge and ran it over Maggie's back. The scented bubbles dripped off the sponge onto his hand. After he scrubbed her back, he pulled her between his spread legs. Her buttocks nestled against his groin. She rested her head on his shoulder as he wrapped his arms around her. With tender caresses, he stroked her breasts, paying special attention to her nipples. When she moaned and rubbed her behind against his arousal, he slid his wet hands down over her tummy and slipped them between her thighs, separating her legs. With the fingers of one hand lifted to a breast and the fingers of the other hand occupied below, Egan teased her until she was breathless.

"Relax, honey, and let it happen," Egan whispered in her ear.

Obeying his command, she allowed his talented fingers to pleasure her. When fulfillment claimed her, shudders racking her body, Maggie cried out. Once the aftershocks subsided, Egan stood, water and bubbles dripping from his big body, and got out of the Jacuzzi tub in Maggie's bathroom. After tying a towel around his waist, he offered her his hand, then lifted her up and out of the tub. He wrapped a large, fluffy towel around her and dried her with slow, sensuous pats. Maggie grabbed her silk robe from the hook on the back of the door, slipped her arms through the sleeves and tied the belt.

Egan led her into her bedroom and over to the bed. After loosening her belt, he spread her robe apart to reveal her beautiful body. She smiled wickedly at him and snatched away his towel.

"Lady, you're asking for trouble," he said.

"Trouble's what I want, big boy." She looked directly at his erection.

"Then trouble is exactly what you're going to get."

He shoved her down on the bed and stood there gazing at her. Lifting her right foot, she stroked his hip, then inched her foot around so that her toes could tap against his sex.

"I'm glad Bent spent the night with Chris so that his parents could work off a little bottled-up tension," Maggie said. "These past two months without making love have been the longest two months of my life."

Egan parted her legs and walked between them, then lifted her hips. With one fast, deep lunge, he entered her. She sighed with pleasure, then straddled his waist with her legs and opened herself completely to his plunder.

"It'll take me years to make up for lost time," he told her.

"Then we shouldn't waste any time, should we?"

They made love with all the passion, all the hunger, all the longing that they had been forced to deny for so many weeks. They shared simultaneous climaxes that rocked them to the core of their bodies.

Sated and happy beyond their wildest dreams, they lay together in Maggie's bed, the night still young and the future spread out ahead of them like a golden dream waiting to be fulfilled.

Maggie held up her left hand and stared at the shimmering amethyst-and-diamond engagement ring Egan had bought while he'd been in Chicago. "I can't believe you remembered that my birthstone is an amethyst." She wriggled around, freeing her arm trapped between them, braced herself on one elbow and leaned across Egan's chest. "I love this ring. It's beautiful. But with all these diamonds it must have cost you a small fortune. I would have been happy with something less expensive."

Egan rose up and kissed her on the nose, then lifted his hand to thread his fingers through the damp, tangled mass of her hair. "I've got more money than I can spend in one lifetime, so let me enjoy myself and spend it on you and Bent."

"Hmm-mmm. I had no idea I was marrying a millionaire," she teased.

"You're marrying a man who loves you more than anything in this world and is grateful that you're giving him a chance to spend the rest of his life proving it to you."

"So while you're proving your love to me, what do you intend to do to keep yourself occupied when I'm working? You could always be a househusband."

"I'm going to write more Nage Styon poetry and I just might try my hand at writing a novel. Maybe a murder mystery."

"Hmm-mmm. Uh, Egan?"

"Huh?" He idly caressed her naked hip.

She snuggled as close to him as possible, then forked

her fingers through his chest hair. "Let's get married next week."

"Suits me just fine, but why the big hurry? I thought you women liked months to plan these big shindigs."

"I don't want a big wedding. I'd like something simple. Just you, me, Bent and Janice."

"I want whatever you want, honey. You know that, don't you?"

"Uh-huh. Does that total acceptance extend to *anything* I want?" She looked at him coyly and smiled.

"I'd give you anything in the world you wanted, if I could."

"How about another child?" She nuzzled his chin with her nose.

"You want a baby?"

"I want your baby. And this time, I want you to be with me, every step of the way."

"I can't believe..." As Egan rose into a sitting position, he eased Maggie up with him until she sat on his lap. "I'd be more than happy to oblige and feel blessed if you were to get pregnant. But honey, I'm forty-seven. The equipment still works, but I can't guarantee—"

She pressed her index finger against his lips. "Your equipment works just fine. As a matter of fact...I'm pretty sure that I'm already pregnant."

"What?"

"A little over two months pregnant," she admitted. "I took a home pregnancy test this morning and it came out positive."

"Oh, Maggie, honey. How the hell did I get so lucky?" He smothered her with kisses, then suddenly stopped. His mouth fell open; his jaw went slack. "What are you going to say to Bent? Do you think he'll be upset?"

"I'm going to say, 'You know that baby sister you always wanted when you were a little boy...'"

Egan laughed as he pulled Maggie down on top of him. "I love you, Maggie mine."

"And I love you, Egan."

Epilogue

Christmas at the Cassidy home was an incomparable event. The aroma of cinnamon wafted from the kitchen mingling with the scent of fresh evergreen throughout the house. Twinkling white lights adorned the eight-foot tree, draped the mantels in the living and dining rooms and set aflame the small shrubbery that lined the brick walkway. Red-and-green plaid ribbon laced over and under windows and doors, and huge bows graced every present stacked under the tree.

Shrill squeals and the sound of little feet bouncing up and down alerted Maggie that Bentley Tyson Cassidy had arrived. She checked the sugar cookies in the oven, wiped her hands on the towel and then rushed out of the kitchen and down the hallway. There in the foyer stood her eighteen-year-old son, home from the University of Alabama.

Red-haired, three-year-old Melanie clung to one of Bent's legs and her identical twin sister, Melinda, clung to the other. Egan reached down and lifted first one and then the other daughter away from their beloved big brother Father and son stood side by side, each six-three and broad-shouldered, although Egan possessed the bulk of a mature man while Bent still retained the lankiness of youth.

"Mama!" Bent hurried toward Maggie, lifted her off her feet and whirled her around and around, then set her back on the floor. "The house looks wonderful and boy, something sure smells good."

"Cookies," Melinda said.

"Sugar cookies," Melanie clarified.

"Come on you two little demons. Y'all can help Mommy in the kitchen." Maggie gathered up the twins and herded them down the hallway. "Lunch will be ready soon," she called back to her men. "Put your bag in your room, Bent, then by the time you and your father wash up, I'll have chicken and dumplings on the table."

After picking up Bent's suitcase, Egan draped his arm around his son's shoulder. "It's good to have you here. Your mama's had a difficult time adjusting to your living away from home."

"Mama has, huh?" Bent grinned. "And you haven't missed me, have you, Dad?"

Egan chuckled. "Actually, Maggie's been handling your being gone better than I have. I guess I'll never feel as if I've had enough time with you."

"Yeah, I know what you mean," Bent said. "My little sisters are lucky that you've had the chance to be a part of their lives from the beginning." Bent hugged his father. "But I'm lucky that you didn't give up on me, considering what a stubborn mule I was before you and Mama got married."

"I would never have given up on you," Egan said. "And I'm the lucky one to have you and the girls and Maggie. She's given me a life I never thought I could have."

Fifteen minutes later, the Cassidy family gathered around the kitchen table for their noontime meal. After the twins said a prayer of thanks simultaneously, Maggie glanced across the table at her husband. Egan smiled at her and her stomach did a quivering little flip-flop. She mouthed the words "I love you" and he returned the silent gesture.

"What ya doing, Mama?" Melanie asked, her mouth half-full of dumplings.

"She and Daddy are making faces at each other," Melinda said. "They're always making kissie faces."

"That's because our mother and father love each other," Bent told his little sisters, then spread out both arms, reached over from where he sat between them and ruffled their silky red curls.

"And they love us, too," Melanie added. "Me and her—" she pointed to her sister "—and you." She pointed at Bent.

Everyone laughed. Joy in abundance filled Maggie's heart. She had everything she'd ever wanted—and more. So much more. Three beautiful, healthy children. A happy, contented husband who worshiped the ground she walked on. And the life she'd dreamed of since the first moment Egan Cassidy had walked into her life.

*   *   *   *   *

Look for HER SECRET WEAPON
by Beverly Barton in October 2000.
And don't miss the next book
in Beverly Barton's series,

THE PROTECTORS,

coming in early 2001 from
Silhouette Intimate Moments!

Silhouette invites you to come back to Whitehorn, Montana...

MONTANA MAVERICKS

WED IN WHITEHORN—
12 BRAND-NEW stories that capture living and loving beneath the Big Sky where legends live on and love lasts forever!

June 2000—
Lisa Jackson *Lone Stallion's Lady* (#1)

July 2000—
Laurie Paige *Cheyenne Bride* (#2)

August 2000—
Jennifer Greene *You Belong to Me* (#3)

September 2000—
Victoria Pade *The Marriage Bargain* (#4)

And the adventure continues...

Available at your favorite retail outlet.

Silhouette®
Where love comes alive™

Visit Silhouette at www.eHarlequin.com   PSMMGEN1